Jelly's
Big Night Out

Patty Campbell

ISBN: 978-1-955784-79-5

Published by Satin Romance
An Imprint of Melange Books, LLC
White Bear Lake, MN 55110
www.satinromance.com

Published in the United States of America.

Cover Design by Ashley Redbird Designs

This book is dedicated to my dear friend and author, Molly Jebber. She and I have been critiquing partners for many years. I write contemporary love stories and Molly writes Amish/Christian love stories. We have come to depend on each other's straight talk and honest editing to improve our novels. Of all my books, Jelly's Big Night Out has always been Molly's favorite.

I also want to give a shout-out to Ashley Redbird, my creative and tireless cover artist.

Chapter One

Simi Valley, California
Tuesday, 7:30 a.m.

"What? I have a conference with your teacher this morning?" Jelly looked at her kid sister. "I swear, Martha Elizabeth, you keep pulling this kind of baloney, one of these days I'm going to..." She mimicked a choking motion with her hands and scowled.

Emi stood glaring at her, her usual defiant stance. She was clearly trying for a mean look, but her sweet face at fourteen still had some rosy baby fat. The oversize Jonas Brothers tee shirt hung almost to her knees over faded jeans. Jelly struggled to keep a straight face.

"Don't call me that! My name is Emi. Go ahead and kill me if you want to. It must run in the family. Then you can go up to Folsom and share Daddy's cell."

Jelly heaved a sigh. "Let's leave Daddy out of it for today, all right?" She turned back to the mirror to finish her hair. "You must have known about this teacher conference for days. Why are you telling me now? Are you in some kind of trouble?"

Hands on her hips, Emi yelled, "No! I just forgot, okay?" She flashed her big sister a look of disapproval. "You can't go see Mr. Henry looking like that. You wear way too much makeup and stuff."

"Look, kiddo." Jelly turned from the mirror and pointed at her face. "This is the way I look. This is the way I dress. Live with it. At least I don't go around looking like I live in a homeless shelter." She dropped her brush on the counter. "You know that today is the biggest sale of the year for Big Night Out. I've planned and advertised it for weeks. How am I supposed to take off for an hour or more in the middle of the morning? My new girl started yesterday. I haven't even had time to train her." She closed the door on the medicine cabinet with a sharp snap. "You make me nuts, Emi."

"I know the feeling."

Jelly mimicked her posture. "You know the feeling? Tell me, please, what is it that I've done so wrong in the past twelve years? I quit school to take care of you when Daddy went to jail. We were lucky this house was paid off, or we'd have been on the street.

"Aunt Martha helped to keep the Child Welfare people from putting both of us in foster care. I don't even have a life to call my own!"

"Thank you, thank you, thank you, Jelly. Wait right here while I get the violin so I can accompany the sad story I've heard, like, a bazillion times all my life."

"Don't even think of touching Mom's violin. I told you it was off limits unless you agreed to take lessons."

"And play that dumb boring stuff you listen to?"

"Paganini is dumb and boring? Oh, well, how would you know? You're probably deaf from that ear splitting crap you listen to." She sighed again. "You're such a smart ass." Jelly finished with the hairspray and put on her shoulder length sparkly red earrings, pleased at how great they went with her russet hair and purple silk blouse.

"You care more about that dumb store than you do about me!" The hurt in Emi's eyes was real, even though she bit her lip and did her best to hide it.

She reached out and put her arm around Emi's shoulders. She tried to shrink away, but Jelly wouldn't let go. "You know that's not true, baby. The store is what keeps a roof over our heads and food on the table."

Emi picked up her book bag when the doorbell rang. "Are you coming to see Mr. Henry at eleven or not?"

"Please tell me that's not Marco."

"It's Marco. I'm walking to school with him. Are you coming at eleven or not?"

Jelly nodded. "Of course I'm coming. Don't ask me how, but I'll find a way to get there." She walked with Emi to the front door.

Marco had backed away from the door and stood on the first step. When the door opened, he glanced briefly at Jelly and looked down at his battered shoes. He went dark red in the face and neck. Jelly was sure the kid had never looked directly at her. She shook her head with dismay at his grungy appearance, grateful that at least Emi hadn't pierced her nose or had barbed wire tattooed on her wrists. God, how his mother's heart must sink every time she looked at the little hoodlum. His frayed jeans hung so low on his hips they looked as if they were about to slip off. The only thing Jelly approved of was the colorful retro tie-dyed tee shirt he wore.

"Good morning, Marco."

Face even redder, he gave Jelly a nanosecond glance and mumbled something that might have been an intelligent response. But how could she tell? Emi slung her huge backpack over her shoulder, said a quick, "Bye," brushed past her, and closed the door.

Jelly turned back to the kitchen. The window was open, and she overheard their conversation from the front porch. She peeked out to see Marco and Emi talking while Emi sat on the step to re-tie her high-top tennis shoes.

"Hey," Marco mumbled. His skinny shoulders were six inches above Emi's when she stood with her head thrust down and forward under the weight of her book bag.

"Hey."

"Your sister really looks pretty this morning."

"Pretty? You need your eyes examined, you geek."

"You're the one who needs an eye examination. She's hot. She's beautiful. I'm in love with her." He gave Emi a big grin, which she returned with an incredulous and sour expression.

She shook her head in disbelief. "Huh. Well then, at least she has one guy in love with her. She's never ever had a single boyfriend, you know."

Jelly took exception to that remark and had to stop herself from saying so, thus giving away the fact she was eavesdropping.

"That's because she's so gorgeous she scares them all away. Every time I look at her, I wish I was eighteen."

Jelly shook her head, and a smile bloomed on her face at Marco's words.

"Eighteen! She'd still be ten years older than you. She's too old now to ever, like, get a serious boyfriend. Anyway, she's probably a lez."

What!

Marco flashed another lopsided grin in Emi's direction. "You look a little bit like her, you know."

"I hate you, Marco Roy Rogers."

"No ya don't Martha Elizabeth Swanson. You're just jealous because I'm in love with your big sister. How'd she ever get a goofy name like Jelly?"

This elicited an evil little giggle from Emi. "I couldn't say Julie Lea when I was little. I called her Jelly, and it stuck. Now everybody calls her that."

Marco seemed amused by Emi's self-satisfied remark.

"She dresses like a cheap hooker," Emi grumbled.

"What do you know about cheap hookers?"

"I go to the movies. I watch TV."

"Yeah, like they know."

Jelly watched as the two of them stepped off the porch and headed down the front walk, turning in the direction of school.

Santa Susana Magnet High School loomed into view at the far end of two long blocks. Marco and Emi waved to a couple of kids. Jelly watched them for half a minute more and headed for her bedroom to look for her gold sandals with the ruby red fake gems. Below her pink broomstick skirt with hot pink hibiscus flowers printed on it, they added just the right touch to her outfit.

She wondered where her flamboyant taste in clothing and accessories had come from. Not Mom, surely. She was the quintessential lady. Aunt Martha? No, Aunt Martha was more like Aunt Bea on the old Mayberry reruns that Emi loved.

She gave herself the once-over in the full-length mirror, flipped up the ends of her hair, smiled with approval, grabbed purse and keys, and headed out. She'd have to figure out some way to be out of the store between eleven and one. Maybe ask Sally?

Jelly was a workaholic who ran her store single handedly until she finally gave herself a break and hired her first employee. She spent months acquiring discarded wardrobes of Hollywood's biggest names for her once-a-year sale at the high-end, gently-used clothing store.

Movie and TV stars soon grew tired of their clothes. They had hundreds of pairs of expensive shoes that had been worn once, if at all. Women in the limelight seldom appeared at a fancy function in the same outfit twice for fear of making the front page of *The National Inquirer.*

Sally Lewis, her best friend, owned the travel agency next door to Big Night Out. Maybe she could come to Jelly's store for a couple of hours and help her new girl. Jelly prayed she'd come to her rescue one more time.

Chapter Two

Big Night Out
Tuesday, 9:05 a.m.

After surveying her store one last time to make sure everything looked good for the sale, Jelly locked up. She walked next door to Unique World, Sally's travel agency. Big Night Out didn't open for another hour.

"Morning, Susan. Is Sally in yet?"

Sally's office manager slid back her chair and looked out her office door with a friendly grin. "Hi, Jelly. She just got here. Go on back, I'll buzz her and let her know you're on the way."

Sally smiled as she listened to Jelly's newest dilemma and agreed to send over an employee to help at BNO for a couple of hours so Jelly could go to Emi's teacher conference.

Jelly jumped up and rounded Sally's desk, where she embraced Sally and kissed the top of her head several times. "Thank you, thank you, and thank you. You saved my life."

"I don't think so, but I may be called on to do so one of these days. Go talk to Susan. I have a flight from Burbank

Airport in less than two hours. Go." She stood and smiled as Jelly's face dissolved into a big, relieved smile.

"Love you, Sal."

"Love you, too."

Jelly turned as she was leaving. "See you at the corner at seven thirty tonight?"

"Count on it. By the time I get back from the state capital, I'll need that long walk. Gotta go." She gave Jelly a quick shove. "Beat it."

Santa Susana High School
Tuesday, 11:10 a.m.

Jelly screeched her lipstick-red Mustang to a stop in the student parking lot, grabbed her purse, and jumped out of the car. She slammed the door, catching the hem of her skirt. The only thing that kept her from falling flat on her face was the strong elastic in the waist. She grabbed at the top of the hood, took a deep breath, and unlocked the door. After re-arranging her clothes, she shook her wavy hair, straightened her shoulders, and headed for the school library.

The large room was deserted except for a tall, skinny guy with a mop of black hair reading the bulletin board. His back was to her. "Oh, I'm, uh..." she stammered as he turned to face her.

Time stopped. Jelly stared at his striking angular face with gray eyes exactly the color of her own. She was unable to speak and thought she might be in the middle of a petit mal seizure, not that she would know. Every book in the library took on a glow of bright color, and the windows gleamed in the mid-morning sun. Sparkling, golden dust motes floated in a shaft of sunlight. The chairs and tables seemed to hover just above the plaid carpeted floor. Jelly had been in this library many times but never realized how beautiful and, well, perfect it was. She forgot about her store, forgot about everything.

Henry Palasczewski stood rooted to the floor, stunned by a vision of the most beautiful, sexy woman he had ever occupied the same room with. Except for her soft gray eyes, she glittered from head to toe, a grown-up woodland fairy with perfect breasts, a slender waist, and shapely ankles. Afraid he might be drooling, he swallowed noisily. His Adam's apple bounced. Every one of her perfect toenails was painted candy apple red, her strawberry blonde hair a shining nimbus surrounding her perfect face. She couldn't possibly be real. Could she?

He shook his head, suddenly conscious of his long arms and big hands. He didn't know what to do with his hands, so he shoved them deep into his pockets.

The vision spoke, "Mr. Pal, uh Pala, Mr. Palashhh—"

Henry croaked, cleared his throat, and tried again. "Ms. Swanson?" The dream creature who stood before him couldn't possibly be Martha's mother.

Jelly cocked her head at Henry's deep baritone. "Yes, I'm, uh, Swanson. Julie Lea Swanson, Mr. Pala—How do you say your name?"

Henry extended his right hand, looked at it, quickly withdrew it, and jammed it back into his pocket. Once he began talking, he couldn't seem to stop himself. "Pol-ah-shevski, but everyone here calls me Henry, or Mr. Henry or, once in a while, Dr. Henry. Because almost nobody can, uh, say Palasczewski." A blush crept up his neck and stopped at his jaw line.

Henry was sure his lungs had collapsed when she twisted her bright red lips. Ms. Swanson had the most kissable lips he'd ever seen. Get a grip, man, he told himself. Henry cleared his throat again in an attempt to speak about the reason for the conference. There was a reason he was sure, but it took a moment for him to get his bearings.

Charmed by his blush, Jelly was sorry when he stopped speaking. His mellow, nearly god-like, Sam Elliott baritone echoed deep in her chest. She wished he'd take those wonderful big hands out of his pockets so she could see them again. "I'm sorry I was late. Emi—Martha—she didn't tell me about this meeting until after breakfast today. Is she in trouble or something?"

Henry shook his head with vigor to emphasize that his student was in no trouble. "No, no trouble. She's a wonderful student. I thought perhaps we should talk about her future."

Jelly wrinkled her nose. "Future? She's only fourteen."

"No, yes, uh, shall we sit?" He gestured to the chairs, then sat after she did. Jelly noticed him clamp his big hands on his knees to still his trembling legs.

Yes, she thought, sit before I fall down. What's wrong with me? She pursed her lips in confusion. He's not even a good dresser. Crocs? Faded jeans with a dress shirt? Crooked tie? Not exactly your Armani fashion model. But there was something...

Without Jelly knowing why, they both suddenly burst into relieved laughter and exchanged broad smiles.

Henry spoke first, "I was, ah, expecting someone...older. You look far too young to be Martha's mother."

"That's because I am too young. I'm her sister, her legal guardian." Jelly extended a be-ringed hand toward Henry and left it sticking out there until he clasped hers. "I'm happy to meet you, Dr. Henry." The warmth of that big hand shot right up to her elbow, then her shoulder. Her own legs jittered.

"Henry, please call me Henry." He didn't let go.

He released her and placed his hand back on his knee. "I'm not sure. They seem clumsy and oversize, too big."

"I like them." *There I go again. Think before you speak, Julie.*

I like everything about him, she thought, especially the way his neck goes red when our eyes meet.

Chapter Three

Big Night Out
Tuesday, 5:00 p.m.

The bell above the shop door had not stopped tinkling all morning and afternoon. The place teemed with delighted customers when Jelly returned earlier from her meeting with the dishy, sexy Henry Pala-whatever. Her inventory dramatically reduced, she was just about to close for the day.

Her new employee had left in a state of near exhaustion when the bell jingled again. Jelly put on her professional smile and looked up to see Henry Pala-whatever. He peered around the store. His eyes lit up when he spotted her.

She hung up the dress she had just placed on a hanger and slid the hangers on the chrome bar back and forth to rearrange them neatly. She needed a moment to get her thoughts together, to calm her racing heart. "Henry? What are you doing here?" Her smile was all Jelly this time.

He walked in her direction, swinging those wonderful long

arms, and then raised his hands in a clumsy gesture. "I forgot to have you sign the permission slip so Martha could go on the field trip to the Ventura County Science Fair tomorrow, Ms. Swanson."

Jelly raised her eyebrows. "Are you sure? I signed the slip and left it with you."

His neck went red. "You did? I didn't see it in the file."

Jelly remembered that she had signed a permission slip. He was looking for an excuse to see her again. That was A-OK with her. It saved *her* the trouble of thinking up something for the same reason. "I'm just closing. Would you like to have a cup of coffee and wait while I finish up?"

His smile lit up the room. She'd nearly swooned when he smiled this morning and had been unable to take her eyes from his mouth while he told her about Emi's plant biology exhibit. He wasn't Greek god handsome, but when you put all his distinct facial features together with his great smile, he was just, well, perfect.

"Sure, I'd love some coffee. Actually, I was, uh, hoping you'd be free for an early dinner. There were some other things I wanted to tell you about Martha's class work. I do have to be back at school by seven for a teacher's meeting, though." He shrugged, put his hands in his pockets, looked around, then immediately pulled them out again. "Nice place."

She felt his eyes follow her as she locked the front door and lifted the big sale poster from the window.

Jelly turned. "Henry, can I ask you something?"

His eyebrows went up. "Sure. Anything."

"Did you make up that story about the permission slip so you could see me again?" She hoped she was right about that and not making a complete fool of herself.

Henry's neck reddened some more, confirming her suspicion. "I did. Yes, sorry. Have I offended you?"

She stood in front of him. "Not a bit. I've been trying all afternoon to think of a reason to see *you* again." Her clear, gray gaze locked onto his.

A relieved whoosh escaped Henry's lungs, his grin huge. "You were? God, that's great!" He threw up his arms, his eyes sparkling with happiness. "Isn't it?"

"Here." She placed the sign in his hands. "Yes, it's great, Henry, and can I ask you a favor? Could you call me Julie?"

"I'll call you anything you like. Julie is a lovely name. It suits you." He held up the sign. "What am I supposed to do with this?"

She laughed. "Oh, sorry, would you put it in the back storeroom and turn off the coffeepot after you pour yourself a cup? It'll take me a few minutes to close out the cash register and get the bank bag ready." She turned, had a thought, then faced him again. "There's a nice little coffee bar across the parking lot. They have sandwiches and salads. Would you like to catch a quick dinner there?"

Henry's big feet barely touched the floor all the way to Julie's storeroom. He wasn't surprised to see that it reflected her appearance and personality: sequined garments sparkled, boas fluttered in cloud-like waves as he passed. Open shelves held dozens of pairs of fancy shoes in gold, platinum, satin, and patent leather, many adorned with flashy fake gems. Some had spike heels that would serve quite well as murder weapons. Another shelf of very expensive-looking lady's boots sat next to an old glass topped display case that had been retired because of a large crack in the glass. The top shelf was jam-packed with all kinds of colorful and flashy costume jewelry and hair clips.

Where was that coffeepot? He could smell it but couldn't see it. He propped the sign next to the old display case and pulled back a curtain in the back wall. A mirrored dressing room. He opened another curtain and found the coffee set-up next to a small refrigerator, microwave, and a stack of foam cups, one filled with throwaway stir sticks. He served himself a cup of coffee, then turned off the pot, poured what was left into the small sink. He dumped the coffee grounds into a waste-basket lined with a plastic grocery bag.

Henry paused to wash out the pot. He wiped down the counter with a wet paper towel. Never would he think of leaving a mess for someone else to clean up.

Jelly's heavenly, sexy voice reached his ears, sending tingles up his back and neck as he turned to the front of the store. "Henry, what are you doing back there? Trying on the shoes?" Her voice tinkled with teasing laughter.

"No! My feet are way too big," he hollered, happy and aroused. No woman had ever jolted him like Julie Swanson. From the moment he met her, he began to think maybe the Cupid myth was true. There was an arrow right through the middle of his heart. No question about it.

Jelly chuckled at Henry's response. "I'm ready, so let's get out of here!" She gave him another big smile when he walked through the door. She picked up the night deposit bag, slung the strap of her beaded suede bag with fringe along the bottom over her shoulder.

He stopped. "Wait a minute." He turned back into the storeroom, dumped the coffee, and threw the cup away.

When he strolled through the door, he had a bright orange ostrich feather boa thrown around his neck. "I love your place, Jel—Julie, so many pretty things to play with." He flipped one end of it in her direction and blushed at his own boldness.

She reached up and tugged the boa off with a slow, sexy slide and dropped it across a clothing rack. "I don't think this suits you." Giving him a little push toward the front door, she added, "Chartreuse is more your color." The warmth of his back lingered on her hand.

They stepped outside and Jelly locked the gold painted front door. "I have to walk over to the bank and drop this bag, okay? Lots of money in here tonight. This was the best sale I've ever had." She took his arm and steered him to the bank branch at the end of the mall.

A small cooling breeze brushed across Henry's face and ruffled his hair, which was good considering he was so aroused at Jelly's bare hand on his arm that sweat beads were forming on his temples. He dare not look at her for fear of uttering something foolish.

The next thing he knew, he was watching her across the table while she ordered a roast beef sandwich with double horse-radish, jalapeno seasoned curly fries, and a large mocha freeze. Henry could see himself as a small kid in a darkened theatre watching a movie that was above the rating his parents would allow him to see.

"Sir?"

"Huh?"

"Are you ready to order?" Pencil in hand, the perky wait-ress cocked her head and widened her eyes in Henry's direction.

"Oh, yes, sure, I'll...have the same."

She put the pencil behind her ear and picked up the menus. "Be right back."

Jelly shook her head and giggled. "Do you even know what you ordered?" Her long, dangly earrings continued to sway like mystical fingers, beckoning him ever closer.

Henry sat straight, told himself to snap out of it. With a serious expression, he answered, "Of course I know what I ordered. I ordered—what did I order, Jel—Julie?"

She crossed her arms, shook her head with a small smirk. "You'll just have to wait and see. I'm not telling." Leaning forward on her elbows she said, "I can see you're having trouble remembering to call me Julie."

He raised his hands. "I'm trying, but I have to tell you, I like Jelly, and it seems to fit. I'll do better, I promise."

She waved a dismissal. "Oh, it doesn't matter. You can call me Jelly like everybody else if I can call you Hank." She winked. "Is it a deal?"

"Hank? You want to call me Hank?"

"What's wrong with Hank?"

He grinned. "Nothing, I love Hank. I always wanted to be called Hank, but nobody ever would."

Her big bracelet jangled when she reached across and tapped his hand. "I'm more than happy to grant your wish, Hank."

Henry was pretty sure that Jelly didn't know what he wished, but *Hank* was a great start.

Their animated conversation continued unabated, half the time with their mouths full, while they practically inhaled the sandwiches and shakes. His eyes watered from the horseradish and she laughed while he pretended it wasn't too hot.

Hank was mesmerized by her expressive hands and amazed that she was interested in hearing all about the science fair; of how he'd been so consumed with plant biology after spending his childhood on the flower farm that he'd majored in science at UC Davis. She'd smiled and nodded when he told her how he'd decided to become a teacher. "I love the magnet school and working with the bright and curious kids, like Martha and Marco."

Jelly interrupted his life story. "She hates that name, you know. She insists everyone call her Emi, as in M.E. She's named after our dad's twin sister. I only call her Martha Elizabeth when I'm mad at her or trying to make a point. She thinks her name is horribly outdated and old fashioned."

Their conversation seemed to go on for hours, but when Hank looked at his watch, it was only six-forty. "Oh, gosh, I've got to go. I can't be late for the teacher's meeting. We're doing the final planning for the bus assignments and equipment transport for the fair. We're pulling out from the school before eight in the morning." He waved the check.

"You have to take it over to the cash register," Jelly said, disappointment in her voice. "I was just getting to know you. Where did the time go?"

18

Chapter Four

Corner of Alamo and Indian Hills Drive
7:30 p.m.

Jelly saw Connie Ramirez and Sally Lewis pace and stretch as they waited for her. They spotted her jogging in their direction along the front of the Indian Hills golf course. She wore a hot pink warm-up suit and neon green sneakers.

Breathless, grinning, and jogging in place, Jelly said, "Am I late?" Her fiery ponytail swung from side to side, brushing her shoulders as she bounced on her sneakers.

Connie ran her hand down the side of her prison-gray sweats. "I look like an inmate. She lights up the place like the Las Vegas strip."

Sally laughed. "They don't need to turn on the streetlamps when Jelly's out after dark, do they?" She cast a look at Connie. "What are we doing hanging around with this kid?" She put both her hands on Jelly's shoulders. "Stop, slow down, and take a breath. You're not late."

Connie laughed when Jelly followed Sally's command to the

letter without losing her happy smile. "What's up Jelly? You look like you just made a killing in the stock market."

"She had a great day at the store. Susan told me that during the two hours she was holding down the fort, the cash register never stopped ringing. There wasn't a minute when there weren't at least three customers in the shop. Right, Jelly?"

"That's part of it. The best sale I ever had. You should have seen the wad of money I put in the night drop. Every single piece I got from that soap opera babe was sold before two o'clock. Some customers didn't even try on things. They were too worried they'd go away empty-handed. Amazing!"

Connie raised her hands and shrugged. "Who fits into that stuff, anyway? The woman must be a size two. I couldn't fit one leg into her jeans, and I only weigh a hundred twenty...five."

Sally and Jelly lowered their chins and raised eyebrows. "Okay, maybe thirty," Connie admitted.

They started up the gentle slope of the sidewalk, golf course on one side and Sycamore trees on the other. It would soon turn into a hard climb. From where they started, it appeared the houses were stacked, one on top of the other, but it was no more than an optical illusion.

Connie grumbled, "Wait till you've had six kids. I weighed a hundred ten when Miguel and I got married. Now look at me."

"I think you look great—for an old lady with six kids, that is." Jelly dodged Connie's smack and jogged ahead of them. "Come on, you laggards! I've got some excitement to work off."

"Should we kill her now or later, Sally?"

"Later. I want to find out what she meant by, 'That's part of it.' As far as I know, all she did today was go to a parent-teacher conference and work at her shop."

Jelly turned around and jogged backward, her grin wider than ever. "I'll tell you, but you won't believe me."

"Why?" Sally and Connie asked at the same time.

"Because I don't believe it myself." She threw her hands in the air and twirled around. "I'm in love!"

"I don't believe you, Julie Lea."

"Who's Julie Lea?" Connie asked Sally.

"Jelly's real name is Julie Lea."

"No kidding?"

Jelly turned and called back over her shoulder, "No kidding, that's my name. I'll tell you the rest when we get up to Maricopa, where it levels off. Come on!"

Sally and Connie grumbled and picked up their pace to keep even with Jelly, who was a good ten years younger than either of them.

Where the street leveled off, Jelly did a little bouncy, side-to-side jog while she waited on the corner for them to catch up.

Sally stopped and bent, gasping for breath, her hands on her knees.

Connie followed on her heels, barely able to breathe. "Let's just kill her now."

"Turn right at the corner, Jelly. We're walking the rest of the way. If you start running again, I'll hold you down while Connie slaps some sense into you."

"That's okay, I'm dying to tell you." She burst into song, "I'm in love, I'm in love, I'm in love, I'm in love, with a wonderful guy!" She finished with her arms wide and twirled in circles, her head tilted back.

Connie frowned. "What's that from?"

"South Pacific, I think." Sally reached out and grabbed Jelly's arm and pulled her toward them. "When did this happen?"

"Today."

"When did you meet him?"

"Today."

Connie raised her hand. "Stop! Just wait a minute. You met

a guy today, and you fell in love with him today? What happened to your last boyfriend?"

"You mean the one I had for two days about four years ago?"

"Yeah, him." Connie furrowed her brow and stared at Sally. "*Dios mio,* was that her last boyfriend?"

Jelly spread her arms and looked around. "Just shut up a minute, you guys. Look west, past the windmill on top of the hill. In about one minute, we're going to have one of the best sunsets of the year."

Jelly stepped forward and put one arm on Sally's shoulder, the other on Connie's. They watched quietly, and true to her word, the sun slipped down past the hills on the western end of the valley, and everything suddenly went golden. Flowers on the Indian Hawthorn along the parkway glowed dark pink when just moments before they were pale, almost white.

Sally sighed. "Wow, I wish Charlie could see this."

Connie reached across Jelly's back and put her hand on Sally's waist, pulling her tighter into the group. "He *can* see this and more, *amiga.*"

Jelly realized she'd jolted her friend into a memory of her husband who died a year earlier. She rested her head against Sally's. "I'm sorry, Sal."

"That's okay, hon." She gave Jelly a squeeze. "Now, I want to know how it's possible you met a man today and fell in love today."

"Yeah," Connie added. "You always said you didn't have time for a man."

"I did say that." Her expression dreamy, she added, "That was before today. I am so, so crazy about him."

"Him, who?" Sally and Connie asked.

"Henry Pola...Pala—whatever. I can't even say his name and I'm madly in love with him. Do you believe it?"

"Nuh-uh," Connie shook her head.

Sally gave Jelly a nudge. "No, we don't believe it. So give with the details. Where did you meet this guy, and when, for heaven's sake? You worked all day, except for the time you were at the high school." Sally's eyes opened wide. "Did you meet somebody at the high school?"

A serene smile, a big sigh, then Jelly said, "Uh huh, Emi's science teacher."

Connie jerked her head, astonished. "Henry Palasczewski?"

"You know him?"

"Yes, Paco's in his class." She shook her head. "You've got to be kidding me!"

Sally grabbed Connie's arm. "Hold on a minute. Can I get in on this? Who is Henry Palasczewski?"

"How come both of you can say his name and I can't?" Jelly asked with a pout.

Connie turned to Sally. "Henry Palasczewski is a tall, skinny science teacher with a brain like Einstein. The only thing he's interested in is looking at flower seeds under a microscope. His long arms, long legs, and big hands would qualify him for a spot on the Lakers if he could play basketball." She snorted. "He looks about as graceful as a gazelle on a trampoline."

Jelly bounced up and down with excitement. "Oh, oh, oh I have to tell you! He has the neatest thing in his classroom. On the wall right beside the door, where you come in, you know? He has a plastic-covered poster with human handprints from a newborn baby all the way up to adult. The first and last prints are his! He covered it with plastic because the kids like to put their hands on the poster and find where they fit. It's so totally cool. I put my hand over his and my fingertips only come up to his first knuckle!"

Connie wiggled her eyebrows and pursed her lips. "You know what they say about big hands with long fingers, don't you?" She gave Jelly a little poke. "No wonder she's in lust—I mean love."

Sally smirked at Connie's racy remark and Jelly's sudden blush. "Connie, do you ever think about anything but sex?"

"Sure I do, I've got six sons and a husband to feed and cleanup after." A lascivious wink transformed her expression. "But I thought about sex enough to get six *hijos*." She smiled and nodded. "There would have been more, but after Paco was born, I wouldn't come home with Miguel. I told him I'd stay with my *mamacita* until he got himself neutered."

Jelly and Sally burst into laughter and shook their heads at Connie's guileless remarks. If you ever wanted the truth, just ask Connie.

"Do you think I'm attracted to him because he has big hands? His voice is uuhhh." Comically wobbling her knees, she went on, "He's got a great smile and he's very funny in an awkward, kind of innocent way. He's a gentleman, too." Hands on her hips sent the message loud and clear: Jelly was definitely ready to do battle in Henry's defense. "I call him Hank. He said he always wanted to be called Hank."

Connie and Sally exchanged smiles.

They picked up the pace of the walk as they turned onto Alamo. The rest of the way was steep downhill and would end a block from Sally's and Connie's homes.

"It's okay to be sexually attracted to the man, Jelly," Sally said in a soothing voice. "You're a grown woman, you're young and attractive, and you've never allowed yourself time to develop any kind of lasting relationship. I think you should explore this and see where it goes."

"I'm really nervous about it. He's so nice, and I don't want to screw it up. I'm pretty sure he's attracted to me. At least he sends the right signals. I get all tingly around him, especially— you know." She stopped and put out her arms to stop their response. "Oh, oh, remember that old Godfather movie where they told Al Pacino that he'd been lightning bolted, or something, when he first saw that Sicilian girl in the village? Well, that's what it was like for me when I met Hank."

Connie shook her head gravely and put her hand on Jelly's shoulder. "You need to get laid, *chica*. And don't let anybody tell you it's not all it's cracked up to be. It is."

Sally winced at Jelly's mortified expression. "She's right, you know. Boy, do I miss sex, having a man around all the time." A soulful sigh escaped her lips.

Connie put her hand on Sally's cheek. "There are dozens of men out there who'd like to jump your bones. Miguel's partner, for one."

Sally squeezed Connie's wrist. "I'm too picky. It's too soon. I know Miguel's the exception, but I really don't think I have the backbone to be involved with a police detective. I'd be worried sick all the time."

"Yeah, well, Bob's been married twice, so he's no bargain."

Jelly spoke quietly, "Connie's right. I do need to get laid." The heat of a blush warmed her cheeks. "I have, uh, a confession. You both have to swear to keep this a secret, cause if you don't, I'll have to kill you."

Eyes wide, Connie and Sally nodded in agreement and anticipation.

"I'm, uh, well, you're not going to believe me anyway, so I might as well just say it." She took a breath and cleared her throat. "I'm a virgin."

"No!"

"Are you serious? You can't be serious!"

"See, I said you wouldn't believe me." Jelly's face crumpled and tears threatened.

Sally reached into her pocket for a tissue and pushed it into Jelly's hand. "Oh, honey, it's okay. We'd never think of telling anyone. Would we, Connie?"

"My little Mexican lips are sealed. They could waterboard

me and I'd never tell." She put her arm around Jelly, and she lowered her head to Connie's shoulder.

"I feel like a freak. I'm twenty-eight years old. I'm practically an old maid!"

Sally and Connie petted and soothed Jelly while she sighed on Connie's shoulder. A neighbor's car slowed as it was about to pass by. He lowered the window and called out, "Hi! Everything okay?"

"Hey, John," Sally said and waved. "Everything's under control. Thanks for stopping, though."

He waved back, smiled, raised the window, and continued down the hill. He turned on the same street that led to Sally's house.

"Oh, great," Jelly groaned. "The first thing he's going to do is go home and tell Mary. I'm doomed. I never should have told you!"

Connie straightened up and grasped Jelly's arms. "He doesn't know anything, and we promised we wouldn't tell. Didn't we?"

"Yes, we promised. Your secret is safe with us. I admit it was a shock, Jelly, because you always look like a luscious sexpot. You had me fooled."

"Do you suppose Hank thinks I'm just some kind of easy lay, some sexpert who'll jump in bed with him if he crooks his finger?"

Hands on hips, Connie said a firm, "No!"

"Absolutely not, no," Sally insisted.

"How can you be so sure?"

Connie jumped in. "We can't be sure, but I've known him as Paco's teacher for over two years. Like you said, he's a gentleman. I've never heard anything but praise from other parents and students. Miguel thinks he's an okay guy, and it's hard to fool a police detective. All right?"

"Wait a minute. I think I know who this guy is." Sally tilted

26

her head and Jelly could practically see the gears going around in her brain. "Do you remember Carol Gratner who used to work for me a while back?"

"No, I don't know her."

"Yeah," Connie said. "The drama queen. Why?"

"I think she was dating him for a short time. Yes, I'm sure it was him. There couldn't be two Henry Palasczewskis in this town." She thought for a minute. "Carol said he—"

Jelly's eyes went wide. "He what?"

Sally looked as if she wanted to bite her tongue off. "Oh, nothing, it wasn't important, and anyway," she blathered on, trying to cover her tracks, "Carol was famous for embroidering stories. I never took much she said seriously. Forget it."

"What did she say? You have to tell me," Jelly implored her, near panic.

Connie put her hand on Jelly's arm. "No, Carol was a big liar. Sally had to let her go for that. Didn't you?" She turned to Sally and put on a stern *shut the heck up* face.

"Tell me."

"No, I—"

Connie reached for her cell phone. "Hold on a minute." She hit a couple of keys. "Miguel? Hi, sugar-pie, it's Consuelo. The gals and I have a tequila emergency. Could you fix dinner for the boys when they get home from football? I put several pizzas in the freezer." She nodded. "You will? That's great; we'll be a couple of hours. What? No, nobody's driving. We'll be right next-door at Sally's. *Si, enamorado.*" She snapped the phone shut. "Margaritas, here we come."

"Great idea, Connie, I've got all the fixin's. I even have a couple of ripe avocados on my tree and chips and salsa. Come on, Jelly, we're going to sit down, drink margaritas, and solve all your problems. Right, Connie?"

Staring glumly into her margarita glass, Jelly took a lick of salt from the rim and a generous swallow. The effect of the tequila tingled in her thighs within seconds. I'm a cheap date, she thought. One drink and I'm your slave. While Connie mashed up avocados for her unbelievably delicious, no-recipe guacamole, Jelly nibbled at the edge of a tortilla chip. Sally turned on the blender to complete the second batch of "good for what ails us."

Maybe it was the alcohol, maybe the inviting warmth of Sally's kitchen, or just the fact that she had friends, real friends, who knew? Jelly perked up. The blender went silent. "Do you think I'm a freak? The way I dress and all?"

Connie stopped mashing. "Don't be silly, *chica*. You're some lucky guy's precious treasure. You're smart, sexy, successful, and a flashy dresser with the cutest *tuchis* in town. Quit feeling sorry for yourself." She added chopped tomatoes and some other delicious ingredients to finish off the guacamole.

Sally grabbed her arm as she picked up the bowl. "Wait. Let me have a bite of that before you take it out of my reach." She grabbed a chip, scooped up a generous dollop, and put it in her mouth. "Mmm-mm-mm, Connie, you have the touch. This is to die for." She reached up to the top shelf of the cupboard and brought down a lovely cut-crystal souvenir pitcher, with the inaugural date and logo of Crystal Cruises' first ship etched on one side. She poured the margaritas into it from the blender cup.

Jelly looked around and leaned sideways to see the stairs going to the bedrooms. "Where's Jenna tonight?"

"Don't worry, she'll be home late. They're in the last week of rehearsals for the senior play. Your secret is safe." She carried the pitcher to the table and topped off their glasses.

Connie raised her glass. "It's in the vault." She put her fingers to her lips, twisted the imaginary key, and tucked it in her bra.

Jelly laughed. "It's not actually so bad now that I said it out loud. I'm a virgin, so what? But when the right guy makes the right move—stand back!"

That remark nearly brought the house down. Glasses clinked and the light from the hanging fixture above the table glinted off the salt encrusted glasses and their laughing faces.

Sally dabbed her lips with a paper napkin. "Details, Jelly. We need details. Start with when you walked into Henry Pala-what-ever's presence until you met us on the corner."

Connie nodded in agreement and mumbled through a mouthful of chips and salsa, "Yesh." She took a swallow of margarita and added, "Leave out nothing. No detail is too small or insignificant. We're experienced women. We can help you."

Tequila-induced grins painted three faces. Jelly had their complete attention as she related her love-at-first-sight story. At the conclusion, she pressed her lips together and sighed. "Maybe I just think I'm in love. You can't fall in love that fast. I have to think about this."

***

Sally's Kitchen
10:30 p.m.

"I can walk. Really, I'm fine," Jelly said, balancing on knees, which were none too steady.

"You are not walking home alone at this hour, drunk as a skunk," Connie stated. "I'm calling Miguel. He'll drive you."

"No, I—who's that?" She turned her head as the back door opened.

"Hey, Mommy, are you having a party?" Jenna walked to the table and hugged Sally. She surveyed the remains of the chips and the empty margarita glasses. "Maybe I should have got home earlier." She picked up the lone whole chip and wiped her finger around the inside edge of the guacamole bowl. "Connie made this. I can always tell."

"You're just in time, sweetie. Could you drive Jelly home? We didn't make any allowance for a designated driver." She tightened her arm around her daughter's hips.

"This is silly, I can walk."

"Barely." Connie dismissed Jelly's declaration with a huff.

Jenna chuckled. "It's okay. I have some papers to give to Emi, if she's still up. Do you have a jacket? It's getting cold out."

"No. It's only three blocks. Anyway, I'm so full of tequila I won't even feel it." Jelly giggled.

"Back in a few, Mommy. Do you need a ride home, too, Mrs. Ramirez?"

Connie smacked Jenna's fanny as she passed her. "Don't forget, I'm married to a cop. I can have you arrested for disrespecting your elders."

When the back door closed and Jelly was seated in Jenna's car, she wondered what it was that Sally's former employee had said about Henry.

Chapter Five

"We can't leave yet. I have a couple of students who aren't here." Henry ran his finger down the clipboard as he stood next to the school bus, double-checking the names. "Joe Morgan?" he shouted through the open door of the bus. "Does anybody know if Joe's coming?"

A student called out, "Here he comes, Mr. Henry. That's his mom's car."

Henry churned his arm in a hurry-up motion as Joe stepped out of the car and trotted in his direction. "Get onboard, Joe. The only student who isn't here is Jeremy, your partner."

"He's got a sore throat. His mom won't let him come."

"Oh, boy, can you manage the exhibit on your own?"

"I think so, Mr. Henry, as long as you can cover for me if I need to take a quick break."

Henry clapped him on the back. "Not a problem. Okay, we can take off." He stepped inside and took a seat behind the bus driver. Turning toward the back, he shouted, "Try and keep the noise down, okay?" He stood. "Make sure you have everything you need. Once we're on the way, you're out of luck if you forgot anything." He scanned the crowd. "Okay, here we go." He tapped the driver on the shoulder and took his seat.

He overheard Emi and Marco in the row behind him. Papers and notes covered their laps. Their entry in the science fair was a comprehensive display with drawings, graphs, photos of microscopic images, and many soil samples. They took the soil samples from several agricultural locations in Ventura County and examined them for any and all chemical and biological dissimilarities, and the differences, if any, from the same crops grown in different locations.

Marco said, "If we win a ribbon today, it's going to be a big plus for me when I apply for scholarships. I hope we packed up everything so it doesn't get damaged on the ride up to the fairgrounds."

"You're such a worry wart, Marco. Jelly gave me so much bubble wrap and Styrofoam it will take forever to unpack and set up. And why worry about scholarships now? We're only in tenth grade."

Henry smiled, remembering his similar conversation with Jelly about Emi's future.

"You gotta start right now," Marco replied, "to get into the university you want. Anyway, I don't have rich parents like you."

"I don't have any parents at all! It's just Jelly and me, and she's not rich. All the flashy clothes and jewelry she wears come from her fancy second-hand shop. She says she's a walking billboard for the store and has to dress that way." A snort followed her remark. "She dresses that way because she likes to. I think her biggest budget item is makeup. She's got no class. She wouldn't even recognize class."

"I don't get why you always talk so bad about your sister.

And anyway, I think she looks great, and so do most of the guys."

Henry eavesdropped with interest. He counted himself among "most of the guys."

"Which guys?"

"You know, kids from school and church."

"Church? Father Ignatius gets red in the face every time he looks at her."

"Yeah, guess what? He's a guy."

"He is not! He's a priest. They're—"

"They're what?"

She mumbled, "Immune to sex and stuff."

Marco chuckled. "You are such a kid. Grow up, Emi."

"Does your mom know you have a Playboy under your mattress?"

Henry suppressed a grin.

"Are you gonna tell her?"

"I hate you!" Emi clamped her lips shut, crossed her arms, and stared out the bus window.

Santa Susana School Science Lab
Wednesday, 4:30 p.m.

Henry and Emi finished packing up the last of the science fair exhibits for storage. Marco had just left, excited to get home to show off their blue ribbon.

"Thanks for helping me finish up here, Martha." He handed Emi a bottle of spring water from the small refrigerator and took one for himself.

He wrestled with himself as to whether or not he should ask questions for answers he was anxious to know. With a shrug, he decided to tread lightly, to come at her from an angle, so as to allay her suspicions.

"Your—sis—Je—Ms. Swanson said that you preferred to be called Emi. Is that right, Martha? I have no problem with addressing you as Emi, if you prefer it."

Emi blushed and ducked her head behind the box she was taping. "Yeah, I like Emi better."

"Okay, then, Emi it is." Now, where did he go from here? "I, ah, dropped by Ms. Swanson's store last night with your permission slip. I forgot to have her sign it when she came here yesterday."

"Yeah, she told me that when she got home from her run all shit-faced." Her cheeks flared up like a furnace when she realized she'd used profanity in front of her most favorite teacher. "I mean, I mean—" She choked on her words as they trailed off.

"She was drunk? Ms. Swanson was drunk?" Henry hardly knew what to say next. "I certainly hope that's not a frequent occurrence."

Emi shook her head vigorously. "No! No, in fact, it's the first time ever! We don't even have anything in the house stronger than Dr. Pepper!"

Emi's revelation was not making any sense to him. "What possibly could have been the reason, do you think?" He hoped it had nothing to do with his visit and their quick dinner together. That made no sense either.

"I dunno." A big shrug, shoulders almost touching her ears. "She and her two girlfriends take walks almost every night after dinner. I think something sad happened to one of them so they went to Mrs. Lewis' house and made margaritas. Mrs. Lewis' daughter, you know the one I'm tutoring in math? She drove Jelly home. It's only about six blocks on the other side of the golf course. It was after ten when they got there. I was starting to worry."

"I should think so." Henry was perplexed that Jelly would leave Emi home alone until so late.

"Yeah, she's usually back by eight-thirty. She doesn't have a boyfriend, so I was pretty sure she wasn't on a date. Anyway, she never stays out late when the next day is a work or school day."

Bells clanged in Henry's brain. "She doesn't have a boyfriend?" Heat rose in his belly, his stomach jittered.

Emi did one of her dismissive, eye-rolling snorts. "Who would be her boyfriend? She had a boyfriend when I was twelve, for about ten minutes. Men don't like her. The way she dresses and stuff."

How wrong could a kid be? Jelly's unique dazzling style was great in Henry's book. Beautiful and sexy, why wouldn't men like her? Maybe through the eyes of an adolescent girl, it would seem that way. But she didn't have a boyfriend! Fantastic!

"She's a lesbian."

The thundering sound Henry heard was his heart slamming into the floor. Unable to breathe or form words, he stood mute as a mannequin.

Emi wagged her head from one side to the other. "I don't know for *sure* she is, but she's getting really old, and the only men ever around our house are repair guys and the UPS driver." She picked up her backpack and hauled it over her shoulder. "I gotta go help Jelly at the store. She's doing inventory after closing today and then we're going to Chi Chi's. She never pays me, just bribes me with Italian food."

"Is your ride here?"

"I'm walking."

Henry's head shot up. "Walking? Emi, that's at least five miles from here!"

"No big deal. I walk to the store all the time. The busses in this town suck."

He saw an opportunity, an unexpected gift. "Leave your backpack. It's too much to carry all that way."

She approached the door. "I got a lot of homework when we get home. I need my books."

"This is nonsense. I'll take you in my truck. I'm going that way, it's no trouble." He took his car keys out of his pocket and turned off the lights in the classroom. "Come on."

Her eyebrows rose with skepticism. She stared at him. "Does the school allow that?"

He turned to lock the lab door. "Allow what?"

"Students to ride in teachers' cars?"

"I don't know why not. Billy Embry rides to school every day with one of our teachers."

Emi looked at Henry as if he'd lost his senses. "Mr. Henry, Billy's mom is a teacher here. Duh."

"Oh, yes, of course." He blushed. "I knew that. Come on." Undeterred, he hoisted her backpack off her shoulder onto his. Why students today carried such heavy bags was a mystery. They had lockers and could leave books they didn't need at school. It couldn't be good for their bone development. Perhaps he would do a study on it, might discover something interesting.

He led the way to the parking lot. "It's at most a ten-minute trip, and I'd like to see your sister's face when you show her that blue ribbon." The truth was he'd like to see her sister's face period.

Big Night Out
5:10 p.m.

Sally and Susan leaned against the counter while Jelly finished balancing the cash drawer. Jelly had pestered Sally earlier that day about what Carol said about Henry until Sally threw up her hands and told her to just get her out of her office so she could get some work done.

"She said his apartment looks like a model that nobody lives in. He's extremely neat, listens to classical music, has a place for everything and cleaned up the kitchen the minute they finished eating. What really convinced her—he never tried to get her into bed, and he drives up to Oxnard to visit his parents every weekend. Ergo, she concluded he was gay."

"I don't believe that." Jelly chewed her bottom lip.

"Me either." Susan looked around the shop. "Wow, Jelly, looks like you really had a big day yesterday. This place looks skinny."

Jelly flashed a weak smile. "Yes, inventory shouldn't take more than an hour at most tonight. Emi's going to help me with it, then we'll catch dinner at Chi Chi's."

"Jelly, Susan and I came over to talk to you about Henry. You should know why we don't believe for a minute what Carol said about him."

Susan shook her head. "Not for a minute. Not at all. If you knew Carol, you would know why. She dramatizes everything and is an accomplished liar. That's why Sally finally let her go."

"That's right. You should have seen her when she came to work 'feeling unwell.' She did her makeup to look like death warmed over and dragged herself around the office like she had one foot in the grave. Finally, either Susan or I would suggest she go home. It was laughable, but not fair to the rest of the staff." Susan leaned closer to Jelly. "She thought she was the sexiest thing on two feet. She just didn't know what to think when Henry didn't try to get her into bed after a few dates."

With a hopeless shrug and sigh, Jelly said, "I don't know. I don't want him to be gay, but if he is, he is. What do I know about men, anyway? Gay men are supposed to be very neat, right? When he got himself a cup of coffee last night while he was waiting for me, he cleaned up the whole kitchen." Jelly had a fleeting thought about any hidden meaning in the boa he'd flung around his neck. "I guess we could be friends, at least."

Susan opened her hands. "Why don't you just ask him?"

"Oh my God, I couldn't do that! He might be in the closet. He's a teacher."

"I don't see what being a teacher—" Sally stopped abruptly when the bell on the shop door jingled, and Henry and Emi entered.

Jelly lit up with a fiery pink blush to her cheeks. "Hank. Emi. What—?"

Except that her hair wasn't pink and sticking straight up, Emi screwed her face around until she was the image of a mad troll. "Hank?" She glared at Jelly and turned to see Mr. Henry's foolish grin directed at her sister. "Hank?"

After some throat clearing, Henry said, "Hank, yes, that's my nickname." He continued the sappy grin in Jelly's direction.

Ever skeptical, Emi asked, "When did you tell her your nickname was Hank?"

"The same time she told me you preferred Emi rather than Martha."

Susan took Sally's arm. "We have to go. See you Monday, Jelly." When they passed Henry and Emi she added, "Have a nice weekend, everybody."

Trying to mask her wariness and disappointment, Jelly put on a happy face. "Hank, what are you doing here? Did I forget to sign something again?"

"Mr. Henry drove me in his pickup truck. He said it was too far to walk with my big book bag, and he wanted to see your face when you saw this." She pulled a ruffled blue ribbon out of her jacket pocket and thrust it toward her sister.

Jelly's eyebrows went up. "What's this?" She held the ribbon and studied the gold lettering. "First place?" Her smile was almost too big for her face. "You won first place?" Jelly hugged Emi and kissed her. "That's great!"

Emi pulled away and rubbed Jelly's lipstick off her cheek.

"It's no big deal." She shoved her hands in her pockets and slouched as if to make herself smaller or even disappear.

Hank stood straight and shook his head vigorously. "Oh, no, I disagree. It's a very big deal." He faced Jelly. "It's a very big deal, Jel—ah, Ms. Swanson. Marco and Emi won first place in the science fair over fifty-two other entries!" His chest puffed out with pride for his students. "It's a very big deal indeed, Emi." His smile wattage increased.

"Yeah, well." She masked the fact that she was proud of her accomplishment by adding, "Are we going to do inventory, or what? I don't want to hang around this place all night."

Hank exchanged a restrained smile with Jelly. "I have an idea. Why don't I help with the inventory? It'll go faster. Then, please, let me treat both of you to dinner. We should celebrate, don't you think?" He cast a hopeful look in Jelly's direction.

"I think that's a fine idea, Hank. Don't you, Emi? I've already got a start on the inventory and the whole job shouldn't take more than an hour."

Emi dropped her backpack in the corner and threw her jacket on top. "Okay, whatever."

Chi Chi's Restaurant
7:30 p.m.

Even though Chi Chi's was a neighborhood family restaurant, the contemporary Italianate hanging fixtures over each table dimmed the lights to a pleasant glow. Hank, clumsy and fumble-fingered, nearly tipped over his water. He knocked the empty breadbasket on the floor attempting to right his glass.

Relieved when neither Jelly nor Emi seemed to notice, he took a breath. "What looks good tonight?" The menu trembled a bit in his hands.

Jelly looked up and smiled. "Tonight's specials are on the back page, Hank. Now, turn the menu around so it's right side up." Emi looked up and giggled, adding to his discomfort.

"So it is." He quickly turned the menu around and chuckled. "I guess I'm still excited over Emi's success today." Unable to concentrate on the daily specials, he asked, "Would you like a glass of wine, ladies?"

"Sure, sounds great," Jelly answered. "I'll have the house red."

Emi jerked her head up from the menu. "Huh?"

"Oh, of course I didn't mean you, Emi, sorry, how about a Coke?"

"I hate Coke. I'll have Mountain Dew."

Jelly grimaced. "Ugh!" and put her finger in her mouth to mime gagging.

Emi bumped her with her elbow. "You don't have to drink it! Anyway, I'd go easy on the wine. After last night I don't think you handle alcohol very well." She cast a satisfied glance in Henry's direction.

Mortified, Jelly's face flared with a hot blush. "How can you say such a thing in front of your teacher?"

Emi pushed out her lips in a pout and scowled. "He already knows."

Jelly turned to Henry. "What do you know, Hank?"

He aimed a disapproving glance in Emi's direction and shifted uncomfortably in his seat. "Nothing. It's not important; you needn't be embarrassed about it, Ms. Swanson."

"Why do call her Ms. Swanson when she calls you Hank? I bet you call her Jelly when I'm not around."

Hank swallowed.

Jelly put her menu down and took Emi's away from her. "You can't hide behind this. You seem to know an awful lot, Martha Elizabeth. Just what do you think you know?"

Emi squirmed. "I know you like each other." She glared at her sister, then Mr. Henry.

Hank put down his menu and leaned forward on his elbows. "Emi, do you have a problem with that? Your sister and I barely know each other. I'd like to be friends with Julie. I'm friends with several of the parents of my students." He tried to appear cool and collected but felt his predictable neck blush flare.

"She's not my parent!"

"You know what I mean, Martha. You're a very intelligent young lady. If something is troubling you, you should discuss it with your sister or me. Not lash out with anger."

Jelly put her arm around her shoulders and Emi shrank down in her seat. "We can't read your mind, Emi. What's wrong?"

"Nothing, except if we don't order dinner soon, I'll be doing homework till after midnight. I don't want to talk about it anymore."

Henry signaled the waiter. "That's a good idea. Let's order dinner. Shall we share a pizza and some spaghetti?"

Jelly smiled. "I'm in. How about you, Emi?"

Following a dramatic sigh, she answered, "Yeah, okay."

After dinner, they walked out to the parking lot together. Henry climbed into his pickup and Jelly and Emi into the red Mustang. They waved goodbye as they went in different directions at the exit. Jelly wondered if gay men drove pickup trucks.

Chapter Six

Jelly's Kitchen
Friday, 7:30 a.m.

The newspaper shook in Jelly's hand, and she cried out, "Oh, my God, Daddy!" She folded the paper when she heard Emi's footsteps and tried to shove it down between the counter and refrigerator.

"What about Daddy?" Emi asked, shocked at her sister's stricken expression. "Jelly? What about Daddy?"

Jelly slumped down in a chair and buried her face in her hands. Determined not to cry, the tears came all the same. Her shoulders shook from the violence of her sudden gasping sobs.

"What? Tell me!" Emi shook Jelly's shoulder as her own tears threatened. "Jelly, please. You're scaring me."

Reaching out to retrieve the newspaper, Jelly said, "I have to go. I have to drive up to Folsom. Daddy's been hurt. Why didn't they call me?" She unfolded the paper and smoothed it with her hands. "I had to read it in the Simi Valley Star. Damn them!"

Emi sat across from Jelly. She reached out and snatched the newspaper. Her face crumpled as she scanned the large headline and the photograph of their father. Horrified, she stammered, "They put—they put it on the front page!" Angrily, she shoved the paper off the table. "I can't go to school today."

"No, no, of course, you'll come with me. We'll leave right away. It takes over six hours to drive up there." Jelly turned off the stove and coffee maker and reached up to retrieve a box of cereal from the cupboard. She placed it on the table and put bowls and spoons out. "We'll only have time to eat a bowl of cereal. We can stop along the way and get something else later."

A horrified look on her face, Emi said, "I'm not going."

"I know you're not going to school. You'll come with me."

"No!"

"Emi?"

Emi stood abruptly, knocking over her chair. "I'm not going up there! I hate him! I hope he dies!"

Reflexively, Jelly threw back her arm as if to slap Emi's face but stopped herself in time. Emi jumped back so hard she fell to the floor, landing sharply on her bottom. Stunned by her action, Jelly dropped to her knees and reached out. "Oh, baby, I'm sorry. I don't know why I did that."

Emi pushed Jelly's arms away and shoved her viciously. "I hate you too! Get away from me." She placed her hands over her face and dissolved into a heap. Her sobs broke Jelly's heart.

Jelly reached out and gently touched Emi's head. "Emi, I'm so sorry. I didn't mean it, honey. I didn't. I would never hit you."

Flailing arms and legs, Emi viciously kicked out, hitting Jelly in the shoulder, and knocking her back against the refrigerator. Stunned and speechless, Jelly gasped. When she caught her breath, she yelled, "What's wrong with you! He's our father, he's been hurt!"

Emi fell to her side and rolled into a tight ball, her arms clutching her head as she moaned, "I don't care, I don't care. My life is ruined."

"Your life is ruined?" Anger filled Jelly to bursting. "You selfish, spoiled brat!" She stood and pounded her fists on the kitchen counter, then whirled around. "How can your life be ruined? How? Answer me!"

The only answer Jelly heard was muffled gasping and choking sobs. Emi rolled to her knees and turned her tear-stained face to her sister. "Everybody will know about him," she whispered. "All my friends will know."

Her knees weak, Jelly held the edge of the sink then slowly slid to the floor, her legs splayed out in front of her like a rag doll. Their father was critically injured, and all Emi cared about was that her friends would know he was in prison. Until this moment, Jelly had never admitted to herself that Emi felt no love for their father. But why should she? Barely two when he went to prison, she never knew him or their mother. Jelly was the only family she had, except for the rarely seen Aunt Martha who lived in Sacramento to be close to Folsom prison.

Jelly had visited Daddy faithfully twice a year for the past twelve years. She brought Emi with her once and he asked her not to bring her again. He told Jelly not to come anymore, either, but she wouldn't hear of it. She knew the truth of why he was in there. He might be in prison, but he was her father, and she wouldn't deny him. She counted the days to the end of his thirty-year sentence, when he'd come home, and they'd be a family again. Now that might never happen.

Emi crawled to her and laid her head in Jelly's lap. Jelly stroked her hair. The only sound was the ticking of the big-eyed, grinning black cat wall clock as the tail swung back and forth, tick, tick, tick.

Emi shuddered. "I'm sorry, Jelly. I didn't mean it."

Continuing to stroke her hair, Jelly said, "It's okay, honey. I understand. I really do. Don't cry any more, it's okay."

Emi reached for her hand. "What are we going to do?"

Delano, California
Friday, 10:30 a.m.

Jelly gripped the steering wheel of her Mustang as she sped north on Route 99. A red warning light on the dash told her she had to stop for gas soon, and she needed a bathroom and a cup of coffee. In her rush to leave, she'd forgotten to eat or throw any snacks in her bag.

She dropped Emi off at Big Night Out with strict instructions to go to Sally when the travel agency opened. Emi could skip school and stay with Sally and Jenna until she got back from Folsom. Connie had offered to keep Emi, but Jelly knew she already had a full house with her six boys. Sally assured her Emi could use Erin's room, because she was away at UCSB, or double up with Jenna. She urged Jelly to get going and not worry about her little sister.

Jelly made good time, but the knot in her stomach would not ease up. She called Folsom, but they wouldn't give her any information other than the prisoner, George Swanson, was in critical but stable condition in the prison hospital.

The story in the Star had no details of Daddy's injuries or how they occurred. Instead, they went into great detail about the murder trial. More than ten years after the sentencing, few people remembered or knew the hideous details of the Swanson family tragedy. Now it was front-page news again.

Golden Arches loomed ahead, surrounded with several tall gas station signs. Jelly pulled off the highway, gassed up the car, used the bathroom at McDonald's, picked up a to-go lunch, and returned to her car. With luck, she'd be at Folsom prison by four o'clock.

Jelly's friends wouldn't recognize her this morning. She dressed with the California Prison System's requirements for visitor attire. She wore black slacks without a belt and a gray turtleneck sweater. Her bra had no under wire and her shoes were plain black flats. No jewelry adorned her ears, neck, or hands. No makeup other than pale lipstick. Her hair lay restrained at the back of her head in a French braid.

She'd made the egregious mistake of arriving in jeans for one visit and was turned away. Blue denim, chambray, or anything resembling inmate attire was strictly forbidden. Her visit had been cancelled, and she'd had to wait more than a month to return. She'd submitted a new visitor questionnaire and sweated it out until it was approved.

Jelly had a special purse she carried when she visited, a small retro, clear plastic envelope style bag. All the contents were visible, and it helped expedite the search procedures. It held her I.D., thirty-one-dollar bills, the maximum amount and denomination allowed. A brush, cloth handkerchief, and her car key, and nothing else, not even chewing gum.

She made sure she had no metal on her body that might trigger the metal detectors. A cheap Timex watch with a leather wristband could be quickly removed and placed in her see-through bag.

As she approached Sacramento, her cell phone rang. She grabbed it from the passenger seat. "Hold on. I'm driving. I'll pull off at the next off ramp." A quick glance told her the caller was Aunt Martha. A half mile ahead, she exited the freeway, drove to a nearby gas station, and parked in the rear.

"Hello? Aunt Martha?"

"Yes, Julie dear, where are you? I haven't talked to you since early this morning. I was hoping to catch you before you got all the way to Folsom."

Heart in her throat, Jelly asked, "What happened? Did something happen to Daddy?"

"There's been no change, but we can't go in today. I've been in touch with Warden Hill and he's arranging an emergency pass for tomorrow morning. You should come here, to my house."

"I'm on my way."

Big Night Out
Friday, 9:15 a.m.

The bell over the golden door jingled as Sally entered the store. She smiled at the young woman arranging garments on one of the rear racks. "Good morning, Jeannie. I came to pick up Emi."

Jeannie turned in her direction. "She went to school. She left this note." Jeannie reached across the counter and handed Sally the note, written on the back of a sales slip.

Jeannie and Mrs. Lewis, I decided to go to school. I'll walk to your house after my last class and do my homework on the back patio until Jenna gets home. I hope that's okay with you. Emi.

Sally looked up and smiled. "She decided to go to school after all. That's good. I think that's best. Thanks, Jeannie. Call Susan if you get swamped or have any problems while Jelly's away. We're right next door."

Jeannie returned Sally's smile. "Thanks, I appreciate it. Maybe Susan can come over after lunch and give me a few minutes to run and get some take-out."

"Not a problem. I'll ask her soon as I get back to the agency." She waved and left the shop.

Big Night Out
Friday, 4:30 p.m.

Henry parked his truck in front of Jelly's store. He'd read the morning paper and debated with himself whether or not he should presume to say anything about it to her. He was concerned about Emi missing her classes and decided to go in and talk to Jelly to make sure everything was okay with them.

When he saw Jeannie behind the counter, he stopped just inside the door. "Oh, sorry if I startled you, I'm looking for Julie and Emi." He saw her hurriedly shove the bank drop bag under a hat. He raised his hands. "It's okay, I'm Emi's teacher. I was worried when she didn't come to school today."

"She didn't come to school? But she left a note for me saying she did. Oh, gosh. I'd better tell Mrs. Lewis. I hope she hasn't left the agency yet. I don't know her home phone number."

Henry pointed to his right. "Is that the lady from the travel office next door?"

Jeannie rounded the counter. "Yes, I think she goes home about now."

"No, you stay here and finish up. I'll go find her."

Entering the travel agency, Henry walked to the reception desk, identified himself, and asked for Sally. The young man at the desk rang Sally's office, then asked Henry to follow him down the hallway.

Sally stood and walked to Henry with her hand extended. "Mr. Palasczewski?" She was clearly puzzled. "How can I help you?"

He shook her hand. "I was concerned because Emi didn't come to school today. I read the morning paper and thought it might have something to do with her father. The clerk in Jelly's shop said Emi left a note saying she was on her way to school this morning."

Sally's face paled. "Oh, dear, maybe she changed her mind and went directly to my house instead. Emi said she'd go there after school and wait for my daughter. She's staying with us while Jelly's up, uh, north." Sally reached for her purse and keys. "I'd better go home and see if she's there. She doesn't have a key, and Jenna won't be home from school yet."

He took a step forward. "May I follow you? I'd like to make sure she's all right."

Sally hesitated for a split second. "Of course." She walked to her desk and reached for one of her business cards. "I'll put my address and cell number on the back in case we get separated. I'm in Indian Hills Ranch, not far from Jelly's house, on the other side of the golf course."

She pointed toward the back door. "I'm parked out back. I drive a green Honda Accord. I'll wait for you at the back lot exit onto First Street."

In less than ten minutes, Sally was unlocking her front door and beckoning Henry to follow. Once they were inside, she headed toward the back of the house to the French doors leading to the outside patio. She opened the door. Emi was nowhere to be seen.

Henry pointed to the table where a piece of notebook paper fluttered around the edges of a small citronella candleholder. "That looks like a note." In two long strides, he reached the table and picked up the paper.

"What does it say?"

He handed the paper to Sally. "She said she's at the Ramirez house and would be back here after dinner. Where is that?"

Sally loosed a relieved sigh. "Oh, thank heaven, she's right next door. Kids—they make us old before our time." She chuckled and turned to her door. "Let's go inside. I'll give Connie a call, just to make sure everything's okay."

Henry sat on a barstool by the kitchen counter while Sally opened the refrigerator and reached for a pitcher of iced tea. She set two glasses on the counter. "This is cold, but I can add some ice if you like. Sugar?"

He shook his head. "No, this is fine, thanks. I don't know how parents manage. I worry about the kids, and they aren't even mine. What will I do when I have my own?"

Sally raised her glass and smiled. "Worry even more, would be my guess." She shook her head slowly. "We do manage somehow, though."

"I was shocked when I read this morning's paper. I had no idea Julie and Martha had been through such an ordeal. It's beyond my imagination."

Sally nodded. "Yes, it was truly awful. First, their mother was brutally murdered. Then George took matters into his own hands when the lawyer talked about getting her killer off with an insanity plea. He calmly waited for the prisoner to arrive for his arraignment at the rear of the courthouse with a crowd of police and reporters. He stepped forward and stabbed the man to death in front of dozens of people."

"My God!"

She shook her head at the gruesome memory, so long buried. "Charlie and I had barely moved into this house when it happened. Both our girls were toddlers. We didn't know the Swanson family. They lived just over there on the other side of the golf course. Jelly and Emi stayed in the house." She tilted her head. "Jelly's mother was a concert violinist. She was on hiatus for a couple of years to take care of Emi, who was only about two. She gave violin lessons in her home, mostly to children, but she had some adult students also."

"Who was the man who killed her? Why did he do it?"

Sally shrugged and shook her head. "He was a local plumber, doing some work in the house, installing a new faucet or something. He'd been there several times doing various repairs. It was completely out of the blue." Sally shuddered and took a swallow of tea. Henry waited for her to continue. "He raped her and beat her and stabbed her to death. God, it makes me sick to think about it."

"It makes me sick to hear about it."

"It gets worse. Jelly came home from school and heard Emi crying from the back bedroom. She called out to her mother and when she got no answer, she headed for her baby sister, then nearly tripped over her mother's body."

"Jesus!"

Sally gritted her teeth and placed her head in her hand.

"Julie must have been about Emi's age when it happened," Henry speculated. "God, I admire how upbeat and intelligent she is. I can't imagine a child overcoming such an ordeal."

"Perhaps I should call Connie and make sure Emi's okay."

Chapter Seven

Sacramento, Aunt Martha's Home
Friday, 5:00 p.m.

Jelly slumped in the overstuffed chair in Martha's living room and rested her head on the back cushion. "I'm exhausted."

"I can imagine. That's an awful drive. You made record time." She pulled a crocheted afghan from the sofa and draped it over Jelly's knees. "It's really cooling off early today. Relax and I'll make hot cocoa. That should perk you up some."

Martha headed for the kitchen. Jelly watched her dad's twin sister with deep affection. She had never married, and Jelly suspected it had something to do with the many months she spent in Simi Valley after her brother's trial. Jelly remembered Martha had a man in her life at the time, but the memory of him was fuzzy. Martha never spoke of him.

Jelly must have dozed off. When she opened her eyes, a mug of cocoa sat on the side table. The marshmallows on top were mostly melted. Martha sat across the room, her crochet hook flying through the yarn creating a baby blanket. The Catholic home for unwed pregnant girls, where Martha worked, never had enough of them. Most girls gave up their babies for adoption, a few would not.

Martha must have sensed Jelly's gaze. She looked up and smiled. "If that's gone cold, I'll make you another one. I didn't want to wake you."

"This is fine, just right. I won't burn my tongue like I usually do on your cocoa." She held the mug in two hands and sniffed the warm fragrance before she took a soothing sip. "How was Daddy before the—the last time you saw him?"

"Oh, you know George. He was calm like he usually is, but I could tell he felt some excitement at the prospect of getting parole granted after all this time." She dropped her work and raised her hands. "Don't get your hopes up, Julie Lea. The reason he never mentioned it in his letters to you was because he didn't want to raise your hopes again." Martha's eyes, the same gray as Jelly's, sparkled with impending tears. "Dear George," she whispered through trembling lips.

Jelly went to her aunt and embraced her. That was all it took for both of them to break down. Jelly knelt with her head in Martha's lap, resting her cheek on the unfinished baby blanket. Martha reached for a box of tissues, pulled some out, took a few, and placed a couple next to Jelly's hand.

After a while, Jelly sat back on the floor cross-legged and blew her nose. "Do you know what happened to Daddy? Did Warden Hill tell you anything?"

"Yes, he called me soon after George was admitted to the infirmary. I'd just been up there a few days earlier to testify at his parole hearing." She removed the handwork from her lap and placed it in a basket next to her chair. "He's very badly hurt, Julie. I won't soften it for you. He has severe head injuries and lost a lot of blood before the guard found him on the floor of the library."

Jelly moaned and placed her face in her hands. "Oh, Daddy,

Daddy." Tears started anew. She grabbed a wad of tissues and pressed them to her eyes. "How—how did it happen? Who did it?"

"Another inmate. He was sitting at a table calmly reading when the guard walked in. He hasn't said a word. They don't know why it happened. The man's been placed in isolation, and they've been questioning him, but so far, nothing."

Jelly wiped her eyes. "What about his parole? Do you think he was going to get it?"

Martha sighed. "It's very hard to tell when you're sitting before that stone-faced panel. The fact that George killed Jessie's murderer at the courthouse before the trial weighs very heavily against him getting early parole. He's resigned to serving his full sentence, you know. That's why he pled guilty."

Wiping once more at endless tears, Jelly sighed. "He always said he did wrong to take the law into his own hands and was willing to pay the penalty, but Aunt Martha, we've all paid the penalty. We haven't been sitting in that horrible prison, but we've paid and paid."

"Yes."

Jelly turned her tear-stained face to her aunt. "Emi thinks she hates him. She told me this morning that she wanted him to die." Her shoulders shook with sobs, her words were barely audible. "I almost slapped her face. God, I'm so ashamed."

Martha leaned forward and rested her hands on Jelly's shoulders. "Don't beat yourself up over it, dear. You've carried the heaviest burden of all of us these past years. George hates himself for what he's put us through, you most of all. Blinded by grief and rage, he didn't consider the consequences to his daughters."

Jelly nodded. "Emi's only fourteen. She doesn't know Daddy. All she cares about is what others think of her."

"You must try and forgive her for that, Julie. It goes with being an adolescent. Some of the pregnant girls I counsel every day are only thirteen or fourteen. Their values are barely formed and when they are...formed badly."

Sitting straight, a hard look on her face, Jelly said, "I was fourteen when Mama was murdered! I never had the luxury of being a spoiled, self-centered brat!"

"That's true. You were slapped in the face by reality, Julie. You chose to accept responsibility for Emi and grew up very fast. Deprived of the years that should have been fun and carefree, you—" The ringing of Jelly's phone cut off the rest of what Martha had to say.

"Hello? Hank? What are you—?" She stood and paced. Throwing her head back, she groaned with disbelief and frustration. "Have you called the police, her friends? What's the number where I can reach you? I'll call you back at Sally's number in a few minutes. Yes."

Martha turned Jelly to face her, her eyes wide with concern. "What's happened?"

"Emi's gone."

Chapter Eight

Highway 99 South
Saturday, 9:00 a.m.

Martha insisted Jelly stay the night and leave the next morning, telling her it was foolish to turn around and make the long drive back home without sleep. She reluctantly agreed and started back at five a.m. Now, after four hours on the road, she needed breakfast and coffee if she was going to be in good shape when she got home.

Connie Ramirez' husband, Miguel, a detective for LAPD, put things in motion. He contacted the local police chief, a personal friend, and they ordered an Amber Alert. Simi Valley police and county sheriff officers were conducting an investigation.

Henry Palasczewski got permission from the high school to form a group of students and teachers who were combing the hills on the north and east side of Simi Valley. The school set up a phone chain to contact all students who may have information that would help the police and the searchers. All Jelly could do now was go home and wait.

Why did Emi run? Where would she go? Jelly's drive seemed endless.

Jelly's House
Saturday, Noon

Henry stood on the front lawn, surrounded by about a dozen students. They studied maps and arranged backpacks with food and water, as well as cell phones and first aid supplies, including snakebite kits. The hills around Simi Valley were rife with rattlesnakes. "You must remain together in groups of three. Fan out and walk as much as possible in a straight line, so that you sweep the area you're assigned to search."

"How long should we stay out?" a student asked.

Henry pointed to the area on the map the group of three was to search. "Try and cover as much of this area as you can by five o'clock but check back by phone every thirty minutes. If we find her before you finish your section, you'll want to know to come in."

He looked up and indicated a white mini-van. "Here's your transportation to the assembly point. You'll start and end at the Flanagan Drive trailhead. The same parent will come back for you with the same vehicle." He patted a student on the shoulder as they walked to the van. "Make sure you have the number programmed into your phones. Okay? Ready? Good luck then. Let's find her."

Teams of other students had fanned out around town distributing flyers with Emi's picture, placing them in windows of every store, and tacking them to telephone poles and community bulletin boards.

Jelly pulled her car into the driveway and parked next to a police car. Her heart pounded at the sight of all the people, neighbors, strangers, and the TV truck. A bank of lights next to a reporter blinded her. Her head screamed for answers. She spotted Hank, felt a rush of relief, and waved.

He trotted across the lawn to her and tentatively opened his arms. The mixture of relief and concern on his face destroyed her resolve. She reached for him. He wrapped his arms around her and lowered his head to whisper, "We're going to find her, Julie. She's going to be all right."

The sympathy and concern in his voice brought a sudden flood of tears. He tightened his embrace while she sobbed into the front of his blue cotton shirt, saturating the fabric. She felt comfortable and natural in his arms. The sensation felt familiar even though they'd never touched, except when they walked from her shop to the bank and coffee bar three days ago.

His big hand on her back guided her toward the front of the house. "Come to the porch and rest while I get the other groups on their way."

She stopped. "No, I have to do something, Hank. I can't just sit and wait."

Sally and Connie looked in her direction when they heard her voice. They stood on the porch next to a female police officer. "Jelly, let Henry do his job. Come, the officer has some questions," Sally called out as she reached for her hand. "Jelly, I'm so sorry. I didn't think to look for Emi earlier. She left a note in your shop saying she was going to school. All of us thought she was at school."

Sally's daughter, Jenna, hugged Jelly. "I'm sure she's not far away. They'll find her. Emi's so smart. She's fine, I'm sure of it."

Jelly pasted a brave but unconvincing smile on her face. "She's probably trying to scare me. We had a nasty argument yesterday morning before I left. Let's see what the officer needs, okay?"

Henry had turned when he heard Jelly's Mustang pull up. He did a double take when she stepped out of her car. For an instant, he didn't recognize her. No makeup, no jewelry, dressed in gray and black, her glorious hair tamed into a tight braid. What surprised him the most was how beautiful she was whether decked out "Jelly style" or conservatively dressed. Her natural beauty couldn't be denied either way.

He was completely taken with her, almost in love with her. What Emi said about her sexual preference was wrong, that's all there was to it, a fanciful notion of a teenager, nothing more. He didn't understand why men weren't flocking on her doorstep, why she didn't have a steady boyfriend, or according to Emi, never had. There was so much more he wanted and needed to know about Jelly. After the immediate crisis was taken care of, he intended to concentrate on discovering the real Julie Lea Swanson.

He left with the last group of students to comb a section of the hills north of the valley, above the golf course. The county sheriff contacted all the landowners to get permission for the search. The foreman of a horse ranch volunteered to go out with a mounted patrol.

Poor Emi, Henry thought. On top of the front-page story revealing the incident of the attack on George Swanson at Folsom Prison, her disappearance was headline news in today's Simi Valley Star. The story had also been picked up by the Los Angeles Times, local and national TV, and radio. If Emi ran away because she was afraid the story of her father would draw unwanted attention, she did exactly the wrong thing. The media were rife with wild speculation.

Jelly's House
8:00 p.m.

Jelly pulled away from Sally. "I can't stand around doing nothing!" She tore the rubber band off her hair and yanked at her braid, pulling it apart. Alive with static electricity, her hair swirled about her head.

Distraught, she went down on her knees and pounded the floor. "What if she's hurt? What if she needs my help? I can't stay here!" She stumbled to her feet and turned as if to leave.

Hank grabbed her arm. "Stop it!" Her knees gave way, and he pulled her against his chest. His hand caressed her back. "Listen to me," he murmured. "Listen to me, Julie. There is nothing more we can do today. At dawn we'll start all over again."

He placed his hands on her cheeks and tilted her head. More than anything, he wanted to kiss her, but now was not the time. Instead, he said, "You need to be calm. You need to eat and rest if you're going out with us in the morning. Are you listening to me?"

She slumped forward against him and brought her arms up from her sides and encircled his waist. "Stay with me, Hank. I need you to stay with me."

He hugged her hard. "They couldn't drag me out of here with the Budweiser Clydesdales. I'm here as long as you want me."

The room went silent. Hank looked to Sally, Jenna, Connie, and Miguel and gave a quick tilt of his head in the direction of the front door.

Miguel cleared his throat. "He's right, sugar. It's time for us to go home. The chief will call me if Emi turns up, but in the meantime we all need rest if we're going to be any good tomorrow." He motioned to Sally and tugged Connie toward the door.

Sally and Connie touched Jelly lightly as they passed. "We'll be back in the morning. We'll find her tomorrow," Sally said.

By the front door, Connie turned. "I left some sandwiches in the fridge. Eat and then go to sleep, okay?"

"We'll do that," Henry said. "See you in the morning."

Jelly forced a weak smile. "Thank you, everybody." She clung tightly to Hank and gave no sign she would let go anytime soon.

In spite of the crisis hanging over them, holding her in his arms was comfortable, natural. He accepted that fact. He didn't try to analyze his feelings.

Several moments passed, their breathing the only sound in the quiet living room. He led her to the kitchen, pulled out a chair, and gently urged her to sit.

He smoothed down her disordered hair. "I'm going to put out Connie's sandwiches. We both need to eat. Okay?"

Leaning back into his hand she said, "Yes, you're right, we need to eat then rest, but first I have to call my aunt to see if she was able to get in to see Daddy."

He took her kitchen phone off the base and handed it to her. "While you're calling, I'll heat some water for tea."

She hesitated. "Hank, do you mind if I go into the living room to speak to her privately?"

"No, of course not, go. I'll have everything ready when you finish." He reached out for her hand and pulled her to her feet. "I'll be right here if you need anything."

She squeezed his hand in response, looked at him with sad gray eyes, and carried the phone into the living room.

Hope, fear, sadness—a range of emotion swamped him as his eyes followed her. He did his best to ignore the snatches of conversation coming from the living room while he filled the teapot with water, set it on the stove, and turned on the burner. Even though he could make little meaning of Jelly's side of the conversation, he sensed the pain and tension in her voice.

Where did they go from here? He replayed in his mind all that had happened in the past twenty-four hours. He must not take advantage of Jelly's distress or assume anything other than her need for a friend to lean on. They knew little about each other, even though his initial strong attraction was present and undeniable. He hoped Jelly felt the same, but now was not the time to press forward on that score. Now she needed a friend, and he would be that friend.

Jelly came back into the kitchen, the phone at her ear.

"I'm doing okay, Aunt Martha. I have a friend here who's fixing dinner for us. No, I won't be alone tonight. I'll eat and get some sleep. Everyone will be back in the morning to look for her. Yes, I'll let you know as soon as I have any more information. Call me tomorrow after Daddy has surgery. Love you, too. Good night."

The last sentences of her conversation finished, she sat at the kitchen table across from Hank.

He filled her cup from the teapot. "How's your father?"

"He's been transferred to UC Davis Trauma Center." She cleared her throat. "For a procedure to drain a large hematoma on his brain."

"That's a good hospital, Julie." He passed her a paper napkin. "Do they know the full extent of his injuries yet?"

She took a sip of the hot tea before answering his question. "Aunt Martha visited very briefly and had a chance to speak to the doctor who took care of him at the Folsom infirmary before they transferred him to the university hospital. Daddy should recover from the other injuries without complications. It's his head injury they're worried about."

Jelly sensed Hank's concern was real, and it warmed her. She had a sincere friend, and she knew in her heart he was dependable. If he were gay—well then, he would be one of her best friends all the same. Was she selfish thinking about romance and love when her sister was missing, and her father so seriously injured? Hank was such a great guy, she hoped.

They both jumped when somebody knocked, then pounded on the front door. Hank pushed back his chair and headed for the living room with Jelly nearly running him over him on her way to the door. *Oh please, let this be good news.*

Hank threw open the door to see Marco, standing on the porch, dirty and disheveled, his agitation palpable. "Mr. Henry, Mr. Henry, I—oh, Ms. Swanson—" His face reddened, and he seemed unable to continue. He swallowed and his Adam's apple bounced in his neck.

Hank reached out and took Marco by the arm and pulled him into the room. "Take a breath and calm down, Marco. What is it?"

Jelly put a firm hand on his bony shoulder. "Has Emi been hurt? Did the police find her? What, Marco, what?"

He gasped, "I think I know where she might be."

Chapter Nine

Simi Valley Police Station
Saturday, 9:00 p.m.

Jelly, Henry, and Marco rushed into the lobby and stopped in front of the desk sergeant. He was on the phone but looked up and signaled he'd be a minute. Jelly paced and wrung her hands.

Finally, the officer hung up. He recognized Henry and Marco because they'd been part of the morning's events. "What's happened, folks? Has the young lady turned up?"

Hank leaned onto the counter. "No, but my student here thinks he may know where she could have gone."

The sergeant stepped away from his chair. "Stay right here, and I'll alert the officer in charge." He walked through an unmarked door and disappeared. In seconds, he opened a side door into the lobby and beckoned them to follow. "Officer Mills will talk to you. I'll take you to her."

They followed him, the room abuzz with phone conversations, officers hunched over computer keyboards, and some conducting personal interviews, to a desk near the center.

"Have a seat. She's with the captain. She'll be right out." The sergeant hauled an extra chair from another desk for Marco and left them.

They sat in silent tension. Henry reached over and placed a hand on her jittering knee. Jelly acknowledged his gesture with a smile and turned to Marco. "Thank you for coming, Marco. I really appreciate all you've done."

Jelly's hand brushed his cheek, and he went scarlet with a hot blush. He ducked his chin into his chest and squeezed his eyes shut. Sympathy for his embarrassment made Jelly happy and sad at the same time. Her heart felt too big for her chest.

"Marco, I apologize for being rude to you in the past. There was no excuse for it. I'm really sorry." She touched his skinny shoulder and marveled at how frail he seemed.

He glanced at her and quickly looked away, struggling for words. "It's, uh, I, uh, don't, it's okay, Ms. Swanson," whooshed from his mouth like a deflating balloon.

Unable to stop herself, Jelly leaned over and gave him a quick hug. "I'm glad you're Emi's friend."

Officer Mills approached them from the rear of the large room. She was the same officer who interviewed them this morning at Jelly's house. A file with Emi's photo attached to the inside front cover lay open on her desk. "What have you got for me?"

Henry indicated Marco. "My student, Marco Rogers, thinks he has an idea where Martha would have gone. Tell her what you told us, Marco."

The teenager squirmed uncomfortably in his seat and looked at the officer. "Once, when Emi and I went hiking, we started on the Hummingbird Trail. We were looking for some rocky soil specimens for our plant biology assignment and we kinda went where we weren't supposed to go."

The officer leaned forward and wiggled her fingers, urging him to continue. "Come on, give me something."

"Yeah, we, uh, kept hiking until we came to the security gate at the Big Sky Movie Ranch." He stopped, his eyes flicked from one person to the other, and he leaned forward nervously, hands clasped tightly between his knees.

Henry reached across Jelly and tapped him on the shoulder. "Just tell her, Marco. You trespassed, you didn't rob a bank."

The officer suppressed a smile and cocked her head to the side. "We'll deal with your felonious behavior later, Mr. Rogers. Tell me what you did and where you think Martha may have gone."

Marco related how he and Emi entered the movie ranch. Because they didn't see anyone around, they kept going farther into the property. After about an hour, they stopped and sat under an ancient oak tree that they were sure they'd seen in the movies. They ate their snacks and shared a bottle of water. It was barely mid-day so they decided to explore more.

Coming over a rise, they were surprised to find the Old West Movie Town. It was partly burned out, but most of the building fronts were intact. They walked down the dusty main street and pretended to be outlaw gunslingers, pointing their fingers and shooting at imaginary townsfolk. Startled when they heard approaching voices and the sound of horses, they ducked down a small alley and hid behind a fake storefront.

The horsemen rode down the main street, stopped not far from where Marco and Emi were hiding, dropped the horses' reins over a rail and walked into one of the buildings. He and Emi hunkered down in the shadows and stayed quiet, scared of getting caught.

Marco was sure it wasn't more than half an hour, but it seemed like an eternity before the men came out, re-mounted, and continued through town and disappeared over a rise. He and Emi waited a few more minutes than crept from their hiding place and ran across the street to the building the men entered. The door wasn't locked. Once inside the dim interior, they could see the room was set up as a storage area for lighting and electrical equipment. There was a desk in the corner with filing cabinets and a telephone.

The phone rang, scaring the daylights out of them. In a panic, they ran from the building, back across the dusty street and into the livery stable. The clean interior looked like a real working stable, with new water hoses attached to faucets in front of each stall. A ladder led to a hayloft above. After scampering up the ladder, they sat against a pile of hay. Giggling with relief, they waited to see if the men would return.

By mid-afternoon, they decided to leave because the hills were too treacherous to navigate in the dark, and they didn't want their parents to know where they'd been all day. The two-hour hike back to the trailhead exhausted them, and they still had a couple of miles of neighborhoods before they got home.

The officer pinned Marco with a serious stare. "What makes you think she would go there?"

"Because when we were on our way back, she said if a person had food and stuff, they could hide out there for a while without being found." He drew up his shoulders in a shrug and raised his hands. "I didn't even remember that until after we finished the search this evening and I was on my way home."

Officer Mills thought for a minute, then asked Jelly, "What do you think? Would she go there?"

Shaking her head, a look of faint hope on her face, Jelly said, "It sounds like something she'd say. I don't know. I hope that's where she is."

Hank spoke up. "Could we go there now, or are there guards or caretakers who might be willing to take a look?"

"I'll give the ranch manager a call, but it's likely we'll have to wait till morning. Sit tight. I need to talk to the captain."

Several anxious minutes later, Officer Mills returned with the police captain, who said, "I've just made a few phone calls. It's not safe to go in there at night. Much of the terrain is treacherous and there're several thousand head of free-range cattle on the property. The ranch is about ten thousand acres, and they're not sure where the cattle are located. A helicopter search would be out of the question."

"But—"

He shook his head. "I understand, Ms. Swanson. We've contacted a private cattle rancher, and he offered to get a horse patrol out at dawn. If she's there, we'll know early tomorrow morning. They'll have the gates unlocked for us in case we need to get emergency vehicles inside."

Jelly's head swam with fear when she heard the words, "emergency vehicles." She gasped audibly.

Hank spoke up. "Will *we* be able to get in there in the morning?"

"I can't promise that. The owner of the movie ranch might not want to accept the responsibility of unauthorized vehicle entry. If you'd like, you can come here at six tomorrow morning and follow one of our patrol cars to the gate."

Jelly slumped with relief. "Oh, thank you. Yes. We'll be here early." She grabbed Marco's and Hank's hands with a hopeful squeeze. "All three of us."

Chapter Ten

Simi Valley Police Station
Sunday, 5:30 a.m.

Fuzzy headed with worry and lack of sleep, Jelly and Hank pulled into the nearly deserted parking lot of the police station. Hank painfully unfolded himself from Jelly's car. He had a crick in his neck and his lower back ached from sleeping on the couch in her living room, which was about two feet short of being comfortable.

She'd tried to convince him to take her bed, or Emi's bed, but he refused, and now he was paying for it. So much for the noble gesture. Jelly needed sleep more than he did, but when he saw the strain in her face over that quick cup of coffee they drank just before they left, he could tell she had a bad night.

He smiled to see that she'd put on dangly earrings along with lipstick and mascara in a muted attempt to get some of the *old* Jelly back. He loved her for that.

In the outer lobby of the police station, a uniformed officer met them. "If you folks would like to follow my car, I'll lead you to the ranch entrance gate. The guard will open up for us. We can drive most of the way to the movie set from there."

An ambulance passed them as they approached the gate off Old Santa Susana Pass Road. Jelly stiffened in her seat, stark fear on her face. "Oh my God, oh my God," she moaned, near panic.

Hank put a big hand on her shoulder. "It might only be a precaution, Julie. Let's try and be calm and not worry before we have to." He squeezed her gently, his own heart pounding with trepidation. He knew he must be strong for her sake.

The officer in the car they were following pulled over to allow the ambulance through the gate ahead of them. Jelly stopped behind the police car and lowered her window as the officer got out of his vehicle and approached them.

"What happened? Did they find her? Is she hurt?" Breathless words, tinged with panic, tumbled from Jelly's mouth.

"The wranglers found her, ma'am. She's injured, but they don't think it's serious. The ambulance was called as a precaution. Keep behind me and we'll be there in less than ten minutes. Okay?"

Jelly and Hank each expelled a big breath of relief. Jelly nodded to the officer. "Okay. Yes. I'll follow you. But hurry please."

He tapped the top of her car. "It's dirt roads from here, ma'am. We'll need to proceed at a safe pace." He stepped back from the car door. "Follow me."

The officer returned to his vehicle. Hank was acutely aware of the sound of his boots on the ground, the squeak of his leather gun belt, and the bobbing of the nightstick swinging from his waist.

Jelly shook as a quick tremble coursed through her body.

Hank leaned close to her. "Are you all right? Do you want me to drive from here?"

Her brave smile was feeble, but reassuring. "No. Thanks, Hank. They found her. I'm fine to drive." She briefly leaned her cheek on his hand and glanced in her rearview mirror when she heard a car approaching. "Oh, look who's behind us!"

Connie and Miguel Ramirez waved when Jelly ducked her head out the driver's side window and Hank turned in his seat.

Jelly pulled ahead as the officer motioned them to follow him to the gate. He paused to speak briefly to the guard and pointed back, two fingers raised, apparently indicating the cars following behind should be allowed to pass through.

The trip to the old west movie town took less time than Hank expected. When the police car came to a stop, Jelly slammed on her brakes and leapt from the car, running toward the ambulance parked outside the livery stable. Hank, Connie, and Miguel followed close behind.

Skidding to a stop when she saw the back doors of the ambulance open and the EMTs pulling out a stretcher, Jelly put her hands to her face. Fearful tears spilled down her cheeks. Hank's arm was around her shoulder, and she turned into his chest. Her knees collapsed, and he held her tight.

Connie stopped to comfort Jelly as Miguel's long strides took him ahead and inside the building. In a moment, he looked out and nodded. "Come on, Jelly. Emi's okay. Come in and see." Connie reached out and pushed tendrils of hair behind Jelly's ears and wiped at the tears on her cheeks.

On a shaky breath, Jelly said, "Yes, she's okay. Let's go."

Lights blazed inside the stable. Large banks of movie lighting lit every corner. The emergency workers knelt next to Emi's small frame, talking to her, fastening a stiff cervical collar around her neck. Her muffled sobs nearly broke Jelly's heart.

Running to her side, she called out, "Emi, my baby. I'm here." She knelt down near Emi's head and gave a beseeching look to the man who was preparing to place a splint on one of her legs.

"What happened? Is she okay? Is her leg broken? Why is this thing on her neck?"

Emi reached out and grabbed her hand. "I'm sorry, Jelly. I didn't mean to—" Sobs wracked her body, and she cried out in pain when the splint was applied. "Ow! It hurts. It hurts."

Jelly squeezed her hand. "It's okay, honey. They don't want to hurt you. But you need to be moved out of here. Hold on tight to me."

Emi looked up to see Hank, Connie, and Miguel hovering over her. She seemed comforted to see familiar faces, but blushed with embarrassment, quickly looking away. Fluttering her fingers, she sighed, "Hi, everybody." Her lips quivered. "I'm sorry." She tried and failed at putting on a brave smile.

A chorus of protests went up at her apology.

"Okay, folks," the police officer said. "Let's back out of the way and let them get her on the stretcher. You can follow them to the hospital."

Clutching Emi's hand, Jelly said, "May I go in the ambulance with her?"

"Sure thing," an EMT said. "Let us get her inside and secured, then you can climb in." A man on each side, they rolled the stretcher the few yards to the back of the ambulance, Jelly jogging close behind.

She turned to her friends. "I'll go with her. I'll see you at the hospital, okay?"

Just as the doors were closing on the ambulance, Hank shouted, "Wait!" He ran up and grabbed one of the doors. "I need your car keys."

"Oh, right." She dug deep into the pocket of her jeans and handed them to him. "Meet me at the hospital?"

He nodded and waved. "You bet."

The waiting area of the emergency room seemed quiet for a weekend morning. A couple sets of parents held crying babies, doing their best to comfort one with a croupy cough while the other tearful infant tugged on its tiny pink ear.

Jelly and Hank held hands as they waited outside the examining room. Her heart took a bounce when she studied her hand lost in his. She remembered holding hands with Daddy when she was small, her child's hand completely invisible inside one of his big mitts, as he called them. No wonder she loved Hank's hands.

Emi was in X-ray. They watched for her return. Miguel and Connie left for home and asked Jelly to call them once the extent of Emi's injury was determined. Connie offered to bring dinner to Jelly's house later, but she thanked Connie and gently refused her gesture.

Hank squeezed her hand. "Look, here comes Dr. Thompson. He got here fast." Hank strode toward the entrance to meet the pediatrician. After a brief greeting, they joined Jelly.

Thompson's smile comforted her. "The attending physician called me. Emi has a closed fracture of the left tibia, but her growth plates are still open, so I expect she'll heal very nicely." He leaned down and placed a hand on Jelly's cheek. "You look as if you need a doctor, Julie."

She stood and gave him a quick hug. "She's my sister, not my child. I'm a basket case."

The doctor returned her hug, stood back smiling, and squeezed her upper arms gently. "You may be her sister, but you're the only mother she knows, Julie."

"Thanks for coming so fast and on a Sunday morning. Emi will feel much better when she sees you."

Jelly explained to Hank that Dr. Thompson had been their family pediatrician since she herself was a baby. He was almost a member of their family.

Dr. Thompson chuckled. "I'm a de-facto member of many Simi families. It isn't because I'm such an outstanding doctor—I was the only game in town twenty-five years ago."

She patted Hank's arm. "Pay no attention to him. He's a wonderful doctor and we wouldn't know what to do without him." She cocked her head in Dr. Thompson's direction. "So, now what?"

They sat and the doctor said he called in a local orthopedic specialist to take over Emi's initial treatment, and he would consult with him on her follow-up care. So far, the case was routine. They were placing her leg in a cast to completely immobilize the knee and ankle joint. She could move about as necessary and put some weight on her leg with help. She'd be able to navigate on her own and return to school. After a while, they'd put her in a more comfortable walking cast.

"Kids are resilient." He patted Jelly's shoulder. "I'll go see what's happening."

Hank reached for her hand. "Let's take a walk, get some fresh air. Soon as they bring her out, I'll hop over to Eggs 'N Things and pick up some take-out breakfast. You need to eat."

Jelly smiled, a big, relieved smile with more than a hint of affection. "You mean we, don't you?"

Chapter Eleven

Jelly's House
Sunday, 2:00 p.m.

Whispering so she wouldn't wake Emi, Jelly leaned close to Hank. "Please don't take this wrong, Hank, and don't think for a minute that I'm not grateful for all your help, but I feel it would be best if Emi and I were alone for a while."

"Of course, you're right. I'll get going. You could use some sleep yourself." He stood, careful not to scrape the chair against the floor. "Call me if you need me for anything, Julie. Anything." She quickly squeezed his hand, and he tiptoed to the back door and let himself out, ignoring the urge to go back inside and kiss her goodbye. A real kiss that she wouldn't mistake as mere friendship.

He didn't want to leave her but realized there was nothing more he could do for now. He never wanted to leave her. Deep in his gut, he felt *she was the one.* For some time he'd been immersed in his job and research, pushing thoughts of a private life onto the back burner, not even looking for anyone, then Julie walked into the school library. Now wonderful possibilities dominated his thoughts.

He started his truck and drove slowly in the direction of his condo. When he reached Alamo, he took a right instead and headed east. The family farm in Oxnard was where he needed to be. He'd spend an hour or so helping at the roadside flower stand, then go to the house and mooch a good Sunday meal. Several of his sisters and brothers would be there with their kids and spouses. It was exactly the right place for him this Sunday afternoon.

Jelly missed Hank within minutes of his departure, but she needed to mend her relationship with Emi more than she needed to develop her budding friendship with a caring gay man —*if* he was gay. She hoped it wasn't true. How could it be? Hank was the first man in memory that stirred those deep yearnings she ignored for so long. If he *was* gay, well, life had played a dirty trick on her. It wouldn't be the first time.

Too exhausted to think, she crept into her bedroom, slipped out of her shoes, and slumped onto the duvet fully clothed, too tired to pull up the quilted throw draped over the footboard. Sleep came quickly, awash in troubling dreams of frantic searches and visions of corpses, her mother's, Emi's, and Daddy's.

Endless rocky hills, climbing, dodging rattlesnakes while visions of vultures circled the endless horizon, brought on a massive headache. Hank whispered soothing words and pointed to an old barn. He pulled her toward it. Just as they reached the rickety weatherworn doors, her father stumbled out, covered with blood, reaching for her hand. He cried out, "Julie Lea, Julie Lea, help your mother. Please, she's hurt."

A small voice in the distance called out, "Jelly, what's wrong! Jelly, are you okay?" A glass hit the floor and shattered.

Jelly sat bolt upright, confused and sweaty. She swung her legs off the bed, stumbled into Emi's bedroom, and stepped on a shard of broken glass. "Ow! Ow! Emi, did you call me?" Holding the edge of the dresser, she stared into the darkness while groping for the light switch.

Emi raised her hand to shield her eyes from the sudden glare. "I heard you crying, Jelly. What happened?"

She took a deep breath, leaned back on the doorframe, and inspected her foot. "I was in the middle of an awful nightmare when you called me. I'm okay except for the glass I stepped on."

"I'm sorry. I knocked it over when I tried to reach the lamp."

"It's all right. I'm going to the bathroom to get the tweezers and a Band Aid. Do you need anything?"

"My leg really aches. Could I have another pill yet?"

"Sure. Give me a couple of minutes to take care of this and get my shoes on. The pills are on your nightstand. I'll bring you some water."

Bodacious Blooms Farm
10:00 p.m.

Henry turned in the front seat of his truck. His oldest brother, Dominik, sat next to him.

"She's beautiful, Dom. She's like sunshine breaking through a dark cloud whenever she enters a room. I never felt this way before." He dropped his head on the back of the seat and groaned. "God, you'd love her. Her smile would stop a train."

Dominik chuckled and slapped Henry on the shoulder.

"Sounds like you got it bad, professor. It's about time you looked at a woman again. So, what's the problem?"

Henry laughed ironically and turned his head to look at his brother. The oldest of the siblings, Dominik, had taken over the day-to-day running of the farm. Their parents were still active in the business but were getting too old to work outdoors from dawn to dusk like they had for over forty years. Dom and his wife were the only ones, besides their parents, still living in the original ranch house now. He and Mollie had four daughters, all attending various colleges. Their other two brothers and two sisters lived nearby and were involved in running the operation on every level. Henry had "jumped the reservation," as his papa liked to say.

"What's the problem, you ask? Other than the fact I'm gaga and have been swept off my feet by the woman of my dreams?" He sat forward and gripped the steering wheel. "I gotta go. I have classes tomorrow."

"You didn't answer me."

Henry cocked his head. "The problem, Dom, is that her little sister, my student and the very same girl who was the main character in the *missing* drama this weekend, told me Julie's a lesbian."

"What!"

He shook his head. "I don't believe it, no, but what can I do?"

"Ask her for crissakes. Put an end to your misery."

Chapter Twelve

Henry's Classroom
Monday, 8:30 a.m.

"Quiet!"

Heads turned in Henry's direction, conversations stopped in mid-sentence.

"Take your seats, please." He motioned toward the lab tables and desks. "You'll have your answers, and then you can stop all the wild speculation and rumors. Okay?"

He walked to Marco, leaned down, and spoke quietly, "I thought you were going to the ranch with us yesterday morning. What happened?"

Ducking his head, Marco whispered, "My parents grounded me. I can only go to school and back for the next week. No TV, no computer, nuthin'."

Henry chuckled and patted him on the back. "A week isn't so long. I got grounded for a month once."

"What'd you do?"

"Some other time."

He turned to his class and related the events of the previous day, knowing there'd be no work done until his kids knew the details. "Then, when she heard the cowboys approaching, she tried to scramble up to the hayloft, lost her footing, and fell down the ladder. She broke her left tibia." He held up his left leg and touched his shin. "She's in a cast and won't be able to attend school for a while."

A freckled arm went up in the back. "Why'd she run away, Mr. Henry?"

He thought for a moment before answering, then decided it was best to tell these kids the truth.

"She was mortified when the story about her father appeared on the front page of the Star. Humiliated, Emi thought her friends and classmates would judge her and shun her when they learned her dad was in Folsom prison."

A clamor of protests rose in the room and Henry raised his arms gesturing for silence. "Okay, okay, but that's what she thought and that's why she ran. If she was wrong, it's up to you to let her know."

One by one, students shouted out questions.

"My mother told me what happened and why he's in prison. Emi was only a baby."

"Why would we be mean to her because of that?"

"Yeah, doesn't she know we were all out searching for her?"

"When I heard on the news last night that she was found, I almost cried."

"Emi's a nice girl. We like her."

"She's really smart, too."

Henry waved his arms again. "Okay, quiet please. Are we going to get any work done here today?" He went to the whiteboard and pointed to the homework assignment, which was to have been completed over the weekend. "Did anybody get their assignment done? A few? Great! Here's what we're going to do —break up into teams of three and complete the work as a group project."

When the class merely stared back, he grinned. "Is that too easy? Would you rather work on it individually?"

His answer was wild scrambling as they broke up into small groups and opened their books. "Try and keep it down, okay? Don't get me into trouble with Mrs. Ransom. I hate being called to the principal's office."

Emi's House
4:30 p.m.

"Oh no, not again." Jelly stood and walked to the front of the living room.

Emi sat forward on the couch. "What is it?"

Jelly peeked out the front window. "I thought it was local TV or the newspaper again, but it's a bunch of kids coming down the street." She tilted the blinds so she could see more clearly. "It looks like most of the same ones who took part in the search."

"Are they coming here?"

"Looks like it."

Emi struggled to a standing position, winced, and sat down hard. "Don't let them in. Pretend we're not here."

Jelly opened the door. "Don't be silly." Behind the group of students, Jelly saw Hank hanging back. She waved. He shrugged and smiled.

"Hi, Ms. Swanson, is Emi home?"

"Can we talk to her?"

"Is she okay?"

Jelly turned in time to see Emi shrink down onto the couch and pull the coverlet up to her chin. "Yes, she's fine. Would you like to come in?" She stepped back and opened the door wide.

Dozens of Emi's classmates crowded into the living room.

"Hey, Emi!"

Jelly stepped out to the front porch and closed the door behind her. She strolled toward Hank. He moved in her direction, met her at the edge of the sidewalk.

"How are you doing, Julie?" He tilted his head toward the house. "Everything okay?"

She reached for his hand. "We're good. Come sit with me."

Hank followed her to the porch swing as she tugged his hand. "Marco wanted to come too, but his parents grounded him. He had to go straight home after classes."

Shaking her head, Jelly sat. "Oh, the poor kid. No good deed goes unpunished, huh?"

He took a seat next to her. "Looks that way. They took his trespassing episode more seriously than the police or the ranch people." He chuckled. "They sentenced him to one week, so you'll be seeing him soon. He's madly in love with you, you know." *Me, too, beautiful.*

Jelly acknowledged his remark about Marco with a small smile and raised eyebrows. "Wow, it sounds like a New Year's Eve party in there, doesn't it?" She stood and pulled him up. "Let's take a walk. I wouldn't dare go inside till the uproar dies down."

They turned to go down the block and she put her arm around his waist. The effect on him was like a sock in the gut. Breathing stopped, he saw spots and nearly stumbled over his own big feet. Flooded with happiness, he put his arm around her shoulder and squeezed her to his side.

Racking his brain for something intelligent to say, he came up with, "Didn't you open the store today?"

"Big Night Out can survive without me for a day." She flashed a smile that melted his insides. "The woman I hired is very good. As long as there's no big sale going on, she can handle it alone. The world won't stop when I get off."

It would stop for me. "I'm not so sure about that."

Jelly gave him a squeeze. "You're a sweetie pie, Dr. Henry. Did I ever tell you that?"

He laughed. "Oh yes, over and over. I'm sick of it by now." He felt her shoulders tremble when she giggled. "Julie, I—"

She stopped walking and interrupted him, "Oh, Hank, great news! Emi has decided to come to Sacramento with me. She'll stay at Aunt Martha's house while I visit Daddy at the hospital. I was speechless when she told me. That's the first time in years she's acknowledged his existence. We're driving up there first thing tomorrow if the orthopedist gives his okay. Emi and I will meet him at the hospital tonight at seven when he finishes his rounds. Isn't that great?"

Santa Susana High School
Tuesday, 8:00 a.m.

Jelly pulled her Mustang into the school parking lot. She cast an inquiring look at Emi, stretched out on the back seat with her leg propped on a pillow. "So where do I pick up your assignments?"

"The counselor's office, I think. Just go to the front desk and they'll tell you."

Jelly grinned. "I can't get over that cast of yours. You should enter it in a graffiti competition if there is such a thing." Emi's classmates spent an hour visiting yesterday afternoon. One of them brought a box of colored markers so they could all "sign" her cast.

Emi blushed with pleasure. "It's so totally, like, cool. I'm going to hate it when the doctor cuts it off. He thought it was pretty cool too."

Jelly opened her door. "I'll be right back."

Emi sat up and pointed out the window. "Look, isn't that Mr. Henry? I wonder who that man is with him."

Jelly turned just as Hank and the man embraced and traded cheek kisses. The breath rushed from her lungs and her chest squeezed when they threw their arms over each other's shoulders and walked toward the far corner of the parking lot. They hadn't seen her. She closed her eyes tight and clamped her teeth together.

"He's really tall, isn't he?" Emi's voice brought Jelly back to the moment. "He looks older than Mr. Henry. He's got gray in his hair. I've seen him around here before."

"You sit tight. I'll be right back." Jelly stepped out of her car and trotted to the front entrance of the school.

Yesterday evening, her heart warmed at the look of disappointment on Hank's face when she told him they were leaving for Sacramento. It only lasted for a flash, but she was sure he was going to miss her. Not in the way she hoped though. It was pretty clear to her now. Hank had a boyfriend. One he was very fond of from the looks of it.

Henry smacked his hand on the roof of Dom's truck. "Thanks for bringing the seeds on your way down to L.A. I've got my class all primed for a new project."

Dom started his engine and shifted into reverse. "No problem. So, are you going to bring your lady friend out to meet the family when she gets back from up north?"

"I'll ask her. Don't want to scare her off, though. Meeting that noisy mob is like a farmer's convention at the county fair." He stepped back from the truck. "I'll let you know."

"Okay, gotta go. They close at noon today." Dom backed out of the parking slot and turned toward the exit. He waved over his shoulder as he left, heading for the 118 Freeway on his way to the Los Angeles Flower District.

Hank turned back to the school building when he caught a

blur of red heading in his direction. Recognizing Jelly's car, he took a step into the parking lot and waved.

The car zipped past him without slowing down. Didn't she see him? She must have, she nearly ran him down. What the—

"Jelly, watch out!" Emi screamed from the back seat. "You almost ran over Mr. Henry."

Turning her car in the same direction the man in the truck had gone, Jelly answered over her shoulder, "Mr. Henry? I didn't see him." She accelerated and the car fishtailed when she turned.

"Are you on crack? We were just talking about him and that tall guy before you went to get my stuff. Stop, Jelly! I want to say goodbye to him." She twisted in her seat and stared at Henry's dumfounded face. He stood with his arms extended as if to say, *what just happened?*

Jelly was crushed by what she just saw. Hank—that man. She grimaced at the taste of stomach acid. A profound feeling of loss overwhelmed her. In the past several days, her hopes had been climbing up and sliding down like a yo-yo on a thin string.

Staring straight ahead, Jelly said, "We've got a long drive ahead of us. We don't have time to stop."

In the rearview mirror, Emi's face glared back at her. "It's a good thing you didn't hit him. I would hate you forever, Jelly Swanson!"

Thanks, Emi, just what I need right now.

Henry, perplexed, walked to his classroom wondering why Jelly hadn't stopped or even slowed down, for that matter. Walking and talking with her arm around him yesterday sent a clear signal she was comfortable with that level of intimacy. She seemed more than ready to move up to the next level. At least, that's what he thought at the time.

Today she wanted to hit him with her car? He understood adolescents a lot better than women.

When she and Emi returned, he'd take Dom's advice and come right out and ask Julie if she had any romantic interest in him. If she didn't, they could still be friends. Maybe.

Chapter Thirteen

Jelly's Car
Friday Afternoon

Emi watched Jelly's face reflected in the rearview mirror. They'd left Sacramento two hours ago and would be home later in the evening.

Jelly glanced up. "Are you getting hungry? It's dinnertime. I'll pull off and get something we can eat in the car."

"I'm hungry."

"Okay, we have Wendy's, McDonald's, Burger King, Kentucky Fried, and Country Kitchen coming up in the next mile. You pick."

"I don't wanna eat in the car. Let's see if one of 'em has outside tables. I need to un-kink myself."

Jelly laughed. "Okay, you got it." She steered the car off the freeway and took a right turn, cruising past Wendy's and McDonald's. "No outside tables here. I'll make a U-ie and we'll try the other side."

Emi pointed. "Look. Burger King has tables outside. Let's go there."

Jelly pulled into the parking area next to the tables and helped Emi out of the car. They found a table in the shade. "I'm going inside to get some wet paper towels to clean this yucky table. Can you stand for a minute?"

Emi rolled her eyes and huffed out a breath. "You're so finicky."

"Yeah, I know. Be right back."

After cleaning up the table and bench, Jelly took Emi's order. She was back in less than five minutes with a tray of food. "Wow, does this smell good! I didn't realize I was so hungry."

They were too busy eating for the first few minutes for conversation. Emi brought a napkin to her lips and cleared her throat. "Aunt Martha told me about that day our mother was murdered."

Shocked, Jelly stopped chewing and gulped a bite of burger. It hurt all the way down, like she'd swallowed a jagged rock. "She did? Why?"

Emi shrugged dismissively. "She said I was old enough to hear the truth." She pinned Jelly with her direct gaze. "How come you never told me you were the one who found our mother all murdered and stuff. You were the same age as me."

On a deep breath, Jelly answered, "I was trying to protect you. I didn't want you to have those images in your mind, like they've always been in mine." Her hunger disappeared.

Emi put down her burger, her eyes swimming. "I feel really bad."

Jelly reached out and grabbed Emi's hand. "She shouldn't have told you. I wish she hadn't said anything about it."

Emi pulled her hand back and dashed away the tears sliding down her cheeks. "Yes! She told me because she thought you probably never would." Her words were angry and accusing. "You should have told me. You're my sister, the only person in the world who loves me. Why didn't you tell me, Jelly? She was my mother too."

Elbows on the table, Jelly sat with her face in her hands. She moaned. Her shoulders trembled with silent sobs.

"I'm sorry, Jelly. I don't want you to cry. I just—"

Jelly wiped her hands across her face and quickly reached out to grab Emi's wrist. "No." She blew her nose on a napkin. "No, I'm sorry. I should have told you. I should have told you long ago."

Cochran Street, Simi Valley
Twelve Years Ago

The tinny school bus rattled down the street. Julie talked excitedly with a classmate as they compared notes on the algebra test. "My mom is going to be so glad when I show her this A. I can't wait to get home."

With a gay wave, Julie hopped off the bus a half block from home. She ran down the street like she had wings on her heels. Bounding up the front steps, she was puzzled to find the door locked. *Mom never locks the door. Maybe she had an errand.*

She considered walking around to the back door, but if the front was locked, that would be a waste of time. Balancing her backpack on the porch railing, she dug through two of the zipper pockets, searching for her house key.

The postal truck stopped in front of the house. Julie waved to the letter carrier they'd had almost forever. Instead of opening the mailbox, the carrier held up the mail and Julie jogged down the front sidewalk. "You're late today, aren't you?

She handed over the stack of mail. "Yes, I'm doing half of someone else's route today. This is my last neighborhood. Seems everybody's been waiting for me. I feel like Santa showing up a day late for Christmas." She laughed and pulled the small truck forward to the next house.

Mrs. Crawford walked down her front steps to meet the mail truck. "Hello, Julie. I've got some cookies in the oven. I'll bring some over in a while."

"Oh, boy!"

Juggling the mail and her backpack in one arm, Jelly put the key in the front door. "Mom?"

The entry hall was dim in the afternoon light. "Mom?" Jelly dropped her backpack on the floor and sang, "Mo-om, where are you? I've got something to show you." She looked toward the kitchen, listened for sounds of dinner in the making. The back door slammed. "Mom? Were you out back?"

A forlorn wail echoed down the hall from the bedroom Julie shared with her baby sister. "Mom? The baby's crying." *Something isn't right.* Hair prickled on the back of her neck. Barely able to walk on legs unnaturally heavy, she crept through the dining room. Her grandmother's handmade lace cloth had been pulled off the table. It lay in a heap in front of the doorway to the kitchen. A vase of flowers was overturned on Mom's treasured mahogany table, fat drops of pooled water dripping off the edge in slow, loud plops.

Too frightened to take another step, Jelly backed into the hall. The baby's hoarse wail grew louder. Unable to move, she trembled with fear. "Mom?" she whispered. "Mom, I'm scared, please answer me."

Baby Martha's cry elevated to a scream. Jelly turned on her heel and ran to the bedroom. Her sister's little face was red and streaked with tears. Sweat soaked her wispy blond hair and chubby arms begged Jelly to lift her from the crib.

Jelly crushed the baby to her breast and covered her head with kisses. "It's okay, sweetie. Big sister's here now. I'll take care of you." Rocking back and forth, bouncing the child while she murmured nonsense, Jelly's own breathing slowed. She rubbed and patted little Martha's back, all the while cooing and humming. Tiny hiccups and sobs nearly broke Julie's heart. "Shush, shush, I've got you. I've got you, baby."

The leaden silence of the house pressed down on Julie. She sat on the edge of her bed, rocking the baby. When her courage returned, she stood and tiptoed to the hall. "Let's go find your mama. I think I heard her go out the kitchen door."

Martha turned up her sweet, blue-eyed face and smiled. "Find Mama."

Jelly hugged her, smiling in return. "That's right, you clever baby. We'll find Mama."

Ignoring the ominous, hollow feeling in her chest, Jelly crept down the hall to the dining room and through the kitchen door. The room was dim and silent. A peculiar, cloying smell enveloped her. Clutching Martha, she reached out with a shaking hand to switch on the ceiling light. She froze at the sight of blood. Blood splattered everywhere. On the floor, the walls, the white cabinet doors beneath the sink. A bloody handprint smeared the refrigerator. Mom's shoe lay in a puddle of shiny red goo. The coppery smell sickened her. She gasped for air, and her stomach convulsed.

Martha pointed. "Je-wee see Mama shoe?"

Overcome with dread at what she feared was beyond the table, Jelly dragged her leaden feet forward, unable to turn or run. Each step thundered in her brain. *No, please, God. No. Oh, please, please.*

A shrill scream bounced off the walls. Jelly fell to her knees in the pool of blood surrounding her mother's twisted, lifeless body. Jessie's long golden hair fanned out, soaking up the hideous puddle on which her head lay. The screams went on and on. The baby stiffened, shrieking in her arms, her tiny hands clutching Jelly's hair and blouse. Jelly rocked back and forth, praying the screaming would stop. *Stop, stop, please, stop!*

From a great distance, a woman's voice exclaimed, "Oh, dear God! Call an ambulance!"

Footsteps thundered down the hall. "What happened here? Jesus God! Where's the phone?"

Someone pulled Martha from her arms. "No! No, don't take her, please don't take her!" Jelly flailed her arm in a desperate attempt to hang on to the shrieking baby.

"Julie?" Mrs. Crawford's trembling voice penetrated the blackness. "Julie? Wake up, dear." The familiar voice was nearly drowned out by the murmur of dozens of other voices, people milling about. *Am I at school? What happened?*

Jelly was on her back. Afternoon sun slanted between the blinds into her eyes. Confused, she rolled her head from side to side on the firm cushion.

"Where—?"

Mrs. Crawford leaned closer. "You're all right, Julie. You're on the sofa. The doctor examined you. You're not hurt."

Bolting upright, eyes huge, a scream built in Jelly's throat. "Mom! Martha! What—?"

A man's strong arms held her down. "Try to be still, Miss. The doctor gave you some medicine. You can't get up yet."

Jelly's pleading eyes searched for her neighbor. "Mrs. Crawford?"

"I'm here, dear. I'll stay right here until your father gets home. Martha is fine. Mrs. Jensen took her home for now. You don't need to worry. Your sister's fine."

Jelly's tongue grew thick and dry. She struggled to speak. The room tilted, the ceiling spun above her. "Mrs. Crawford, I had the worst, most awful nightmare. I came home from school and my mother, she was—" Jelly stared at her blood smeared hand grasped in Mrs. Crawford's. *My mother's blood!* An unearthly howl emanated from Jelly's throat. The light from the window went out.

The next several days were a blur of activity, with officials of one sort or another in and out of their home, full of endless questions and speculations. A crime cleanup crew restored the kitchen. Aunt Martha Elizabeth, Daddy's sister, came to stay. She did her best to bring order and calm to the household. She held them together, fed them, cleaned up after them.

When Daddy wasn't sitting in the corner of the sofa, silent, unshaven, zombie-like, he paced and cried. Inconsolable, he cried endlessly, day and night. He couldn't look at his daughters. He didn't talk to them. His sister had to lead him to the bathroom, to bed, coax him to eat or drink.

Detached, Jelly observed the erasure of all signs of the murder in nightmarish slow motion. She assumed the care of her baby sister. Unwilling to let her out of sight, she brought Martha into her bed at night. Hugging her close, she breathed deeply of her sweet baby smell, taking comfort in her warmth and innocence. *Nothing will hurt this baby. I'll never let anything bad happen to her. Ever! Ever!*

A week after Jessie's gruesome slaughter, Daddy got up, showered, shaved, dressed in a business suit, and had a cup of coffee with his sister. He drove to the Ventura County Courthouse to observe the arraignment of Norman, their plumber. A man who worked in their home over the course of many years, a man they trusted, joked with, who had a family of his own. This same man brutally beat, raped, and slashed to death their beautiful, talented, loving wife and mother. The evidence against him was overwhelming and irrefutable. His blubbery, self-pitying confession was broadcast on the evening news.

George waited, dead calm, at the back entrance of the courthouse in the company of several local police officers and reporters. When the sheriff's car arrived with the prisoner, he stepped forward, faced his wife's killer, and in the presence of a dozen stunned witnesses, stabbed him in the heart and slashed his throat. George would not see the outside of a jail cell for fourteen years.

Burger King, Highway 99, Bakersfield
Present Day

Jelly and Emi exchanged silent glances.

Emi drew in a shuddering breath. "It was so awful. All I can think of is how I would feel if I came home from school and found you all bloody, and murdered, and dead, and everything." New tears glistened on her lashes. "It was really horrible, wasn't it, Jelly?"

Lips trembling, Jelly clamped her teeth together and squeezed her eyes closed against threatening tears. She nodded. "Yes, baby, it was the most horrible thing you can imagine. Sometimes I wake up in the morning and think it was only a nightmare. But it wasn't, it happened."

Emi clung to her sister's hand. "I want you to tell me about our mother. I don't remember anything about her. What did she look like?"

Jelly smiled. "Oh, Emi, she was beautiful. You look like her. I see her every time I look at you."

"I look like her?"

"Yes, except she had blonde hair the color of a wheat field and straight as a ruler. It was so long. She used to let me brush it. Hair like shining silk. It reached all the way down to her waist. She wore it in a tight French twist at the back of her neck. She was very dignified, a real lady."

Emi leaned forward on her elbows, eyes wide. "What else?"

"You have her blue eyes. I have Daddy's eyes. She always wore skirts and dresses. I never saw her in jeans or pants."

"Like that old Father Knows Best they show on Nickelodeon?"

"Yes, just like that. She even wore an apron when she cooked. I thought everyone's mom did." Jelly chuckled at the memory.

"How come we don't have any pictures of her?"

"Oh, we do. I made a big picture album for you. It has my baby pictures, your baby pictures, Mama and Daddy's wedding photo. Everything I could find, so you'd know what your family was like before—uh, the—" Choking on the words, Jelly sipped her lemonade and dabbed her eyes with a napkin.

Emi cocked her head in her curious puppy way. "Where is it? How come you never showed it to me?"

"I was planning to give it to you after we talked about her murder. I didn't think you were old enough. I kept putting it off. I was wrong. I'm sorry."

Emi looked into the distance. After a few moments of silence, she said, "You said 'our family,' but it was really *your* family. Now it's just you and me, isn't it?"

Jelly nodded. "Yes, you and me. But don't forget Aunt Martha and Daddy. They're family, too. They both love you."

At the mention of their father, Emi's face clouded. "Daddy. I don't know him. How could he love me? I was only two when he was arrested."

"Emi, Daddy loves you very much. The first thing he always wants to know is how you're doing. He's seen lots of photos of you and all your report cards. He told me your pictures bring him happy memories of Mama."

"How come he never wanted me to visit him?"

"He was sad and ashamed and didn't want you to see him in that awful place."

"But didn't he care if you saw it?"

Jelly reached across the table and tucked a curl behind Emi's ear. "He didn't want me to come either, but Aunt Martha told him he couldn't deprive me of a father after losing Mama." She sighed and shrugged. "Finally, he agreed to let me come."

"I remember Aunt Martha lived with us for a while when I was little. How long did she stay at our house?"

"On and off for three years, until I was seventeen and graduated from Simi High. I got a swing shift job so I could be home with you most of the day. I asked her to let us try to make it on our own. She was afraid to leave us at first, but I'm pretty stubborn."

"You?" Emi opened her eyes wide, mocking Jelly's statement.

Jelly laughed. "Be careful there, little girl. There's no way you can get away from me with that cast on your leg. Finish eating. We need to get on the road."

Emi mumbled through a mouthful of cold fries. "What does Daddy look like now?"

"Don't talk with your mouth full of food."

"Quit picking on me all the time!"

Jelly raised her arms. "Okay, let's call a truce. I'll try not to be so bossy, and you try not to be so touchy. Deal?"

"Yeah, I guess. I gotta pee now. Will you help me to the bathroom?"

All the way home, Emi grilled Jelly on every detail of her life with their mother and father. The mother she didn't remember and the father she thought she hated.

It was dusk when they approached their house. Hank's truck was parked in front.

Chapter Fourteen

Jelly's House
Friday, 6:30 p.m.

Hank jumped up from the porch swing as soon as Jelly pulled into the driveway. Jelly's weak smile and small wave signaled there was still something going on, something he hadn't figured out yet.

Opening the door to the back seat, he helped Emi out of the car and supported her while she gingerly made her way to the porch. He sat her down on the swing and turned to help Jelly carry in the luggage.

He took the largest one from her hand. "I missed you, both of you. How was your trip?"

She stopped and looked up at him. After her long heart-breaking talk with Emi about their mother's murder, she couldn't also face her disappointment over the fact that Hank wasn't going to be the love of her life.

"Hank, I'm really sorry, and please don't take this the wrong way. Emi's very tired, and I want to get her comfortable with a snack in front of the TV before I meet with Connie and Sally."

"Do you want me to leave?"

"Yes, please." Jelly lowered her eyes and took the bag from Hank's hand. "Could I call you tomorrow? We'll talk then."

The dark hurt on Hank's face was like a blow to her chest. She hated herself for being the cause of it. She and Hank could never have the future she wanted so much. Images of him with the man at school were driving her to distraction.

"All right then." He nodded to Emi, turned abruptly, went to his truck, and drove away without looking back.

Jelly stepped up to the porch. She dropped the suitcase by the door and dug into her green suede bag looking for the keys before she remembered they were in her pocket.

"Come on, Emi. I don't have much time to change. I'll get you a snack, then I'll be off for my walk."

Emi struggled to her feet. "What's the matter with you, Jelly Swanson? Why were you so mean to Mr. Henry? Couldn't you see how happy he was to see us?" Her sweet face clouded with fury and frustration. "Go change. I can take care of myself!" Hobbling to the open door, she shoved herself ahead and reached for the light switch.

Jelly followed her inside. "Emi, you don't understand."

"Yeah, I know. I'm just a stupid little child. I'm too dumb to understand the complicated world of grown-ups." Anger flared on her face and in her words. "One thing I do understand is how bad you made him feel. He was waiting for us."

Jelly took her by the shoulders and Emi yanked herself away, nearly falling with the sudden violence of her action.

"Please listen to me, Emi."

"No! Change your clothes and go meet your girlfriends." She crossed her arms and flung herself against the back of the couch, wincing with pain. "Stay out as late as you want. Get drunk again if you want. Stay out all night if you want. I don't care if you ever come home!"

Jelly understood Emi's hurt and anger. There was no point in trying to explain. Throwing up her hands, she went to her bedroom and closed the door.

Corner of Indian Hills Drive and Alamo
7:10 p.m.

Sally waved. "Jelly, we missed you. You okay? Emi?"

"I'm fine. Can we just walk for a while? I have to unwind, and I don't feel like talking."

Connie started up the hill. "We're not talking, we're walking. Okay by me, *chica*."

Jelly grabbed the back of Connie's sweatshirt. "Connie, wait. I'm sorry, really. I'm in a bad mood, okay? I'll get over it."

Sally quick-stepped to stay even with them. "We don't know what to do with you when you're in a bad mood, Jelly. We're not used to it."

A rueful chuckle escaped Jelly's lips. "You're doing it already. I can't stay in a bad mood when I'm around you guys." She linked arms with Connie and Sally. "Come on, let's get pooped going up this hill. Then I'll be fine."

They set off at a quick pace. All of them were in good shape, but three quarters of the way up Jelly was tugging at them to keep up with her.

"Who turned on the heat?" Connie gasped. "Fifteen minutes ago, I was complaining to Sally that it was getting cold earlier. I'm sweating!"

"Me too," Sally said. "We know it's good for us, Jelly, but genteel old ladies like us aren't used to so much of it. Slow down."

"If you want to hear about the disaster my life has turned into, you'll have to keep up. That's the only way you'll get it out of me."

Once they reached the top of the steep hill, Connie stepped into the street and plopped down on the curb, gasping for breath. "Whatever you have to tell us better be good, or I'll have to kill you, and right now I'm too winded."

Jelly pointed to her left. "Let's go that way tonight. It's longer, but flatter."

Sally sat on the curb next to Connie. "Rest first."

"*Dios!* I gotta start going to Curves again. This fat butt is slowing me down."

Sally slapped her on the knee. "Connie, you do not have a fat butt. Has Miguel ever said you have a fat butt?"

She cocked her head and rolled her eyes. "Whadda you think? He wants to live to a ripe old age."

Jelly put her hands over her face in an attempt to stifle her laughter. It was useless. She soon doubled over then sat down next to her two friends. "Jeez, can't I enjoy my misery for even a few minutes? You're awful. Stop making me laugh."

Sally put her arm around Jelly's shoulder. "That's what friends do. I'm pretty sure." She gave Jelly a squeeze. "Am I right, Connie?"

Connie nodded and raised her hand in an okay sign. "You got it." She leaned forward so she could see Jelly's face. "Now, what new disaster has been visited upon you?"

Jelly stood and pulled them to their feet. "Come on. First, I'll tell you the good news, then the bad news."

Sally and Connie struggled to their feet. They walked in the opposite direction from their homes. The long flat walk along Yosemite would lead them around the top and back side of the golf course and eventually to Jelly's neighborhood.

"Jelly," Connie said, "you know that if we walk this way,

you'll have to drive us home, don't you? We're looking at nearly five miles going this way."

"I'll drive you. Come on."

Sally threw up her arms. "What is this? Misery needs company?"

"Something like that. I have a lot to tell you."

The pace picked up as they headed north on the flat sidewalk. Jelly recounted the trip to Sacramento. Her father's improvement. The U.C. Davis neurosurgical team had skillfully removed the blood clot on his brain. He was out of the drug-induced coma and being treated for a stubborn staph infection. After waiting an anxious day, she was able to visit for a few minutes and speak to him.

Jelly told them that while she was at the hospital, Aunt Martha took it upon herself to tell Emi, in frank detail, what had happened when Emi was a baby. Jelly had withheld the details, and Martha thought Emi was old enough to know what they'd all been through. She told Emi her adolescent anger was misplaced and damaging her relationship with her sister.

"Gosh," Sally said. "That must have been a lot for her to take in all at once."

"It was. We had a long talk on the way home. I should have told her myself. I didn't do her any favors by protecting her from the truth all this time."

Connie put her hand on Jelly's arm. "You never told us any of this either, Jelly. Miguel knew the details but warned me not to mention it until you were ready."

Jelly sighed. "It was a relief to finally talk about it with her. She's still upset that I didn't trust her enough to tell her what happened. I guess I didn't want her to have to live with those memories, like I have."

"It's so hard to know what kids are capable of absorbing," Sally said. "Charlie died so suddenly, when the two of us were on vacation, I didn't know what to do about telling Erin and

Jenna. I couldn't bear the thought of them learning about it over the phone."

"I remember when your mother came over to our house that night after she'd told them," Connie said.

"My folks came cross country to stay with the girls while Charlie and I were overseas. Their joy at spending time with their granddaughters turned to a nightmare the instant I called. They had to break the awful news to them. At least the girls were in school, and Mom and Dad had a couple of hours to absorb it before they got home."

"Sally, once the initial shock was past, Erin and Jenna were more worried about you being in Europe, dealing with it alone," Connie said.

"I know. It was a double whammy for them. I'm so proud of the way they handled it. They weren't much older than Emi is now." She took Jelly's hand. "As much as you'd like to, you can't protect your kids from life."

"Yes, I'm glad Aunt Martha took the initiative. Things were going from bad to worse between Emi and me." She sighed. "I'm still dealing with an angry teenager, though. She told me she wouldn't care if I never came home tonight."

"What now?" Connie asked.

Jelly stopped. "Hank was waiting at the house when we got home. He was so happy to see us. I asked him to leave. I hurt his feelings, and Emi saw it too."

Sally was stunned. "Jelly, why, for heaven's sake? What could he have done to deserve that?"

"Nothing. He didn't deserve it, but when I saw him walking to the car with that big smile on his face, it nearly broke my heart. I'm still—I'm—" Unexpected tears sprang from her eyes. Her hands flew to her face.

"What?" Connie asked, "You're still what?"

Furiously dashing tears away, Jelly mumbled, "I was hoping we could be more than friends, you know? I really like him."

Sally jerked back, dumbfounded. "And that's a reason to send him away? I don't get it."

"Me neither," Connie added.

Jelly threw up her hands. "He's gay! I wanted him to be *the one,* and he's gay." She shook her head and stepped ahead of them, walking at a rapid pace.

Taking long steps to catch up, Sally said, "How do you know that? Did he tell you he was gay?" She grabbed Jelly's arm. "Jelly, stop for goodness sake. Tell us how you know."

"He didn't tell me. He didn't have to. I saw him with another man."

"Wait a minute, wait a minute," Connie said. "Exactly what did you see, and when? I don't believe it. This is *loco.*"

Sally shrieked and jumped off the sidewalk into the street. "Oh my God, look at the size of that tarantula. It's as big as my hand!"

Connie grabbed Jelly's hand and pulled her into the street next to Sally. They stared mesmerized by the giant, hairy brown spider sitting between two shrubs next to the block wall along the sidewalk.

Sally and Jelly grabbed the back of Connie's sweatshirt as she leaned over and looked at the fat, gruesome creature. Connie said, "I bet that's Gordo. Paco's been looking everywhere for him." She pointed a few feet down the sidewalk. "Get that McDonald's bag over there. I'm going to try and catch him."

"You're what!"

"Quick, Sally, get the bag before he gets away. Hurry!"

Sally ran along the gutter and picked up the discarded bag. She shook out a crumpled napkin and extended her arm as far as she could toward Connie.

"Give it to me!"

"I'm not coming any closer to that horrible thing."

Jelly reached out and took the bag from Sally. "Oh, for heaven's sake, it's just a spider. What's the big deal?"

"Just a spider? You could put a saddle on that thing."

Connie reached for the bag, expertly scooped the spider inside, and twisted the sack closed.

Gordo, if that's who it was, scrambled, bounced and scratched inside the paper bag.

Jelly jumped back and shouted, "Yikes!"

Sally pursed her lips and stared at Jelly. "Just a spider, huh? You're scared of it too, smarty pants."

Connie started walking back in the opposite direction. "Come on, we're going back the short way. I'm not carrying this thing around for the next hour."

Sally followed her. "Okay, but you go ahead. We'll follow behind. I'm keeping a safe distance from that hideous thing."

She reached back and grabbed Jelly's arm. "Come on, 'It's just a spider.'" She felt Jelly shudder and couldn't help the giggle that rose from her throat.

"Very funny, Sal."

"Sorry, Jelly, but it is funny. That thing's almost as big as Connie and she reached right out and scooped it up. I'm still trying to figure out how you did that, Connie."

Glancing back over her shoulder, Connie said, "I got six *hijos,* remember. Those boys got all kinds of creepy crawlies living at our house. Adapt or die, that's what Miguel says."

Sally and Jelly stared at each other.

"Now she tells us."

"I'm never going in that house again."

Connie laughed. "See, that proves it. What you don't know can't hurt you. Anyway, what were we talking about before Gordo showed his ugly face?"

"My broken dreams of perfect love," Jelly moaned. "Somehow I've been shocked out of my deep black mood."

Sally snickered. "Wonder how that happened?"

"Come on, you cowards," Connie said, "I'll drop off Paco's baby and we can get back to the important stuff while we walk Jelly home."

After a thorough inspection of Connie's front entryway, Sally and Jelly sat down on the glider and waited for her to come back outside.

Paco stuck his head out the door. "Hey, thanks Mrs. Lewis, Ma said you found Gordo for me."

"Not by choice, Paco. You can be sure of that."

"Ah, he's nice and gentle. He wouldn't hurt you."

"That's what you say. Just promise me something, okay? If he ever escapes again, I don't want to know about it. I might have to start packing a gun when we go out walking."

Jelly shuddered. "Eek, now I'm really scared."

Paco laughed. "Girls are funny." He shut the door.

A minute or so later, Connie stepped out. She sat in the wicker chair across from them. "Now where were we?"

Jelly stood. "Let's head in the direction of my house. I don't want anyone to overhear."

"Okay," Sally and Connie said. They went down the front walkway to the sidewalk and headed west toward the golf course.

Half a block further on, they reached the intersection. Jelly finally spoke. "I, uh, oh, this is so awkward. I saw Hank kissing and hugging a man. They were very familiar and affectionate. They walked quite a way with their arms on each other's shoulders, like little boys do, you know? Then the other guy got in a truck and drove away."

Sally slowly shook her head. "I can't get my mind around this. Where did you see them?"

"At the school parking lot, when Emi and I were there to pick up her class assignments on our way out of town."

"Wow," Connie said. "That sounds kind of risky. You know—the school parking lot. Someone could have reported it."

Jelly shrugged. "They didn't seem to be concerned about hiding anything."

"God," Sally said. "I hate to think Carol was right about him. He's so...manly. What a shock."

Jelly shook her head. "I can't get the images out of my mind, no matter how hard I try."

Connie touched her shoulder. "Me neither."

A mournful sigh escaped Jelly's throat. "I feel so sad. Devastated, you know? When I saw him at the house tonight, I had such mixed emotions. I wanted to run and hug him. At the same time, I felt betrayed. Boy, did I ever misjudge his friendliness. Even Emi thought he was sweet on me."

Sally looked up and down the street as they stepped off the curb. "I'm really sorry, Jelly. You think the right man has come along, and then this happens." She raised her arms and let them fall, as if trying to come to grips with what Jelly told them.

Jelly stopped when they reached the other side of Indian Hills Drive. "I'm going the rest of the way alone. I need to think of a way to make up with Emi. I don't know what to tell her."

Chapter Fifteen

Emi's Front Porch
8:30 p.m.

Emi nudged Marco. "Uh oh, here comes the dragon lady."

Jelly stopped and put her hands on her hips. "Very funny." Emi had moved out to the porch swing and was resting her leg on a kitchen chair. Marco must have carried it outside for her. She was pretty sure Emi couldn't have managed it on her own.

Emi crossed her arms and clamped her lips tight together in an angry pose just in case Jelly forgot how mad she was.

Jelly suppressed a smile. "Hello, Marco." She leaned against the porch railing to catch her breath. "Nice to see you. How'd you know we were home?"

"I called him," Emi snorted. "There's nothing wrong with him being here!"

"Of course there isn't. He's welcome any time." Jelly went to the front door. "It's getting chilly out. Why don't you both come inside, and I'll make some cocoa."

Marco grinned and jumped to his feet. "Really? That's

great, huh, Em?" He carefully lifted her leg from the chair and extended a hand to help her up.

She glared at him. "I can do it myself." Standing gingerly, she supported herself on the back of the chair, then hobbled to the door.

Marco raised his shoulders and hands. "Whatever," he said and looked up in time to see Jelly wink. He rolled his eyes, grinned, and shared a secret moment with the woman of his dreams.

Jelly laughed and followed him inside. "You two get comfortable. I'll get the cocoa going."

"Can I help with anything?" Marco asked hopefully.

"No, I got it. Won't take long."

The kitchen door was propped open, and Jelly could hear the conversation from the living room.

"What are you so mad about now, Emi?"

"I'm mad about two things. First, I'm mad because I get mad so easy."

"I noticed that. So, what's the other thing?"

"I gotta figure out a way to grow up and quit being such a baby. Jelly takes good care of us, and all I ever do is act like a brat."

"I noticed that too, Em."

"Do you ever eat anything, Marco? If you get any skinnier, the kids are going to start calling you Invisible Man instead of Thin Man. Jeez, does your mother know how to cook?"

"My mom says I'm eating them out of house and home. I don't know why I'm so skinny, except I grew four inches since school started in September. I'm taller than my big brother, Sam."

"How come I haven't seen Sam in a while?"

"He joined the Marines. He's stationed at Camp Pendleton. He wants to learn to be an air traffic controller. We're going to the base to visit him in a couple of weeks. I'm really anxious to talk to him."

"Don't you get any ideas about joining the Marines!"

Jelly walked in with a tray of fragrant, steaming mugs. "Marco's joining the Marines?"

Marco jumped to his feet and took the tray. "My brother, Sam. He joined weeks ago." He set the tray on the coffee table, picked up a mug, and handed it to Emi. "Ow, hot, hot. Grab the handle, quick."

Emi took the mug of cocoa and sniffed. "You make the best hot chocolate in the world, Jelly."

Jelly's eyes opened wide with surprise. "Why thank you, Emi. Aunt Martha taught me a long time ago."

"Hers is good, but yours is better."

Marco held his cup close to his nose and inhaled. "I gotta agree with Emi, Ms. Swanson. Yours is the best. My mom just heats milk in a cup in the microwave with powdered cocoa. It's okay, but not as good as this." He sipped very carefully from the edge of the rim, slurping loudly to avoid burning his tongue.

Emi and Jelly laughed when his face turned red, and he made in-and-out whooshing sounds.

Jelly felt good sharing a moment of laughter with her sister at Marco's expense.

He laughed with them and put the mug down on a side table. "Better let that cool down some. It's hot!"

Emi blew on her cocoa. "That's why they call it hot chocolate, dopey." She turned to Jelly. "We got any cookies in the house? Marco needs to fatten up."

Near midnight, Jelly lay awake deciding whether or not to go to Big Night Out in the morning. The evening with Emi, even after Marco left, had been so unusually agreeable she thought of taking another day off and spending it at home.

Sun on her face woke her. Stretching like a cat, she groaned and rolled over to look at the bathroom wall clock past her bedroom door. Seven thirty, her usual time to rise, seven days a week, rain or shine. Stepping quietly on bare feet, she crept to Emi's door and watched her sleeping soundly, arms and legs flung in all directions, blanket sliding toward the floor.

She walked across to the window and quietly tipped up the wooden shutters to darken the room. Emi stirred but didn't wake.

After the coffee was ready, Jelly poured herself a cup, took her cell phone and went out to the front porch. Her chenille bathrobe and furry slippers were welcome in the early morning chill. She called Henry Palasczewski.

He answered on the second ring. Jelly loved the deep tenor of his voice on the phone. His friendship was important to her.

"Palasczewski here."

"Someday I may learn how to say that without tripping over my tongue."

"Julie?"

"Hi, Hank."

"Hi."

"I, uh, I called to see if you'd like to come have dinner with me and Emi this evening."

"Dinner, oh, I don't, uh—"

"Hank, please come. I'm sorry about yesterday. I didn't mean what—I'd really like you to come."

His hesitation seemed endless. Jelly waited.

"Okay. I'd like to come. What time? May I bring something?"

Guilty weight lifted from her chest. "I'd ask you to bring a bottle of wine, but I don't know what I'm cooking yet." A happy breath, then, "Come at six. I'll cancel my walk with

Connie and Sally. We'll set up the Scrabble board after dinner. Emi would like to see you."

"Emi?"

"Me too, of course, I'd like to see you." She silently cursed herself for her awkward words. "Emi's still asleep. I haven't talked to her yet, but we both want you to come."

"All right, I'll be there at six, and I'll bring a bottle of red and a bottle of white." His chuckle warmed her heart.

"Great! I'm going into my shop this morning, then I'll take the afternoon off and dream up something delicious. I'm so glad you're coming, Hank. Really."

"Me too, Julie. Six then. Goodbye."

She snapped off the phone and took a long drink of the cinnamon flavored coffee she loved so much. She smiled.

Hank was coming to dinner.

Chapter Sixteen

Jelly's House
Saturday, 5:45 p.m.

Jelly called from the kitchen, "Emi, what are you doing? I hear you thumping around in there."

"I'm setting the table for you. You're never going to get to it. Mr. Henry will be here any minute. What's taking you so long?"

"Please get off that leg! Go sit and wait on the porch. Stall him for a few minutes. I'm almost finished in here. I'll set the table."

Jelly grabbed the meat thermometer out of a drawer. She opened the oven door and jerked back when moist heat blasted her face. "Dammit!" She gingerly pulled the rack out and stabbed the thermometer into the roast.

Hearing a thud, thud, thud, Jelly looked up to see Emi hobbling to the kitchen door. "It isn't Christmas dinner, you know. Why the roast prime rib?" She held out her hand. "Hand me the steak knives and I'll put them on the table. Hurry up, Jelly."

Waving her hands to cool off her heat-flushed face, Jelly pleaded, "Please don't give me a hard time, Emi. I've almost got everything ready. I just have to watch the temperature and then take the roast out and let it rest a few minutes."

Emi sniffed the air like a hungry dog. "Wow, it sure smells good."

Jelly waved her off. "Go on. Wait out on the porch swing. You can keep him out there a few minutes while I finish up here."

A deep masculine voice asked, "Keep whom out on the porch?"

"Hank!"

"Mr. Henry!"

He held up two wine bottles. "I knocked, but nobody heard me. Am I too early?" He took a deep whiff. "My, oh my, something smells good." Setting the wine bottles on the kitchen table, he turned to face Jelly. "Almost as good as you look, Julie."

Emi rolled her eyes to the ceiling. "How mushy. Yech!"

Hank turned to Emi. "You're looking very good yourself, Emi. You've got color back in your cheeks. It won't be long before you'll be back in school if you keep this up."

Jelly pulled three everyday goblets from the cupboard. "I was going to put out the good dishes and crystal, but I got behind schedule. I could use a glass of that red wine right now."

Reaching into his pocket, Hank pulled out a corkscrew and flourished it aloft. "At your service, ladies." With dramatic flair, he picked up the bottle and expertly whipped off the heavy seal and twisted the screw into the cork.

Emi smirked. "It looks like you've done that a few times."

Henry chuckled. "Ah, yes, a few times."

Jelly flashed her a warning stare.

The minute timer sounded off and Jelly bent to look in the oven window. "It's done. Back away, Hank. I need some room here."

He set the bottle on the table. "Here, let me do that." He took her oven mitts, lifted the sizzling roasting pan from the oven, and stood looking around for a place to put it.

"Here," Jelly pointed to the countertop. "Set it on the trivet." Her eyes followed the pan. "That looks perfect." She smiled at Hank and Emi. "Doesn't it?"

Grinning, Hank answered, "Yes, it's perfect. I haven't had prime rib since last Christmas."

Emi piped up from the doorway, "We haven't either. Jelly's trying to make you think she can cook." Devilment sparkled in her eyes. "She had to empty the cash register at her shop to pay for that hunk of meat."

"Emi!" Jelly flushed.

Hank went back to the wine bottle and pulled the cork. "It's working, Emi. I'm impressed." He poured out two glasses and handed one to Jelly. "Here's to the best looking cook in Simi Valley."

The warmth of the wine coursed through her bloodstream even though she hadn't taken a sip yet. It wasn't the wine; it was Hank. Happiness and sadness formed a whirlpool in her thoughts. *He's so perfect. Almost.*

"Hey, you guys. Where's mine?" Emi reached the table and held up her empty glass.

Jelly opened the refrigerator. "It's cranberry juice for you, young lady."

Emi put a silent-screen-vamp pout on her lips. "Party pooper."

Hank poured the juice into Emi's glass. "I should hope so."

Jelly flipped her hands. "Okay, you two. Please get out of the kitchen and let me finish up in here. Emi, show Hank where the dishes are. He can set the table."

Hank carried his and Emi's glasses through the door. "We're on it."

Hank sighed with contentment and leaned into the back of his chair. "That was great! I'm stuffed." He held out the wine bottle. "There's not much left. Shall we polish this off?"

Emi groaned and tried to stand. "I gotta go sit on the couch and put my leg up. It's starting to ache."

Hank stood and held her chair, then before she had a chance to react, he scooped her up and carried her to the sofa. "Here you go." He plumped up the cushion, lifted her legs, and placed a pillow under them.

Emi grinned at the masculine attention. "Gee, I feel like a queen. Thanks, Mr. Henry."

"Your servant, ma'am." His exaggerated courtly bow evoked laughter from Emi and Jelly. Unable to remember when he'd had a more pleasant evening, he returned to the table, sat, and raised his glass. "A wonderful dinner, Ms. Swanson, thank you." He looked directly into Jelly's eyes but couldn't read anything clearly from her gaze. She seemed mellow and happy, but conflicted.

Jelly sighed and leaned forward on her elbows. "You're very welcome, Mr. Henry." She stood. "If you'll keep Ms. Emi company, I'll carry this wreckage to the kitchen."

Hank set down his empty glass. "Let me help you."

"No, please. I'll just be a minute. The dishes can wait till morning. We promised Emi a hot Scrabble challenge. She'll tell you where to find the set." Jelly made a shooing motion and carried the meat platter to the kitchen.

Front Porch Swing
11:00 p.m.

"I don't know how she stayed awake so long." Jelly rested her head on the back cushion of the swing. "I thought she'd never wind down."

Hank put his arm across the back of the swing. "She's quite a competitor, isn't she?"

Jelly lifted her head and smiled. "You don't know the half of it." She paused for a moment. "It's probably time for us to say goodnight, too, Hank. I'm bushed. I've got to drive to Los Feliz in the morning to look at a wardrobe collection that's up for grabs. If it's as good as I suspect, it'll be great for Big Night Out's inventory."

He stood and extended his hand. "Walk out to my truck with me." Jelly took his hand and followed him.

Leaning against the side of the truck, Hank put his hands on her shoulders. "Julie, may I kiss you goodnight?"

Embarrassment and pain clouded her face. Before he dropped his hands, she reached up and caught them, holding them to her shoulders. "Hank, oh, this is so embarrassing. I have to ask you something, and it's terribly personal."

He cocked his head. "What?" He couldn't keep alarm from his voice.

Unable to utter the words, Jelly stood mute. She ducked her head and cleared her throat. "Hank, are you, uh, are you—?"

"Julie, what is it? Am I what?"

"Gay?"

"What!" His astonished shout of laughter was so loud she reached up to put her hand over his lips.

No amount of shushing could stop his laughter. He tilted his head back and gasped for breath. When he stared at her, tears of amusement clouded his gray eyes. As answer to her dumbfounding question, he grasped her tight and planted a serious kiss on her lips.

Jelly melted into his embrace. Her arms went around him, and she held on tight.

Lifting his mouth from hers, Hank reached down and pressed her hips against his. "Does this feel like gay to you, Julie?" But before she could answer, he kissed her again and again until she was breathless.

She rested her head on his chest. "Oh, Hank, I'm so glad."

"Whatever in the world made you think I was gay?"

Jelly looked at his angular face and grinned. She brushed a wisp of curly black hair from his forehead. "I feel so stupid. I should have known there was a logical explanation, but I heard some things and then I saw something."

Hank took her arm and led her around to the passenger door. "Get in, Julie. We need to sort this out and do it where we won't be overheard."

"Where are we going? I'm not leaving Emi alone in the house."

"We're not going anywhere, we're just getting inside." He took a lingering look at her trim bottom when he helped her step up into the cab of his pickup. A few long strides led him to the driver's side. He opened his door and sat inside. "Now, tell me what you heard and what you saw, Julie."

She sighed and embarked on the events that led her to suspect he might be gay. First, Sally's former employee, Carol, claiming he had to be gay, because he never tried to sleep with her. And then finally, Jelly saw him kissing the man at school the day she and Emi left for Sacramento.

"Well, that explains why you nearly drove over me in your haste to get out of the parking lot. I wondered about that."

He shook his head and continued. "As to Ms. Gratner... I was not physically attracted to her, intellectually either, for that matter, and had no interest in pursuing a relationship."

He put his hand on her knee. "Julie, the man you saw me with was my big brother, Dominik. He brought me some specimens from the flower farm for my botany class. We happen to be an affectionate family."

"Your brother?" She grasped his hand on her knee. "You kiss your brother?" Her astonished eyes were wide in the dim truck cab. "Hank, that's wonderful."

Resting his head on the back of the seat, Hank laughed again. He turned to face her and shook his head. "You're not going to believe me, but when I told Dom about you he said the family was beginning to wonder why I had showed no interest in women for the past couple of years."

"You told your brother about me?"

"Yes, I told him I was falling for you, Julie. But I didn't know what to do about it because Emi said you were a lesbian."

Bolting upright, Jelly turned to him, disbelief written across her features. "She told you what!"

"Now don't get in a snit over it. She said it as pure adolescent speculation, because you never had any serious boyfriends —then she thought better of it and said you probably weren't."

"I can't believe she'd say such a thing. I could throttle her. It's because of her I've never, uh, that is, never had—when have I had the time for any kind of romantic life?"

"Never?"

"Oh, I had a man interested in me a couple of years ago, but that didn't last long. He didn't care at all about getting to know me, he just wanted to, uh, you know. He thought I was easy. Ha!" She clamped her lips and jerked a disgusted shake of her head.

Hank said nothing. He gazed at her, not sure he understood what she'd told him. He suspected he was misreading her. She was no kid. She was twenty-eight years old. It didn't seem possible that she—no.

"Julie, please excuse me, but I'm not sure I understand what you're saying." He reached his hand to her chin and turned her face toward his. "Julie?"

"I have to go in, Hank." She put a hand to her throat, reached for the door handle, and stepped out of the truck. Both hands to her cheeks, she ran into the house. Instantly, the porch light and living room light went off.

Stunned, Henry sat like a stone, hands gripping his knees. What had she told him? Had she told him anything?

After a few moments, he sighed deeply and started the truck. He backed out into the street before turning on his headlights and heading home. On the way, he reviewed the entire evening. Julie's reaction to his query was odd and unexpected.

He went over and over their conversation, trying to remember if he said anything to cause her sudden mood swing. Something was going on with her, but he was damned if he could understand what it was.

Chapter Seventeen

Big Night Out
Sunday, 4:00 p.m.

The wardrobe collection from the recording artist's home in Los Feliz was huge, varied, and all sized ten to fourteen. These garments would fit more local women than many of Jelly's previous finds. The best thing of all: she picked the lot up for a song. The thought made her smile. Song —recording artist.

The woman had generously given her a few signed photographs with permission to advertise from whose wardrobe the garments came. Everything was dry cleaned or laundered and ready to sell. She was a surprisingly thoughtful woman, in Jelly's estimation. She looked forward to doing business with her in the future.

Back at the store, Jelly sorted, tagged, hung, and folded for three hours. She took a cup of coffee and sat at her computer to put together print ads for the Ventura County Star. She would have a teaser ad appear in tomorrow's edition, then a half page with the singer's photograph in the Wednesday shopper edition, announcing the special sale beginning Friday. She composed a blast email to her customer list.

When she left the woman's palatial home with the last load for her car, a maid ran after Jelly and handed her a collection of *Biggest Hits* CDs. Jelly planned to put them on the stereo in the store beginning the next day.

Her cell phone buzzed. The screen displayed her home number.

"Hi, baby, is everything okay? Yes, I'm just finishing up here; it took a lot longer to sort through this treasure trove than I thought." Jelly hit the send button on her e-mail to the newspaper. "We can have leftovers tonight, or I can stop at Don Cuco's and pick up Mexican. What do you want?"

Jelly cocked her head in confusion. "He what? When?" Her head dropped back, and she pressed a hand to her eyes. "Yes, I'm here. No, he didn't say anything about it to me last night. I don't know if I can. Well, you should have called me first before you accepted the invitation, Emi. Okay, okay, calm down. Yes, we can go. I'm on my way home."

Henry's Condo
4:30 p.m.

Henry stepped out of the shower and toweled his hair and body. He didn't know what to expect when he arrived at Julie's. He felt a little guilty about calling her house to invite her and Emi to go to his parent's home in Oxnard for Sunday dinner when he knew she wouldn't be there. Nothing he could do now but show up and keep his fingers crossed.

Dom told him nearly half the family would not be at the farm this evening. That would still leave a good crowd for Sunday dinner, without counting Henry, Jelly, and Emi. More than enough Palasczewski siblings and their offspring to over-whelm them.

Hank made Dom promise to plead with everyone to be on their best behavior. He was serious about pursuing Jelly and knew how daunting his raucous family could be. He was already in trouble for going behind her back to get her up to the farm.

Jelly's ill humor grew more pervasive with every mile on her drive home. Why would Hank go around her? When he called her house, Emi must have told him she was at the shop. He should have called *her* to extend the invitation. Not Emi! He knew better than that.

Exasperated when she pulled into the driveway, she put her car into park and almost yanked off the emergency brake handle. Ready to take on the world, she stepped out of the Mustang and slammed the door. Trudging up the front walk-way, she grumbled to herself, "Damn him, I have a good mind to make up an excuse not to go."

The front door burst open, and Emi hobbled out. Her face glowed with rosy color and her big smile greeted Jelly. Emi wore a skirt and blouse and had pinned her hair up on the sides. Her uncharacteristically feminine appearance brought Jelly to a halt. There was no mistaking the child's excitement at the prospect of going to Mr. Henry's family farm for dinner.

How could Jelly possibly disappoint her? She took a deep breath and rearranged her countenance from indignant to cheerful. It wasn't easy.

Emi held the door open for her. "Jelly, Jelly, guess what?"

She stopped and put her hands on her hips. "You look very nice, Emi. I like your hair that way." Jelly noticed the mere hint of lip color. Something she'd never seen on Emi's mouth before. Every day, she looked more like their mother, Jessie.

Emi brushed away the compliment. "You didn't guess."

Hand to her chin, Jelly put on a furrowed brow expression

of deep thought. "Hmm, let me see. The Jonas Brothers answered your email?"

"No! Quit teasing me."

"Well, what is it then? I give up."

"Mr. Henry invited Marco to come with us. He's picking him up on the way here. You'll have to sit in the back seat with Marco, though. I'll never be able to get in there with this cast on my leg." She thumped back inside the house.

Jelly followed, closing the door behind them. "There's a back seat in his pickup?"

Emi pursed her lips and shook her head. Her expression clearly told Jelly she thought she was clueless. "Jeez, it has an extended cab with jump seats. Didn't you notice that?"

"When would I have noticed that?"

"When you crawled in the truck with him last night, after playing suck face in front of the whole world?"

"After I—?" Astonished at what Emi said, Jelly was struck dumb.

With an imperious tilt of her chin, Emi said, "You really shouldn't make out in front of the whole neighborhood, Jelly."

Jelly grabbed a handful of her own hair in each fist, tilted her head back, and screeched, "You were watching us?"

She turned abruptly and headed for her bedroom. "I have to change. We'll have a serious talk about this later, young lady!" Jelly slammed her bedroom door so hard it rattled dishes in the dining room sideboard.

Emi smiled and turned when the doorbell rang. "Come in, Mr. Henry. It's open," she sang.

Jelly's loud voice and the sound of the slamming door reached Henry and Marco, but when Emi invited them in, she wore a wide smile. Hank noticed the sly look she flashed in his direction. Uneasiness cramped his belly. He'd made a strategic error and already regretted it. There was nothing to do now but soldier on.

Marco wore a startled, big-eyed expression. "What was that explosion we heard? I thought we were having an earthquake." He took a second look at Emi. "Wow, you look nice, Em. I like your hair like that."

Henry jammed his hands in his pockets and gritted his teeth. He was in it now.

Emi pointed to the living room. "Let's sit down. My leg aches." Once she arranged herself on the sofa, she looked up with a foxy smile. "Jelly will probably be a while. She was in a bad mood when she got home from the store. I think she's mad at you, Mr. Henry."

Hank's belly roiled. He squirmed in the small side chair, unable to get comfortable. "Mad at me? I don't know why, I haven't seen her today." He folded his hands together and dropped them between his legs, then sat straight and put them on his knees. He knew very well why Julie was miffed. He definitely should have extended the invitation to Jelly, not Emi.

Emi wasn't going to let up; he could see that. She turned to Marco. "Mr. Henry had dinner with us last night. He was still here when I went to bed. I don't know how long he stayed, but it must have been reeeaal late."

Marco crinkled his brow. He looked from Emi to Henry and back. He was about to say something when Jelly appeared in the doorway.

Dressed in a silky hot pink, low-cut blouse over a burnt orange gypsy skirt with a fringed green sash around her hips, she was a razzle-dazzle vision. Curly auburn hair formed a circle of radiance about her head and long, shiny black beaded earrings brushed her shoulders. The small black sequined bag in her hand matched gleaming black high-heeled sandals. Hank swallowed at the sight of her slender ankles.

"Hi everybody, sorry I'm late. Shall we go?" Her tone was chirpy, even for her.

Henry saw Marco's goggle-eyed expression and hoped he

wasn't wearing a matching one. Always flashy, this time Jelly had outdone herself. Dumbstruck, he mumbled something that even he couldn't comprehend, stood, and gestured toward the front door.

The three of them started out, when a petulant voice called, "Hey, you guys, what about me?"

Marco turned back and helped Emi to her feet. "Sorry, Emi, I, uh—"

She shook off his arm. "Oh, just forget about it, doofus. Let's go."

Chapter Eighteen

Henry's Truck
Sunday, 5:30 p.m.

Sitting knees to knees on the jump seats behind Hank and Emi, Jelly felt sorry for Marco's obvious discomfort. At the same time, she got a kick from the effect she had on his teenage libido.

To quote Aunt Martha: The poor kid was twitterpated.

She caught a couple of nervous glances from Hank in the wide rearview mirror. Each time, she stared steadily back. He was in trouble with her, and he knew it. Good!

The back road through Simi Valley, Moorpark, and Camarillo was charmingly countrified, even though many of the old farms were slowly giving way to housing. The urban sprawl from Los Angeles north to the San Fernando Valley, then over the mountains into Ventura County, showed no sign of letup.

At least here on the former agricultural lands, the new homes were mostly situated on one acre and larger parcels. The cookie-cutter look of the two valleys did not prevail on this narrow back road. Most of these homes were custom-built and varied widely from California Ranch style to gaudy Moorish mini-castles.

Emi chattered away in the front seat, thoroughly enjoying the discomfort of Jelly, Hank, and Marco. Jelly had to admit she admired the clever, conniving way Emi'd set everyone up. The kid was a survivor, like her. *I must have done something right in the past twelve years.*

Her plan was to enjoy the meeting and dinner with Henry's family and conduct herself in a friendly manner, even though she'd been railroaded.

Hank took a left turn at the end of the last usable country road and went the short distance to pick up the Ventura Freeway for the rest of the trip to Oxnard. Traffic was light. Jelly figured it wouldn't be much more than twenty minutes before they reached Bodacious Blooms Farms. She had a vague memory of passing it on her way to Santa Barbara last year.

Hank turned the truck off the freeway onto a frontage road, past a closed flower stand, and down a long dirt track that finally led to a lovely sprawling farmhouse surrounded by various outbuildings, greenhouses, and sheds.

Jelly was impressed. *Some farm.*

Emi pointed. "Who's that?"

Three kids, two adolescents and a skinny teenager, ran toward their truck.

Hank smiled and waved. "My nieces." He pulled to a stop.

Varying in shades of sun bronzed skin and hair, the three girls ran to greet them. "*Tio Henry, tio Henry!*"

Henry stepped down from the truck and picked up the two youngest girls, then bent to kiss the teenager on top of her head. "How are my favorite girls?" The two he held screamed and giggled as he swung them around. The youngest were barefoot and dressed in frayed overalls and tee shirts. The older girl wore a freshly ironed dress, her hair neatly braided.

Henry set them down. He waved a pedantic finger at the

two youngest. "We have company for dinner. You look like rag pickers!"

"Their mama told them take a bath and get dressed," the tall girl said with disgust.

Leading them toward the truck, Henry lifted Emi from the front seat to make introductions once Marco and Jelly stepped down from the back. "These are my friends, Julie Swanson, Marco Rogers, and Emi Swanson." He indicated the two giggling youngsters. "These two miscreants are Thelma and Phoebe Ruiz, and this lovely young lady is Sharla Palasczewski."

The two little girls ran to the side of a shed and pulled a nursery cart back to the truck. Sharla ducked her head self-consciously when introduced. She extended her hand to Emi, then Marco. "Hi."

"Hellos" were exchanged all around. The two younger girls returned with the nursery wagon. "We washed this nice and clean," claimed Phoebe or Thelma. "You can ride in it to the greenhouse, Emi. We want to show you something."

Hank, still holding Emi, asked her, "Okay? It looks clean enough." When she nodded her ascent, he set her gently down on the big-wheeled cart. Turning to the Ruiz girls, he said, "Now don't wear her out. Bring her to the house as soon as you've shown her whatever it is. Okay?"

The two girls tugged the big handle on the front of the wagon. "Okay, tio Henry." Emi grabbed the sides as they pulled her away from the truck. Marco followed alongside, joined by Sharla.

Henry watched them, then turned toward Jelly. He raised his hands as if to say something, stopped, stuck them in his pockets, and looked skyward. Jelly remained silent, waiting for whatever he had to say. "Nice evening," was all he managed.

The front door of the house opened, and a tall blonde woman beckoned them to come in. "Henry, bring your friend in. Dom is pouring wine, and you know how fast it disappears around here." A warm, inviting smile glowed from her face.

Jelly smiled in return and walked toward the house. She chuckled inwardly as Hank did a quick two-step to catch up with her. "You must be Mollie," Jelly said. "I'm Julie Swanson, but everybody calls me Jelly sooner or later, so you might as well start now."

Mollie took her hand. "Yes, that's me. How nice to meet you at last. I love your nickname."

Jelly felt Mollie's appraising eyes and, for a second, wished she had toned down her flamboyant choice of clothing.

"Come in. Henry told us all about you, and you're just as beautiful as he said." She looked past Jelly's shoulder. "Don't just stand there, Henry. Get Jelly a glass of wine."

They stepped aside so Henry could pass into the wide hall-way. "If you'd like, hang up your shawl and purse on one of the hooks here." Mollie pointed to a long row of wrought iron hooks on one side of the hall, holding an assortment of caps, hats, jackets, and sweaters. An ancient looking umbrella stand stood just inside the door, stuffed to bursting.

Terra cotta tiles on the floor reflected the cheery light cast by three wrought iron chandeliers along the high ceiling. The wall opposite the coat hooks was one long hand-painted mural with a jumble of themes from Mexican cowboys to a fancy dress ball. A colorful depiction of the roadside flower stand exploding with colorful blooms graced the middle.

Jelly's eyes were wide as she stepped back to have a good look at the artwork. "Wow. This is something! Who painted it?"

Mollie chuckled and pointed to several sections while she rattled off a string of names, only a few of which Jelly recognized. "We've all had a hand in it at one time or another. It's a moving feast. One of these days, somebody will paint over this part and put up something new. It's our very own diorama."

Jelly nodded her wonderment and approval. "It certainly beats refrigerator art."

Mollie laughed and took her arm. "Oh, never fear, we have plenty of that, too." She indicated a wide double door beyond the coat hooks. "Let's join the others, shall we? It's like a boarding house around here—every man for himself. Food and wine disappear faster than we can set it out on Sunday evenings. Ah, here's Henry with our drinks."

Hank headed to the doorway as they entered. He carried three ordinary kitchen water glasses, each half full of red wine, two in one hand and one in the other. He smiled and handed one to his sister-in-law and one to Jelly, then raised his in a small salute. "The kitchen smells wonderful, as usual, Mollie. Looks like we got here in time to grab a seat at the table. Who else is coming?"

"Everybody who's coming is here. I think about half the kids and their parents are in the greenhouse looking at Pele's latest litter of calico kittens. They're just getting their eyes open and beginning to stand without wobbling."

Jelly grinned. "Kittens? How many?"

"She had five this time. This will be her last litter. We had Old Tomás altered, and all our other cats are females."

Jelly's eyebrows went up. "All your others? How many cats live here? And why are they all females?"

Another woman beckoned to Mollie from what was probably the kitchen. Mollie waved back. "I'll let Henry explain everything to you. Looks like they're putting the final touches on dinner."

She turned as if to go, then stopped. "Oh, Henry, I should warn you. Speaking of cats, your ex-fiancée, the Lovely Linda, showed up unannounced. She's staying for dinner. Steel yourself. She hasn't changed."

Henry's face went stark white. He took a big gulp, downing

his entire glass of wine. His Adam's apple bounced as he swallowed. "Oh, my Lord," he uttered, "Why tonight? Why, God?"

Clearing her throat, Jelly cocked her head, taking in his obvious distress. "Your, um, ex-fiancée?"

His answer was a mute nod, forehead wrinkled, an expression of pain in his eyes.

Working to maintain her composure, Jelly shrugged. "Well, she can't be that bad."

"You have no idea what—oh, Lord, here she comes."

Chapter Nineteen

7:00 p.m.

The woman swooped down on them in the manner of a bird of prey, or maybe more like Cruella de Ville. "Henry, darling, you don't look well. Are you ill?" The tall, dark-haired woman honed in on Hank, completely ignoring Jelly. Her hand in the crook of his arm, she tugged him away. "You need some air. Come with me."

Jelly stood paralyzed. A jolt of embarrassment gripped her gut. Hank cast a helpless look in her direction, then followed the woman without so much as a mild protest, leaving Jelly standing alone, wine glass in hand, feeling like a chump. She wasn't sure what to do. Stand there? Follow them? That can't be why Hank brought her out here, actually tricked her into coming out here. No, he wasn't like that. He wasn't the kind of man to deliberately hurt her like that.

A man's voice from behind startled her so much she slopped wine out of the glass onto her hand.

"Oh, I'm sorry." He handed her a paper napkin. "Didn't mean to scare you. I see Linda's up to her nasty old tricks." His smile was full of sympathy. "I'm Dominik, Henry's brother. You met my wife, Mollie. Call me, Dom."

Jelly took a breath, unable to summon up a response. The glass shook in her hand. Dom reached out and took it from her. "Why don't you come to the kitchen with me? The women are about to bring out the buffet. You and I can lend them a hand."

Jelly took a breath and touched him on the arm. "Thanks. Yes, I'd like to help. I recognize you from one morning at the high school. I didn't know then you were Henry's brother." She turned a withering look in the direction of the doors that opened onto a patio at the side of the dining room. The doors the woman had pulled Hank through. "What's with her? She seems very rude."

"Yes, Linda's in fine form tonight. She's best friends with one of my sisters, Danuta. Dani must have mentioned Henry would be here tonight. Linda has perfect timing, perfect in the same sense as a fly in the gravy boat. Henry is well rid of her, and he knows it. Had all of us worried for some time, I can tell you."

"It doesn't look to me like he's 'rid of her.'"

Dom raised his eyebrows. "Oh, he is. She's determined to make his life hell, whether they're together or not." He placed his hand on the small of Jelly's back and directed her toward the kitchen door. "You have nothing to worry about."

Jelly raised her chin. "I'm not the least bit worried. In fact, I'm not particularly happy with Henry myself at the moment." She pasted a big, friendly smile on her face as they went through the door.

Dom didn't comment. He introduced her to his mother, Anka, and his sister, Dani Ruiz. Mollie passed them with a large platter of aromatic, steaming roast beef. "Grab that bowl of potatoes, Dom. Don't let your mother carry it. It's hot and heavy."

Henry's mother took Jelly's hand. "Hello, my dear Julie. I'm so happy to meet you. I hope we get a chance to visit a bit later. Right now, we have to get this food out. Would you carry this?" She reached behind her and handed Jelly a platter of fragrant, roasted yellow squash, gleaming with a caramelized burnish.

Dani brushed past, carrying a stack of plates. She whispered, "I'm really sorry about Linda. We've been friends since second grade. Today, I could kill her."

"Don't give it another thought," Jelly answered. "She doesn't bother me a bit." *That's a big fat lie. I'd like to kill both of them!*

Once the food was placed on the side buffet, things moved fast. Without ceremony, those present picked up plates, piled on the food, and carried them to the table. They took seats at random.

Dom walked out to the patio, where Jelly presumed Henry and his "ex-fiancée" were ensconced, and hollered for the kids to, "Come and get it."

Soon, a clatter of shoes and bare feet sounded in the hallway. "Oh, no, you don't!" Dani barred the door to the dining room. "Go wash those hands! And where are your guests?"

Thelma or Phoebe pointed to the front door where Emi and Marco were making their way down the hall. "Come with me," Dani told them. "You can wash the kittens off your hands in here." She directed Marco and Emi to a small guest bathroom at the end of the hall.

Back in the dining room, Anka urged Jelly to take a plate for herself. She did and found a seat at the table between Dom and a dark-haired man to whom she hadn't been introduced.

Dom pointed. "Jelly, this is my brother-in-law, Joe Ruiz, Dani's husband. Thelma and Phoebe are their daughters. Joe's our general manager."

Joe's frank appraising smile was wide and infectious. "I see Henry's taste in *senoritas* has dramatically improved. Happy to meet you, Jelly. Is that your real name?" They shook hands.

Joe's dazzling white smile contrasted with a well-tanned, very handsome face. Antonio Banderas came to mind.

Unable to resist his flattering remark, Jelly's mood lifted. "No, it's Julie Lea, but my little sister couldn't say it when she was learning to talk. So, I'm stuck with Jelly."

"It is a tongue twister, Julie Lea, even for me. Jelly conjures up all sorts of sweet images. So, Jelly it is." He picked up his fork. "Dig in. Food disappears fast around here."

The three girls, joined by two boys Jelly hadn't noticed when they arrived earlier, pounded into the dining room. Sharla took Emi's arm and had Marco take two plates, one for himself and one for Emi. Sharla indicated various dishes on the sideboard and loaded up their plates for them. When they reached the end of the buffet, she nodded in the direction of the patio and they proceeded outside.

Jelly leaned in and asked Dom, "Where are the kids going?"

He tilted his chin. "Mollie has a table set up on the covered patio for the youngsters."

"Oh, I hope they don't get cold."

"No, we have an outdoor heater. It's very pleasant out there."

As the kids carried their plates out to the patio, Henry and Linda entered the dining room. Henry cast a furtive look around the table and flashed a brief, embarrassed smile when he spotted Jelly. Linda, still grasping Henry's arm, tugged him over to the buffet, a smug smile on her striking face.

Jelly couldn't help watching them. Linda was almost as tall as Henry. Her long raven hair hung below her shoulders in soft, heavy waves, as black and shiny as a new pair of patent leather shoes. That hair reminded Jelly of the impossible to believe shampoo commercials. Until this moment, she didn't think anyone actually had hair like that.

As far as Jelly could tell, Linda wore no makeup. Her high cheekbones and slightly slanted coal dark eyes hinted of

Hispanic or Asian genes. She had a generous mouth and a long slim neck. Unlike Jelly, she was dressed very plainly in a white western style shirt and tight faded blue jeans. Well-worn cowboy boots on her rather large feet finished the picture. She exuded understated elegance, in spite of her clothing. But there was nothing understated about Linda. On the contrary, she was as stunning as a runway model.

Aware of her own showy style by comparison, Jelly's food suddenly became hard to swallow. It stuck like glue in her throat. She reached for her glass and sipped some wine. Why did she care anyway? Hank had abandoned her the minute that woman came into the room with claws bared. *I hate him! No, I don't. My life is over.*

Chastising herself for such self-pitying and dramatic thoughts, Jelly concentrated on the two charming men on either side of her.

Anka leaned across and pointed to her husband at the head of the table. "Janusz! This is Henry's very special friend, Jelly. You were in the seed shed when they arrived. Say hello."

The old man lifted his heavily thatched gray head and beamed a high wattage smile down the table to Jelly. "Halloo, be-you-ti-ful girl! Henryk, he's good boy bring you here." He saluted her with his wine glass.

Jelly raised her glass and returned his smile. When she looked at Henry's mother, the old woman winked a sparkling brown eye and nodded ever so slightly.

"Dad always had an eye for the pretty ladies," Dom said as he bumped Jelly with his elbow.

"Did he say Henryk?"

"Yes, that's Henry's birth name. We all have traditional Polish names. Dominik, Aleksy, Stanislaw, Danuta, Henryk, and Zofia. We're first generation Americans, and we broke tradition. All our kids have American names. Pop's still not happy about that." Dom cast an affectionate look at his father.

"Henry told me your parents still work full time here."

"Yes, they're a couple of old warhorses. Takes all of us to rein them in. Pop's out there every day making the rounds, checking up on us. Mollie tries to keep Mama busy in the house and out of the hot sun. So instead, Mama spends most of her day over a hot stove! Wait till you see what she made for dessert!"

"What?" Jelly smiled with curiosity. "What did she make?"

Dom leaned in close and whispered, "It's supposed to be a secret because she made it special for you. Poppy seed makowiec."

"For me? Makovsk—makoviks?"

"Close enough."

"I never heard of it."

"She only makes it for special occasions and holidays. But when she knew Henry was bringing you to meet the family, and what that meant, we couldn't keep her away from the kitchen."

Stunned and surprised that Henry's mother had gone to so much trouble for her, Jelly chastised herself for second guessing Hank's motivation. Maybe he *was* sincere in his feelings for her. Maybe the "Lovely Linda" *had* shown up unexpectedly. Here she sat, surrounded by Henry's big family, so different from her own. She couldn't get her mind around how nurturing and safe it must be to grow up in a family like this one.

Chapter Twenty

Halfway Back to Jelly's House
Sunday, 10:30 p.m.

Emi got a second wind during the drive back home as she chattered on and on about the calico kittens and Sharla. "She said when they get eight weeks old, they'll be big enough to leave their mother. She said I could pick any one of them I want. I liked the one that had a big orange spot on one eye and a big black spot on the other, like a Halloween mask. You know the one, Marco? She has a black tail with a white tip."

Marco leaned forward. "I liked the twins with different colored stripes and white boots."

Henry chuckled and glanced in the rearview mirror. "They'll look different the next time you see them." His gaze was directed pointedly at Jelly. She looked away out the side window.

Emi turned in the front seat with difficulty, so she could see Jelly. "Can we have a kitten, Jelly? Please, please, please?" Her hopeful, wide-eyed expression melted Jelly's heart.

"Oh, I suppose so. Why not? But you'll have to take care of

it. Feed it and clean up after it. A pet is a living responsibility, not like a book you can put on a shelf."

A shriek of joy erupted from Emi, surprising the others into laughter. Jelly was unable to nurture her bruised feelings. It wasn't in her nature, anyway. She leaned back against her seat and winked at Marco.

"I'll have my cast off by the time she's old enough to come home with us," Emi said, full of excitement. "I have to think of a name. Can you think of any good names, Marco? Mr. Henry?"

Hank smiled. "How about Katarzyna? It's a good Polish name. Means pure. She's pure calico."

Marco chimed in, "Yeah, you could call her Kat for short."

They all laughed, and Emi groaned.

"Or maybe she's Mexican. You could name her El Cato." Marco's joke brought on another eruption of laughter followed by boos and groans all around.

Jelly noticed Hank's glance in the rearview mirror. She rewarded him with a small smile. The look of relief on his face was pathetic. They definitely needed to talk. If she could manage it, that is.

Hank pulled into Marco's driveway. He exited the truck and escorted Marco to the door as Jelly and Emi shouted their good nights. The porch light on, Marco's dad opened the door. After a brief conversation with him, Hank returned to the truck, got in, and backed out.

"I apologized for bringing him home so late on a school night," Hank explained.

"Was he mad at you?" Emi asked.

"No, he was fine with it. I called before we left the farm so he knew about when to expect us." He turned the corner. "Now it's past your bedtime, too, young lady."

Emi sighed, shoulders drooping. "Yeah. I'm pooped."

At Jelly's house, Henry came around to the passenger door,

lifted Emi out, and carried her to the front porch. After setting her gently down, he turned to Jelly. "Julie, can we have a word?"

Jelly unlocked the front door and reached inside to turn on the living room lights. "Could you wait out here for a couple of minutes?" When he nodded his assent, she helped Emi inside to her bedroom.

The second she stepped outside the front door, Hank reached for her. "Julie, we need to talk. I want to explain."

She gave him an imploring look. "Hank, yes, but does it have to be tonight? It's late and I have to help Emi with her sponge bath so she can get to sleep. Tomorrow is a school day, remember?"

He straightened and stuck his hands in his pockets, obviously disappointed. "Okay, sure, you're right. Tomorrow then?"

"Isn't tomorrow night Parent-Teacher Open House?"

"Oh, right. Well, uh, then maybe we...?"

"Hank, I'm going in now. I'll see you at school tomorrow evening."

He shrugged and sighed. "Okay then." He turned to leave.

Jelly stepped forward and touched his arm. "Hank, thank you for taking us to meet your wonderful family. I had a real nice time, really, I did. In spite of—"

She smiled at his sigh of relief.

"Julie, may I kiss you goodnight?"

Chapter Twenty-One

Santa Susana High School
Monday, 7:00 p.m.

Henry's classroom was abuzz with voices. Students and parents milled about examining projects and exhibits, some waiting their turn for a short conversation with the teacher.

Henry looked up whenever he had a short break between parents. Jelly and Emi hadn't appeared yet.

Marco and his parents stood next to the science fair exhibit for which he and Emi had brought home the blue ribbon. When Emi and Jelly arrived, Marco hopped off a high lab table stool with wheels and pushed it over to the door. He and Jelly each took one of Emi's arms and helped her to sit. Jelly took the crutches while Marco pushed Emi over to the project table, where his parents waited.

Heads turned at the sound of the wheels rumbling and bumping over the linoleum floor. Several of Emi's classmates smiled, waved, and called greetings.

Henry nodded in their direction and flashed a happy and relieved smile.

Jelly wore sleek-fitting gold-hued pants and a long-sleeved brown cashmere sweater with a deep V at the neckline. The garments could have been painted on, and they showcased her figure to perfection.

Hank shifted uncomfortably in his seat and returned his attention to the parents and student he conferred with. His heart tappity-tap-tapped like the snare drum section of the school marching band.

The three minutes left in his immediate parent conference seemed to drag endlessly. Finally, he stood and shook hands with the parents and patted his student on the shoulder. He called out the next name on his sign-in sheet.

Jelly chatted with Marco's parents. After a moment, Mrs. Rogers pointed to Henry's desk. Jelly nodded and walked to the front of the classroom. Marco and Mr. Rogers both gazed longingly after her retreating figure.

Henry worked at putting on a professional face. "Ah, Ms. Swanson, glad you could make it. If you and your student would like to confer with me, please sign in and I'll call you when your name comes up." He handed the clipboard to Jelly.

Jelly looked at the form and pointed a shiny red nail sporting a small gold heart. "Here?"

"Yes," Henry croaked and cleared his throat. "Right there, after Mrs. Droguette." He noticed the father sitting across the desk from him give Jelly an admiring once-over. Henry was determined he would not watch her as she walked away, to no avail. He felt his neck heat with a blush he couldn't stop.

The man wiggled his eyebrows and said, "Quite a looker."

"Rudy!"

"Dad!"

"What'd I say?"

His daughter leaned toward him and said in a stage whisper, "Ms. Swanson is a very nice lady, Daddy."

"Yes," added his wife. "I shop at her boutique and she's always very professional and polite. Shame on you."

Rudy sat back and raised his hands in a helpless gesture. "Sorry, I didn't know a sincere compliment was disrespectful."

Henry picked up the student's file. "Perhaps we should get back to Keri's progress report." He winked at Keri's dad.

After Keri's conference ended, Henry stood. "Swanson?" He waved his clipboard in the direction of Jelly and Emi. The room had mostly cleared out; just one more student and his parents waited to speak with him.

Jelly and Emi sat at Hank's desk and the brief and unnecessary conference proceeded. The three of them had spent enough time together the past week that there was little to discuss about Emi's progress.

Once they finished speaking, Jelly leaned forward. "Hank, why don't you come by the house when you finish up here? Have dinner with us. Nothing fancy."

He'd already had dinner and wasn't the least bit hungry. "I'd love to have dinner with you ladies. I should be done here in another thirty minutes. Is that too late?"

Jelly helped Emi stand and handed her the crutches. "No, not at all. We'll see you shortly, then?" She extended her arm.

Henry grasped her hand, liking the way hers nearly disappeared inside his. He held on a beat longer than necessary, feeling fuzzy warmth inside.

He stood and gestured to the last parents. "Mr. and Mrs. Wilson?"

Henry's gaze followed Jelly's every step as she left his classroom. With heroic effort, he got his mind off Julie to concentrate on the Wilson family student conference.

During dinner, Emi mentioned her follow-up appointments with Dr. Thompson. He wanted to see her next week, then every week. The appointments were all on Mondays, all at four p.m.

Jelly groaned. "Oh, wouldn't you know? I just worked out Jeannie's new hours and gave her every Monday off. Can you change them to another day? I'd have to close the store to take you."

Emi rolled her eyes and flashed a look of frustration in Jelly's direction. "No, I can't change them to another day. The nurse said they had to be on Mondays and that's, like, the latest appointment of the day. Jeez, it's not my fault."

Jelly shook her head and stared at Emi. "I'm not blaming you. If I'd known before, I would have given Jeannie a different day off, that's all."

Hank put down his glass. "I can take Emi. Classes are over before four. We can leave right from school."

Jelly gave him a skeptical look. "Oh, I don't know if that's a good idea, Hank."

"Why not? Dr. Thompson's office is between the high school and your store. I can take her to the doctor and drop her off at your place after she sees him."

Emi's eyes flicked from side to side as if watching a Ping-Pong match.

"Look," Hank said in a calm, logical voice. "I'll take her next week. We'll see how it works out. It's no problem for me."

"I hate to impose on you, Hank. It's so nice of you to offer, but I'm sure you have other things to do."

"Julie, friends do favors for friends. It's that simple." He raised his hands with an end-of-discussion gesture.

Emi smiled at Jelly's shrug of resignation.

Big Night Out
Monday, 5:30 p.m.

The register was balanced, the bank deposit ready in the drop bag, the CLOSED sign flipped over, but still no sign of Emi and Hank. This was just too much time for him to spend ferrying Emi between school and the doctor. Not his responsibility. It made her uncomfortable, obligated. She spent a few minutes lining up shoes and rearranging the costume jewelry case. *Where are they?*

In the back room, Jelly set up the coffee machine for the next morning. She tied the plastic trash bag and put a fresh one in the waste container. *What's keeping them?*

The sound of a key in the front door followed by the jangle of bells got her attention. Emi called out, "Jelly? We're here. Mr. Henry picked up a pizza for dinner. Are you here?"

"Yes, I'm here." She pushed back the curtain and strolled toward them. "Pizza? I was wondering why you were late." Hank's appreciative gaze slid from her head to her toes, his grin so big she returned his smile with a resigned shake of her head. She tingled in all the right places whenever Hank smiled. *When did I give up control of my life to this man?*

"Yes, I, uh, thought if I picked up something, you'd have more time to relax and eat before you go walking with your friends. Emi said you go almost every evening at seven."

Jelly pursed her lips and cast a smirk at her conniving little sister. "That's very thoughtful Hank. You'll join us for dinner, won't you?"

Sally's Front Porch
8:00 p.m.

Connie pushed her foot against the concrete walkway, rocking the glider while sipping iced water. "Looks like he's using every excuse to spend time with you, chica. Gotta give the guy credit for persistence."

Jelly shrugged and shook her head. "I'm not so sure it's okay for Hank to be driving Emi to Dr. Thompson's every week."

"I don't see why you're so concerned." Sally handed her a frosty, dripping bottle of water and sat beside her.

Jelly put the bottle against her forehead. "Is it hot tonight or is it me?"

Sally and Connie chuckled, both answering, "Yes."

"You guys are a great big help."

Sally nudged her. "Come on, we're always on your side, you know that. I just don't understand why you can't just relax and enjoy his attention."

"'Bout time you had a regular guy." Connie winked. "You're not gettin' any younger."

"I can always depend on you to cheer me up, Connie." Jelly stuck out her tongue, extended her leg, and kicked Connie's foot.

"Watch it!" She dodged the kick and laughed. "That's what friends are for. Right, Sal?"

"Right."

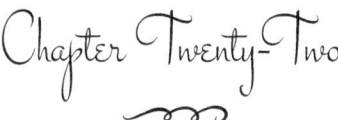

Chapter Twenty-Two

Big Night Out
Two Weeks Later, Monday, 4:45 p.m.

Jelly carefully wrapped the green Irish wool cape with plush red lining in tissue paper. All she could think about was Hank. Hank in the morning, Hank in the afternoon, and especially Hank every evening. *Breathe, Julie, breathe.*

"Is your sister doing well?"

"Yes, thanks for asking, Mrs. Miller. Emi's doing very well. She's got a knee-high, removable walking brace. Now she can bathe on her own." She handed the bagged garment across the counter to her customer. "That's important to a girl her age."

The elderly woman took her package, looked at the receipt, and smiled. "I happened to be in Dr. Thompson's office when she and her teacher came in for her appointment this afternoon. Did you know my niece is the receptionist there?"

Jelly cocked her head to one side. "No, I didn't know that, Mrs. Miller. Emi's appointments are at an awkward time for me. Mr. Palaszczewski has been very kind to take her after school. He should be dropping her off here any time now."

Mrs. Miller put the receipt in her bag. "Such a nice looking young man, that teacher, and so solicitous of your sister. They seem to enjoy each other's company, don't you think? While waiting for the doctor, they had their heads together studying a textbook, chattering away, laughing and smiling."

Something in Mrs. Miller's comments unsettled Jelly. Hair prickled on the top of her head. She cleared her throat and put on a professional smile. "Thank you for your business, Mrs. Miller. Do come again."

Quiet in the shop now, Jelly worked to shake off the unpleasant feeling by rearranging some inventory in the costume jewelry case. Customers often noticed a piece merely because she placed it in a different location on the black velvet background.

The bell above the door tinkled. Jelly automatically raised her head with a welcoming smile. The smile quickly faded when Henry's ex-fiancée, Linda, strode into the shop. Endless legs in tight faded jeans.

Linda ignored Jelly. She pushed hangers back and forth on one of the clothing racks across from the jewelry counter. Jelly stood rooted to the floor. With difficulty she said, "Hello, welcome to Big Night Out," and was mortified when her voice took on an unattractive squeak.

Clearing her throat, she added, "You're Linda." *You sound like a Class-A moron, Julie Swanson.*

Linda made a slow imperious turn and looked down her perfect nose. "Do I know you?"

What a bitch.

Jelly pulled herself up to her full height, still a good five inches shorter than Linda. Without a hint of warmth in her professional businesslike smile, she said, "No, I don't believe you do. We weren't introduced two Sundays ago at the Palasczewski home. I'm Julie Swanson." Jelly extended her hand.

Linda raised her perfect cleft chin. Her face took on a phony, puzzled expression. She reached around the back of her perfect neck and pulled her perfect raven hair across her perfect right shoulder, exposing her perfect left ear. Pursing her perfect lips with false confusion, she studied Jelly with her perfect ebony eyes. Raising her perfect jet-black eyebrows, she said with false warmth, "Oh, yes, now I remember. You're Henry's little friend. How nice to meet you." She took Jelly's hand in a perfectly cold and perfectly limp handshake.

Double bitch.

Jelly rounded the jewelry counter. "May I help you find something? Pants are out of the question. You're much too tall for anything I have in the shop right now." She appraised Linda with a saleswoman's eye. "I do have dresses, skirts, and blouses in your size. Twelve, is it?"

A cold stare. "Ten."

Jelly looked pointedly at Linda's feet. "Ah, yes, I do have a rather large inventory of size ten and eleven dress shoes. Were you looking for something in particular? Special occasion perhaps?"

Linda, her perfect lips clamped and white, looked around the shop. "I doubt you have anything to my liking. I was looking for something more, shall we say, tasteful."

Indignation prompted a nasty jolt of acid reflux to the back of Jelly's throat. "Yes, I do recall that you dressed very plainly that evening, as you are now. Perhaps you'd like to try something, shall we say, feminine?"

Take that, bitch.

The door flew open. "I'm here early!" Emi called. "Mr. Henry just dropped me off. Look how good I'm walking." She quick-stepped across the shop, stopped, and flashed a pleased-with-herself smile.

"Hello, Emi," Linda said.

Surprised, Emi stopped abruptly. "Hi, Linda, what are *you* doing here?"

Linda's smile was a bit warmer when she answered Emi. "I'm looking for something different to wear. Henry's taking me out to dinner tonight. It's my birthday."

Jelly's stomach roiled. Hank was taking her to dinner for her birthday? She wasn't sure whom she wanted to smack more— Hank or Linda.

Emi's eyebrows went up and her face brightened. "Oh, that's why he was in such a hurry. Linda, you know what would look great on you? One of these lace tops from over on that rack. It would look so cool with jeans." She hobbled a few racks over and motioned for Linda to follow.

Emi pulled a hanger off the bar, then put it back. "No, not this one. Jelly, where's the top with the cap sleeves and the little bit of lace ruffle around the neck? It would look, like, excellent on Linda."

"Sold it."

"Oh, too bad. But here's another one almost like it." She held up the blouse for Linda. "See, it's even your size. Ten, right?"

Linda cast a sidewise smirk in Jelly's direction. "Yes. How did you know?"

Appearing oblivious to the tension between the two women, Emi happily went on, "Oh, I learned from Jelly. She's so good at judging sizes."

"Really. How nice for you to learn from an expert."

Emi waved her hands with excitement. "Oh, oh, oh, you know what? One of those antique hair combs would look great. Jelly has one that looks like lace with garnets in it. I'll show you."

Linda followed Emi to the glass top display case. "There are so many. Where did they all come from?"

Emi slid the back of the case open. "Jelly bought a whole

collection of them from the estate of an old time movie star. Rhoda, Rona, what was her name, Jelly?"

Through gritted teeth, Jelly managed, "Rhonda Fleming."

"Yeah, her." Emi pulled out the comb she had mentioned. "Here it is, Linda. Isn't it awesome?"

Linda smiled. "Totally." She turned the bejeweled comb over and over in her hand, glancing quickly at the price tag. "I love it. Show me how to wear it."

Emi grinned and pushed a pedestal mirror to the middle of the case. "You, um, pull up your hair on the side and... Sit down, I'll show you."

Linda sat on the pink velvet vanity stool. Emi came around the counter, stood behind her, and peered into the mirror. Picking up a handful of Linda's perfect hair, she gave it a twist and expertly fastened it behind the comb. "How does that look?"

Linda admired her perfect self in the mirror, turning her head this way and that. "I love it. Is there a matching one?"

"Oh, they don't have to match. That's the cool thing about the hair combs." Emi hurried back to the other side of the case. "Here, try this one on the other side." She held up a tortoise shell comb inlaid with mother of pearl.

Linda, aware of Jelly's seething anger, smiled sweetly at Emi. "Would you put it in my hair for me? You seem to have the knack."

Emi happily complied. "Let's go back behind the curtain, and you can try on the blouse and see how it all works together. It's going to look great on you, Linda."

When did this kid become the super-saleswoman-fashion-expert?

Jelly took a long swallow of bitter cold coffee from the cup next to the register. She shuddered as much from the taste as she did from trying to take in the fact that Hank was taking this cunning, long-legged *femme fatale* to dinner. Something he'd conveniently failed to mention while cozying up to her the last evening they were together.

Ex-fiancée, my whatchamacallit!

Linda and Emi chattered and laughed behind the try-on drape, sounding like giddy rock band groupies.

Jelly clamped her jaws so tight her teeth ached. She wanted to scream and pull her hair.

The curtain slid open, and Emi pointed. "Look, Jelly. Doesn't Linda look great?"

Linda strolled out on her perfect legs and did a perfect model's turn, a smug smile on her perfect lips.

Jelly had the urge to kick her perfect ass. Instead, she forced a smile. "Yes, she looks great, Emi. You have quite the eye."

Linda admired herself in the full-length mirror and purred like a cat full of clotted cream, "I'll take it."

Emi went behind the counter. "Let me ring it up, Jelly. Okay?"

Jelly shrugged and moved aside. "Go right ahead. It's your sale."

Emi tapped away on the adding machine, mumbling to herself. "Let's see, that'll be fourteen dollars for the lace top, hmm, good price, and thirty dollars for the shell comb, and forty-five dollars for the antique garnet comb." She looked up. "That's eighty-nine dollars, Linda. What a bargain, huh? And with tax, it comes to ninety-four dollars and seventy-nine cents. We'll just round it off to ninety-five." Emi tilted her head. "Will that be cash, check or credit card?"

Linda reached into the back pocket of her jeans. "Check, if that's okay."

Emi folded the shirt Linda had worn into the shop and put it in a shocking pink Big Night Out bag. "I'll need to put your driver's license number on it."

Linda, suddenly stone faced, pushed her open billfold across the glass counter. "It's right there." She made quick work of writing the check.

Emi extended her hand. "Could you remove the license from your wallet? It's store policy to make a copy of the license and the check." She put a sweet smile on her adorable young face, took the license and check, placed them on the glass of the copy machine, and punched the button.

When the copy came through the slot, Emi reached for the license, studied it, and handed it to Linda. "Happy thirtieth birthday and do have a lovely evening with Dr. Palasczewski. We appreciate your business." She handed over the sack holding Linda's purchases.

Expression cold in her perfect black eyes, Linda snatched the bag and quickly left the store.

Jelly raised her eyebrows. "Since when is that store policy?"

Emi grinned. "Since that scheming witch walked in here."

Jelly whooped with laughter and hugged her. "How did I ever get you for a sister?"

Emi leaned her elbows on the glass countertop and rested her chin on her fist. "You're just lucky, I guess."

Jelly tapped her on the head. "You're so right about that."

Emi stood straight. She cast a sly glance at Jelly. "Now, what do we do about Mr. Henry—the big stinker."

Meet-up Corner
Monday, 7:00 p.m.

Connie chuckled, astonished. "She said what?"

Jelly stepped off in the direction of the hill. "She said he was a stinker."

Sally was a step behind the other two. "I don't know, Jelly. First, you might be in love. Then he's gay. Then he shows you how *much* he is *not* gay and takes you to meet his family. His old girlfriend shows up and still has her hooks in him. Now the old girlfriend tells you he's taking her out for dinner." She paused for a breath. "You have a very interesting life."

Jelly picked up the pace, in spite of Connie tugging her shirt in an attempt to slow her down. "Too interesting."

"Yes," Connie chimed in. "Every once in a while, I remind myself how nice and comfortable it feels to be in a long uncomplicated marriage rut."

"Miguel is a prince," Jelly stated.

"In his own mind," Connie answered, chuckling.

Sally poked Connie's shoulder. "Come on, you know he is."

"Yeah, you're both right. I got lucky with *mi esposo*. He's a prince for sure." She glanced at Sally. "Charlie was, too."

Sally blinked and took a deep breath. "That he was." She quickly got in step with Connie and Jelly. "Now, what sage advice do we two older, more experienced women offer young Jelly? Or maybe we shouldn't."

"Yes," Jelly said. "Help me out here. What should I do? I'm mad at him, I'm mad about him. I think about him day and night. God, he's a great kisser! For the past two weeks, it's been all I can do to keep from falling on my back, if you know what I mean. I never had any of these feelings before. Now, tonight, he's on a date with *her!*" She waved her fisted hands and screeched.

Connie's eyebrows went up. "Uh oh, have you told him you were, um, inexperienced?"

"No! How can I tell him that?"

Sally shook her head. "Jelly, were you planning on him finding out by accident? That's not fair to either of you. If you want him, he needs to know. You can't have secrets."

"So what if I want him? Looks like Linda still has him. Why else would he be taking her out? He never told me he was engaged before. He has secrets, too."

"Look, chica," Connie said. "You want the man. We know you want the man. You know you want the man. You gotta fight for him. There're a lot of women out there who're trolling for good men. It doesn't stop them just because he happens to be yours."

Sally said, "Boy, don't I know it. Charlie had a secretary once who—never mind." Sally took a couple more steps before she realized Connie and Jelly had stopped.

"Never mind?" they said.

"No way do you get away with 'never mind.'" Connie faced Sally with hands on hips. "Give." Her chin raised in challenge. Jelly mimicked her posture.

Sally threw up her hands. "Oh, it was nothing, really. It's just, I could tell from the day he hired her that she wanted to get something going with him. I told Charlie. He thought I was acting nutty and paranoid."

"Sally," Jelly asked, "what did you do?"

Connie took a step forward. "Yeah, what?"

"Well, if you must know, I invited her out to lunch. Told her I knew what she was up to and suggested she back off and do what she was hired for, which didn't include vamping Charlie."

"Wow," Connie said. "Nothing like taking *El Toro* by the horns, eh?"

Admiration glowing in her wide gray eyes, Jelly said, "Sally, you're so brave. What happened?"

Sally shrugged and smiled. "She turned out to be a very efficient secretary and ended up going after one of the divorced men at Charlie's company. They got married and moved to Denver. I didn't tell Charlie what I'd done till years later."

Connie shook her head and chuckled. "What did he say?"

"He was amused, and I think, secretly flattered that I made a preemptive strike to avoid a full-out war." Sally sighed at the memory. "Jelly, it's a great ego boost when your man knows you're willing to fight for him."

"Miguel knows I'd fight for him," Connie said. "And he also knows I'd cut his heart out after."

"Connie, you have absolutely nothing to worry about. Miguel worships and adores you." Sally waved them on. "Let's get going. It's getting late."

They walked in silence for several minutes, rounded the corner on Yosemite and headed down Alamo toward the finish line. When they reached the street that led to Sally's and Connie's, Jelly continued alone on Alamo.

She walked backward several steps and held up her crossed fingers. "I got my work cut out for me."

"Yes, you do, chica."

"I'll tell you what happens after I talk to Hank."

Sally called after her, "I'll be at your store the minute you open tomorrow. We know you'll figure it out."

Jelly waved over her shoulder. "I'm glad you know. I sure don't."

Chapter Twenty-Three

Henry's Condo
Wednesday, 11:30 p.m.

S hifting nervously from foot to foot on Hank's doormat, Jelly jumped when the porch light went on.

Hank opened the door, shirtless in pajama bottoms. His hair tousled, his eyes wide with surprise. He took a step back.

I probably caught him in the act.

His eyes widened in alarm. "Julie? What's wrong? What are you doing here?" He looked at his watch and realized he wasn't wearing one. "What time is it?"

"Are you alone?"

"Of course I'm alone. What are you—?"

Okay, so I didn't catch him in the act.

"Hank, we need to talk."

He stepped back again and pushed the door open. "Come in."

She shook her head. "No, I can't. I left Emi alone. She's asleep. I have to go right home."

He raised his hands and shrugged. "Then how can we talk? What's going on, Julie?"

"Did you go out to dinner with Linda tonight?" She sounded like a homicide detective grilling a suspect. All that was missing was the bright light blinding him.

"Yes, but it wasn't what you think."

"You don't know what I think, mister." *Who am I? Magnum P.I.?*

Hank threw up his hands. "Enlighten me. What *do* you think?"

Tears welled in her eyes. "I don't know what to think." She gave the tears an angry swipe of her hands. The last thing she wanted to do was stand on Hank's doorstep weeping like a pathetic betrayed lover.

He opened his arms and took a step toward her. "Julie. Talk to me."

She put her hands up to ward off his embrace. "No, I changed my mind." She turned to leave.

"Oh, no you don't." Hank grabbed her arm. "You can't ring my doorbell late at night, say we have to talk, and then change your mind. What in holy hell is going on here, Julie? If you have something to say, say it!"

She yanked her arm free. "Okay. I'm a virgin. There, I said it." She turned and ran down the walkway to her car, jumped in, and tore down the street.

Henry wondered how long he'd been standing in his doorway after Jelly left. He turned to see his young bachelor neighbor, Gary, unlocking the front door to the condo next to his. Henry shivered. He was barefoot, his front door open. Was he in the middle of a bad dream?

"Doc, what's happenin' dude?"

"What?"

"It's cold out here, pal. What's up? You hear something?"

"Yes. She's a virgin."

"Like a Virgin. You got it wrong."

"I got what wrong?"

"The song, 'Like a Virgin.' You said, 'She's a Virgin.'"

"What are you talking about?"

"Madonna. The Song. 'Like a Virgin.'"

"Huh?"

"You okay, Doc? Why are you standing out here?"

"I'm fine. I just thought I—God, it's cold out here. What time is it?" He grabbed his upper arms against the chill air.

"I don't know, close to midnight, I guess. I got off work at eleven thirty. Are you sure you're okay?"

"Yeah, I'm good. Night, Gary." Henry stared at his perplexed neighbor for a couple of seconds, then went inside and closed the front door.

Running his hands through his hair, he took long strides to his bedroom, muttering to himself. "This is nuts, this is completely nuts." He picked up a sweatshirt and sweatpants from the floor of his closet, pulled them on over his pajamas, and grabbed his keys and wallet from the dresser. Before he stepped out the door, he slid his feet into an old pair of Crocs.

Five minutes later, he pulled his pickup into Julie's driveway, hopped out, and jogged to her front door. He rang the bell and waited. And waited. The porch light popped on and Julie peeked around the shirred curtain covering the window in her front door.

She opened the door, but kept the screen latched. "What do you want, Hank?"

"What do *I* want? Are you kidding me?"

"It's late."

"I know it's late, Julie. You woke me out of a sound sleep, blindsided me with half a dozen words, then left me standing on my doorstep like a dazed fool." He raised his hands. "What's going on? Can I come in?"

"No."

"Then you come out."

She stood still, her face an obstinate mask. "It's too late."

"Let's not go through that again, okay? Open the door, Julie."

"Hank, it's really late and—"

"Open. The. Damn door. Now, Julie."

Unmoving, she stared stubbornly at him for a couple of seconds, then unlatched the screen and stepped back. "Okay, but be quiet." She turned and pointed through the dining room. "We'll go in the kitchen."

Once inside, she closed the door and turned to face him. He paced, ran his hands through his hair and down his face. Finally, he stopped and stood in front of her, legs apart, arms akimbo.

"Julie, you owe me an explanation. What is going on with you?"

She mimicked his posture. "I don't owe you an explanation. You tell me why you took Linda out to dinner. She came to my store this afternoon to make sure I'd know."

His mouth agape, he said, "She did what?" Raising his fists, he pressed them to his temples. "What did she say?"

"She said it was her birthday, and you were taking her out to dinner. Why, Hank? Are you seeing both of us?"

He grabbed her shoulders. "Julie, I'm not seeing Linda. I have no interest in her, she's ancient history." She tried to pull away. "No, listen to me. Dani wanted to take her to dinner. Joe got roped into going because Dani doesn't like to drive after dark. He called and practically begged me to go along. He was going crazy at the thought of spending hours listening to the two of them yak. He wanted backup, so I did my brother-in-law a favor. That's why I went."

She sighed and looked into his face. "Oh."

Hank embraced her. "Julie, Julie. How could I possibly be interested in any other woman but you?" He put his hands on either side of her face, ran his thumbs over her ears, and brushed her lips with a soft kiss. "I'm crazy for you."

She rested her forehead on his chest. "Oh, Hank, I'm sorry. I was so green-eyed with jealousy that I was pulling my hair out. My brain hasn't worked right ever since the day I met you. You're all I think about."

He chuckled and hugged her. "What do you suppose we should do about that?"

She pushed back. "Hank, what I said, uh, you know, that I'm a—well I am. I'm a freak, and it really scares me."

He rocked her from side to side and kissed the top of her head. "I can fix that, you know." His groin tightened when her arms went around his waist, her hands on his back. "Julie, I'm mad about you."

"Oh, Hank," she turned up her face. "I don't want to mess up things when we're just getting started. I'm an overage babe in the woods."

His heart squeezed and thumped. He wanted her. "You can't mess anything up, my darling Julie." He pressed her back against the door, his lips to her ear. "I'm dying to make love with you. Will you let me? Say yes, Julie." He ran his hand up her sides and caressed her breasts. Groaning, he bent and kissed her neck.

The door suddenly shoved inward, slamming her against him.

Emi's sleepy voice called out, "Jelly? Who are you talking to? Is anything wrong? Open the door."

Hank backed up, his neck and chest flushed with heat. He turned Julie and pulled her back against his chest to hide his obvious and now ill-timed state of arousal. His arms encircled her shoulders.

Emi opened the door farther and stood staring at them.

Julie mumbled some lame explanation. Hank's mouth went dry. He drew himself up and worked on a convincing smile.

Emi looked from her teacher to her sister and back again. "Were you kissing again?"

Julie opened her mouth, but nothing came out.

Hank thought the truth was the better way to go, so he said, "Yes, Emi, we were kissing again."

She grinned. "Okay then. No problem. I'm going back to bed." She turned and gave them a conspiratorial wink. "Nighty night."

Jelly slumped against him when the door closed. "Hank, we can't..."

He held on tight. He never wanted to let go of her. "I know, I know. But we need to find a way, Julie. Soon."

She placed her hands on his forearms and tilted her head back against his shoulder. "I'll think of something." She turned around in the circle of his arms. "Kiss me again."

Chapter Twenty-Four

Big Night Out
Thursday, 10:30 a.m.

Jelly hung up the phone when Sally entered her shop.

She returned Jelly's happy smile. "Hey, I'm glad to see you looking like your old self this morning. Were you just talking to Henry?" Sally placed her hands on the counter and leaned against the edge.

Jelly did an excited little bounce. "No, it was Aunt Martha. I'm so happy, Sally. I can't believe what's happened."

Sally straightened. "Tell me. Is it good news about your dad?"

Jelly was so full of warmth and tingling joy she could barely get her thoughts together. She hugged herself and twirled around.

"Jelly, for heaven's sake. Tell me."

Arms high above her in exaltation, Jelly said, "Daddy's going to be as good as new. He's been transferred back to the infirmary at Folsom, and best of all, he might get parole sooner than we expected. Can you believe it? I'm so happy I could float, Sally. I can't think straight."

"That's wonderful news. When will he be home?"

Jelly shook her head, shrugged, and rolled her eyes. "Who knows? Aunt Martha said the paperwork takes weeks, and anyway he won't leave Folsom till he's fully recovered."

Sally grimaced. "I wonder how Emi will feel about it."

"I don't know, but one thing's for sure, she has to hear it from me before she reads it in the paper. Soon as she gets here this afternoon, I'll tell her."

"Don't you remember? She's going to my house after school for her last tutoring session with Jenna. Emi's staying with us for dinner."

Jelly placed her hands on her cheeks and rolled her eyes. "I forgot about that. I guess I'll wait to tell her when she gets home from your place."

"You could join us for dinner."

"No, that's not a good idea. I have to tell her in private. I have no idea what she's going to feel about it."

"Yes, I see your point." Sally turned as if to leave and stopped. "See you at our usual place this evening?"

"No, you and Connie go ahead. If Emi's going to be at your house, I think I'll go over to Hank's place. We were right in the middle of something when Emi interrupted us last night."

Sally gave her a sly grin and widened her eyes. "Really?"

"Not that!"

"What then?" Sally asked.

The doorbell jangled and two customers entered the boutique. Jelly put a welcoming smile on her face. "Welcome to Big Night Out, ladies. Feel free to browse and let me know if you'd like any assistance." She flashed a small frown and shrug in Sally's direction.

Sally silently mouthed, "Later," waved, and left.

Santa Susana High School
3:30 p.m.

Jelly silently watched Henry from his classroom door. He sat at his desk grading papers. A warm glow filled her chest when one of those hands she loved pushed through his mop of black hair. She remembered the feel of his hands on her breasts last night, her knees trembled, and the warm glow in her chest migrated downward.

She made a small cough. He looked up and grinned broadly when he saw her.

"I hope I'm not interrupting, Hank."

He stood, rounded his desk, and they met halfway. "Interrupt me any time you like, Julie." He took her hands, brought them to his chest. "I know it looks like I was getting some work done, but I was thinking of you. I can't concentrate on anything."

"Me either." She ran her hands to his shoulders and down his arms. He was so warm. His muscles twitched at her touch. This feeling she was experiencing—was it what romance novels call sexual tension? *Must be.* Touching him like this, she could barely breathe.

He sighed. Shook himself like a wet dog. "God, we need to get a room," he said with a painful chuckle.

She ran a finger down the buttons of his shirt. Staring into his eyes, her face heated, she said, "I was planning on coming over to your place. There's something I'd like to leave there."

Hank's Condo
3:45 p.m.

Hank pulled into his garage. Jelly parked in the driveway behind him. She watched him jog to the kitchen entry as the roll-down garage door closed. She walked to his front door, and he was already there. If he smiled any bigger, she thought his face would crack.

He reached out, took her hand, and pulled her inside. Before she could catch her breath, his mouth covered hers. He kicked the door closed without interrupting his kiss. A kiss so filled with passion she nearly swooned.

Fighting against her rising tide of excitement, she pushed back and gazed into his eyes. "Hank, I'm so nervous. I don't know what I'm supposed to do."

His embrace tightened again. "I know what *I'm* supposed to do." He walked backward down his hallway toward the bedroom, taking her with him. It was the absolutely sexiest dance she could imagine. Every part of his body from his knees to his chest touched her. Every part.

When they reached the threshold to his bedroom, he swooped her into his arms with a shout of happy laughter. Overcome with shyness, she rested her head on his shoulder.

He set her on her feet and held her at arm's length. "You are the most beautiful, the most honest, smartest, and sexiest woman I have ever known, Julie. I've loved you from the day you walked into the school library."

"Me too," she said and felt her blush rising, her scalp tingle. "No, not me, you, I mean." She giggled with nervousness. "Um, what do we, um, what should I—?"

Hank tilted her chin up. "You should only do what feels right, what feels good." He kissed her, and she began to cry. She slumped against him. Alarmed, he asked, "Julie, what's wrong? It'll be okay, I promise."

Snuffling, she raised her face and smiled through her tears. "I'm just so happy, Hank. I don't know why I'm crying. I'm fine, really. I am." She raised a hand to his cheek and ran her fingers down his neck, enjoyed the warmth of his skin, anticipating how it would feel against hers. "I'm ready," she whispered.

He took her hand and pressed his lips against her palm. "Let's start by taking our shoes off."

The unmistakable gleam in his eyes excited her. Her cheeks heated. "I'm sure I can manage that part." She kicked off her shoes. Hank sat on the bed to untie his. She watched, unable to take her eyes off him when he unbuttoned his shirt and pulled it off. She stood still as a marble statue, not breathing.

He reached up and took her hand. "Sit here, next to me."

She sank down on the side of his bed, a bit unnerved when he stood, undid the buttons on his jeans, and pulled them off. His readiness was unmistakable. She closed her eyes when he knelt in front of her, placed his hands beneath the hem of her skirt, and slid them up her bare, trembling legs. "Relax," he whispered.

Jelly reached for the buttons on her blouse. Hank's hand flew up and grasped hers. "No. Please, let me." With controlled slowness and trembling fingers, he opened her blouse button by button.

A silly thought bounced around her brain about her choice of clothing. Why did she wear this blouse with so many buttons? She knew it would be coming off, didn't she?

Hank buried his face between her breasts and murmured over and over, "Beautiful, beautiful, my beautiful Julie."

She put her arms around his neck and held him close. "Hank, my heart is pounding so hard. Can you feel it?"

He nodded and pushed the blouse off her shoulders.

"Stand up, Julie." He pulled her gently to her feet and tugged down her elastic waist skirt.

At least I made one good choice, she thought, suddenly feeling vulnerable, standing there in front of him in panties and bra. Nothing stood between them now except a few flimsy pieces of nylon and lace. "Hank, I..."

He put a finger to her lips. "Shhh, I want to look at you. My God, just look at you."

She stared back at him, noticing for the first time that he wasn't skinny at all. His shoulders, chest, arms, and legs were well muscled on his lanky frame. How could she ever have thought of him as skinny? "Hank, you're so, just right. I want to put my hands on you."

He laughed. "I wish you would." He stood stock still when she reached out with both hands and traced her fingertips over his naked chest and arms. His head fell back, and he groaned with pleasure. He took one of her hands and pushed it slowly down his belly. "Touch me here, Julie."

Barely touching him, her eyes widened in surprise. "Oh. Wow." She giggled and withdrew her hand. "Take off your shorts, Hank. I want to see you." They were off in a flash, and she reached out again with tentative, feather-like touches, marveling at the silky smoothness of him.

The muscles in his belly tensed. "Stop."

Alarmed, she snatched her hand away. "Did I hurt you?"

Hank shook his head and chuckled. "Far from it, you amazing woman. My turn now." He slid the bra straps off her shoulders and ran his hands over the lacy garment, all the while sighing with pleasure. His thumbs traced down her sides and slipped beneath the elastic of her panties. He pushed them down to her ankles. Kneeling, he embraced her hips and planted a kiss on the fluffy red hair he revealed.

Jelly caressed the back of his head and shuddered. "Hank, I'm dizzy. I have to lie down."

He stood, tossed her bra aside, and picked her up with his beautifully strong arms. "See, you do know what to do. That's the logical next step," he murmured and laid her gently on his bed. He stretched out at her side. "See how easy this is?" He kissed her face, neck, ears, and breasts while holding his hand firmly on that mound of curly hair between her legs. His fingers explored her.

Without consciously doing so, Jelly opened herself to him. She pulled his face to hers and kissed his lips as he rolled on top of her. *This has to be heaven.*

Hank raised his head. "We should slow down."

"No, I don't want to. I'm about to scream, I want you so much." Her gray eyes implored him. "Do it, Hank. We can do it again, slower—after—can't we?"

"Yes, we can."

And they did.

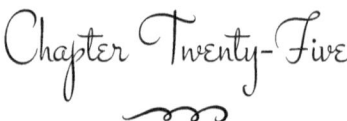

Chapter Twenty-Five

Sally's House
Thursday, 8:30 p.m.

Jenna opened the door, "Hey, Jelly. Did you come to get Emi? I was going to drive her home."

Jelly gave Jenna a peck on the cheek. "I was in the neighborhood so I decided to save you the trouble. Is she ready?"

"Yep, we just helped clean up the kitchen. Have you had dinner? We have lots of leftovers. Mommy made lasagna."

They walked through the entry hall into Sally's family room. "No, thanks. I had dinner. Hi, Sally."

"Hey, what are you doing here? The girls were just about to leave for your place." Sally ripped off a paper towel and wiped the kitchen counter. "Jenna, go upstairs and turn down that music, please. Tell Emi Jelly is here."

In no time, both girls were pounding down the stairs. Jelly winced as Emi hurried down, not the least slowed by her brace.

Emi stared at her sister and cocked her head. "What's with

the happy face, Jelly? Your cheeks are all rosy, like natural rosy, not makeup rosy."

Jelly gave Emi a quick hug. "I do have some great news to share with you."

"What? Tell me."

"It's family business. Say goodnight to Jenna and thank Mrs. Lewis for dinner." She turned Emi toward Sally and smacked her on the bottom.

Jelly couldn't stop grinning. "I've got something to tell you, too, Sally, but it'll have to wait till tomorrow. I've got business in Beverly Hills all morning. Shall the three of us meet at the usual place?"

Sally smiled. "I'll tell Connie. We wouldn't think of missing our walk." She gave Jelly a knowing nod. "Tomorrow; same time, same place." She followed them to the front door and gave Jelly's arm a surreptitious squeeze. Leaning close to Jelly's ear, she whispered, "You're not fooling me."

When they got in the car, Emi said, "What did Mrs. Lewis mean, 'you're not fooling me?'" She tugged the brace to straighten out her leg and shifted her bottom in the seat.

Stumped for a moment, Jelly said, "Oh, just a silly bet we had on something from our walk the other night. A private joke, you know?"

"Private. Meaning you have no intention of telling me." Emi crossed her arms and pouted.

Jelly laughed and tousled Emi's hair. "Don't ever change, sweetie. I love you."

Emi pulled in her chin, turned to face Jelly, and scowled. "Something must be going on. You're acting like a kid." She pointed a finger at Jelly's nose. "I'll find out, you know."

"Can't I have any secrets?" Jelly started the car and pulled away from the curb. She knew her chuckling annoyed Emi, but she was so happy she didn't care. This was one of the best days of her life and nothing was going to spoil her good mood.

Emi shook her head. "Humph."

When they got home, Jelly said, "How about some cocoa? I'm in the mood for cocoa. Oh, and we have some cookie dough in the fridge. Let's make some cookies to go with it. We can eat them while they're warm. How does that sound?"

Emi opened her car door. "It sounds like you're smoking hard stuff. You never allow me to eat sweets just before bedtime." She slammed the door and did a quick hobble step to the front door.

Jelly was right behind her. "This is a special occasion."

Emi stopped and Jelly reached around her to unlock the door, then held it open for her.

Emi paused just inside. "Why are the lights on? Did we forget to turn off the lights?"

"No, I, um, took a shower before I came to get you and decided to leave them on. Come on. I'm going to start that cocoa." She went straight to the kitchen and reached into the cupboard for the jar of solid chocolate chunks she used to make her specialty. "I'll turn on the oven. You can get the dough and a cookie sheet. Let's have a party."

"Jelly, you're acting weird. Stop. What family business were you going to talk about?" She pulled out a chair and sat at the table. "I don't want to bake cookies."

Jelly took a deep breath and put down the chocolate. She had to settle down for Emi's sake, if not her own. "I'm sorry, it's just, I'm so happy."

She pulled out the chair next to Emi's, sat, and took her hand. "It's about Daddy. He's going to mend as good as new, and the best news of all—he might be granted parole. He's going to get out of that awful place, Emi. We're going to get our father back."

Emi withdrew her hand and put it over her mouth. Her huge blue eyes looked stricken and fat tears rolled down her cheeks. "Jelly, I'm—I'm scared," she choked, "I don't know him." She grabbed her sister's hand again. "I'm all mixed up about him. When is he getting here?"

Jelly reached out and hugged her. "Oh, honey, it could be months before he's released." She smoothed Emi's hair and grabbed a napkin to dry her tears. "Emi, Daddy's going to live with Aunt Martha when he gets out. We can see him whenever we want. You'll have plenty of time to get to know him. And later, if it's the right thing for all of us, we'll decide together whether or not he'll come home."

The look of relief on Emi's crumpled pixie face was so pathetic Jelly had to work hard to swallow back tears of her own. "We'll take it slow and easy, okay? That's the way Daddy wants it."

Emi nodded mutely. Pulling another paper napkin from the holder on the table, she wiped her eyes and blew her nose. "Okay," her whisper barely audible as she nodded.

Jelly looked into her eyes. "I have some other good news."

"What?"

"Hank's really is in love with me. He told me today. What do you think of that?"

Emi rolled her eyes. "I think it's about time he told you what everybody already knows."

Jelly straightened her back. "Everybody?"

"Uh huh, Sharla told me his whole family talks about you and him every day since we had dinner there."

"When did you talk to Sharla?" This was news to Jelly.

"We talk on the phone all the time. She's taking care of my kitten till we come pick her up."

"What did she say?"

"She said she's real sweet and lively."

Jelly waved her hands and tried to tone down the impatience in her voice. "No, I mean, what did the family say about me and Hank?"

"They say he's the luckiest guy in the world, and he better not let you get away or he's kicked out of the family."

Jelly's hands flew to her face. Delight fluttered in her chest. "No. They didn't."

Emi nodded and mimicked Jelly's gesture and tone. "Yes. They did. I told Sharla I thought *you* were the lucky one." She lowered her hands and cocked her head like a puppy. "Jelly, are you going to make that cocoa or not?"

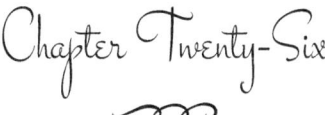

Chapter Twenty-Six

Hank's Condo
Friday, 4:45 p.m.

Her head rolling on the pillow, Jelly stretched languidly in Hank's bed. She sighed and turned to face him. "Was that as good as I think it was?"

His hand grazed her stomach. "Better."

"Hank, open your eyes and talk to me. I have to leave soon, so I can relieve Jeannie and close the store."

"Why can't I just lie here and think of all the ways I plan to make love to you day after day and week after week for the rest of my life?" He rolled over, opened his eyes, the grin of a hungry predator on his lips.

"Why don't you tell me what you plan to do?" His hand slid lower. She grabbed his wrist. "Not that I don't want to. I do. But I have to leave in the next half hour."

"No problem. I'm a teacher. I can teach you the 'Wham, bam, thank you, ma'am' quickie. It comes in very handy when pressed for time."

Jelly twisted her lips and slapped his hand. "What I'd like to know is where you learned all this stuff." She sat straight and pushed her back against the headboard.

Hank tugged the sheet, leaving her breasts exposed. He planted a hungry kiss on the one that brushed his face when she moved. "Yum, yum. You taste like all my tomorrows, Ms. Swanson." He pulled her on top of him.

Laughing, Jelly grabbed his ears and kissed him hard, then softer when his hands caught hold of her bottom. She squirmed and was rewarded by his immediate physical response. A moan escaped her lips.

Hank kicked away the sheet between them with his feet. They were pressed skin to skin. "Sit right here you wild woman." He pulled her knees up, seating her in just the right place.

"Yum yum, indeed." Rising on her knees, she slowly lowered herself. "Oh, that feels good, doesn't it? How many more fabulous, sexy sensations am I in store for?"

"Holy something-or-other!" He gripped her waist. "You're a quick learner. You'll be way ahead of me in no time."

Minutes later, she fell back in sweat-shined exhaustion. Flapping her hands, she fanned the hot blush rising from her chest. "Hank, I feel, I don't know—wonderful."

"You are wonderful, Julie." His face was close to hers, his head resting in his hand. He stroked her face and neck. "I love you. I want you to marry me. Will you marry me, Julie?"

Eyes wide, warmth unabated, she sighed. Niggles of worry fluttered in her chest. "Oh, Hank, I love you too, so much. But we've only known each other for a few weeks. You can't be sure you want to marry me. You don't even know me—who I am, really."

"I know all I need to know. I want us to be married. I can't think of living without you. We were made for each other."

Lips brushing his hand, she sighed. "Do you really think so?"

"Yes, Julie, I do."

"Yeah, me too."

Big Night Out
Friday, One Week Later, 2:00 p.m.

"Oh, you're back." Jeannie picked up her purse. "You want anything from the coffee bar? I'm going to grab some lunch."

"Yes, I'm starving. Bring me a tuna sandwich and an iced tea, please. Lunch is on me. Take it out of the register. Get a receipt."

Jeannie smiled. "Thanks, boss. I'll be right back."

Jelly waved as Jeannie opened the door and held it for a couple of her regular customers. Friday afternoons were always busy. Some of the ladies came to find something special for the weekend. She smiled to herself, for their *big night out.*

By four-thirty, Jelly was beginning to worry about Emi. She was usually never later than four. She and Jenna had finished with the math tutoring. She racked her brain. Had Emi told her she had plans for this afternoon?

She breathed a sigh of relief when Emi came through the door. "Where have you been? I was getting worried." Emi puffed and her cheeks were rosy. "Did you take the bus? Where's Hank?"

Emi plopped down on the pink vanity stool and swallowed some water from the bottle she carried. "I took the bus. Mr. Henry wasn't at school today."

"He wasn't? Why didn't you call me? I would have come to get you."

"I was going to, but when I went outside after class, the bus

177

was there and I jumped on." She dropped her backpack and stretched out her leg, wincing as she rubbed her knee.

Jelly took a deep breath and shook her head. "Emi, you know you shouldn't be walking so much until the doctor says the fracture has healed. You might hurt yourself."

"Jeez, it's only a block from the bus stop to here."

"Well, I don't want you walking around the store today. There isn't much to do, anyway. Jeannie just went home, and I'll close at five thirty. We'll get some dinner. I'll call Hank and see if he'd like to join us."

Emi pushed sweaty hair off her brow. "Something fishy is going on at school, Jelly. About Mr. Henry, I mean."

Jelly's pulse pounded in her ears. A hollow feeling filled her chest. "What are you talking about?" She came across the shop and stood before her sister.

"I'm not sure, but the school psychologist called me to his office and—"

The doorbells jangled and two of Jelly's best customers entered the shop. Jelly greeted them with a smile, turned to Emi, and said, "Don't move. Stay right there."

Even though the two women spent almost three hundred dollars, Jelly was anxious for them to leave. Her face was stiff from smiling, and the forced small talk had given her a headache. She felt slightly panicky by the time they waved their goodbyes and left, delighted with the treasures they scored.

She turned to Emi. "The school psychologist asked you what?"

"He asked me weird stuff, like why did Mr. Henry drive me around in his truck. I pointed to my cast and said, 'Duh.'"

Tilting her head, Jelly said, "Was that it?"

"No, they asked me how much time I spent with him and if he'd, uh, he'd—"

"He'd what!" When she didn't answer immediately, Jelly

bent forward and tilted Emi's chin up so she could look into her eyes. "What?"

"I'm trying to remember!" Emi's eyes were bleak, and her lips trembled.

Jelly's hands flew to her head. The emotional elevator she was on dropped about ten floors. "Oh, my God!" She locked the door to the shop and flipped the sign in the window to *Closed*.

Her hands pressing her chest, Jelly feared Emi's answer. "Did he?" *Please, please, tell me he didn't.*

"No! Are you crazy?"

Relief flooded her heart like cool rain. "Why did the psychologist ask you that?"

Her eyes hard, Emi flashed a frustrated look at Jelly. "How do I know? I told them he never touched me, except to help me in and out of his truck. I said he was our friend."

Ready to pull her own hair, Jelly said, "What are they after? I don't get it." She reached for the phone. "I'm calling Hank."

After four rings, Hank's answer machine picked up. It played his usual message: I'm not home, please leave your name and number, I'll return your call as soon as possible. Jelly left a brief message and slammed the phone onto its base. She paced back and forth and reached a decision.

"Come on. We're going to his place."

"Aren't you going to close the register?"

"No, come on, I'll put the bills in the wall safe and do it in the morning." That took no more than a few seconds. She retrieved her purse, grabbed Emi's backpack, and unlocked the door.

Henry's truck was not in his driveway, but that didn't mean he wasn't home. He might have parked it in the garage. She rang the doorbell, then knocked and peeked through a side window.

A man's voice called out, "You looking for Doc?"

Her head turned in the direction of the voice. "Yes, do you know where he is?"

"Nope. He hasn't been back since he left for school this morning. Is everything okay? You look worried." The youngish neighbor gave Jelly an appreciative once-over and walked across the postage stamp sized patch of lawn separating the condos. "I'll tell him you were here if I see him."

"Thanks. Tell him Julie was here. I already left a message on his phone."

The neighbor shrugged. "No problem. I hope he's okay. He was wigged out several nights ago." He reached for his wallet and pulled out a business card. "Call me if anything's happened, okay?"

She scowled with puzzlement. "Wigged out?"

"Yeah, when I got home from my gig, he was standing out here on the porch in his pj's. I never saw him do anything like that before." He chuckled. "Maybe he was drunk." He gave Jelly a flirty smile.

"Oh, I doubt that." She studied his card. *D.J. 4 All Reasons & All Seasons.* "Thanks, uh, Gary, I'm sure everything is fine." She turned and walked back to her car where Emi waited, a troubled look on her face.

Jelly got in the Mustang and started the engine. "He's not there. His neighbor hasn't seen him since he left for school this morning."

"He wasn't at school, at least I didn't see him there. He wasn't in homeroom *or* science class." She touched her sister's arm. "I'm worried, Jelly. What if something happened to him?"

Chapter Twenty-Seven

Alamo Street and Maricopa Drive
Friday, 7:30 p.m.

Connie and Sally waved at Jelly's approach. When she didn't return their smiles, Connie said, "Uh oh, something is making our Jelly unhappy."

Jelly affirmed her comment with a nod.

Sally nodded, hands on her hips. "I was hoping you and Henry would have everything sorted out."

Connie walked to meet Jelly. "You don't look happy, chica. *Que pasa?*

Swallowing back her fear, Jelly said, "Something weird is going on at the school. Hank wasn't there today, and the counselor asked Emi some very unsettling questions."

Sally heard the last part of Jelly's statement. "Henry wasn't where?"

"At school. And I've left messages on his phone, and he hasn't returned my calls." Her cheeks reddened. "I even went to his condo. His neighbor said he'd left at his usual time this morning."

Connie cocked her head. "That's strange."

"It gets worse," Jelly said. "His neighbor said Hank was acting peculiar late one night, standing out on his front step, he seemed disoriented." She heaved a sigh. "I'm worried about him."

"Gosh, I hope he isn't sick or something." Sally said. "Did you call his mother or brother?"

"No, but if he hasn't called by the time I get home, I will. Come on, let's walk. I need the exercise to work off my worry."

Connie kept up with Jelly. "Was his car there, at his house?"

"His garage door was closed, so I couldn't tell."

Sally patted Jelly's shoulder, but it didn't make her feel any better. Jelly thought of every horrible thing she could imagine might have happened to Hank. He had a heart attack, and they took him away before school started, but for some reason didn't tell the kids. He felt ill, went home, and he's lying there alone, dying with nobody to help. He went to the farm and on the way got in a horrible car wreck. He eloped with Linda. But none of that made sense. "What really concerns me is the questions the counselor asked Emi. And maybe some other kids."

Wide eyed, and sounding as if she'd absorbed some of Jelly's concern, Sally asked, "What did the counselor ask her?"

"He asked why she'd been riding in his truck with him."

Connie crossed her eyes. "Duh, she has a broken leg."

"That's exactly what Emi told him."

Sally said, "There has to be more to it than that, Jelly."

Arms pumped with vigor as they started up the steepest part of the hill. "Oh, there's more. She asked Emi if Henry had ever touched her inappropriately."

Connie stopped abruptly. "*Dios mio!*"

Sally and Jelly nearly tripped when they stopped and turned to face Connie. Connie covered her face with her hands. "No, I can't believe it. No."

Jelly said, "Connie? Connie, what? You're scaring me!" She grabbed Connie's shoulders and gave her a little shake. "What!"

Connie took a breath and raised her hands. "Okay, okay, let's not panic. It's just those are code words for 'did the teacher molest you?' Somebody told the school they either saw or suspected it."

Hands on top of her head, Jelly walked in a nervous circle while her stomach did flip-flops. "That's crazy. That's the craziest thing I ever heard. I don't believe it. That's nuts."

Sally said, "Connie, how do you know this?"

"Before Miguel got promoted to homicide, he was involved in some investigations where allegations of improper conduct had been made against teachers. That's what counselors ask kids. They can't say it plainer because of potential liability to the school."

Fingertips at her temples, Jelly said, "I'm going home. I have to call Dominik and Mollie. I have to find out what's going on." She jogged down the hill, leaving Connie and Sally speechless.

"Mollie?"

"Yes."

"This is Julie Swanson. I'm trying to find out where Henry is and if he's okay."

"Henry's here, but I don't know about okay. I better let you talk to him. Hold on while I see where he is."

"Thanks, Mollie." Jelly drummed her fingers nervously while waiting. She heard conversation and footsteps. Hank picked up the phone.

"Julie?"

"Hank, why didn't you call me? I've been so worried about you. Are you all right? What's going on?"

"I'm sorry, sweetheart. I'm still trying to come to grips with what happened and I'm not having much success. I have no idea who could have done that."

"Done what? Hank, what's happened? Emi and I are like two caged cats. We've been looking everywhere for you. Are you sick? Did you get hurt?"

She heard a big sigh. "God, how I wish I was sick or hurt. This is much worse. Somebody, I don't know who, told the principal at my school that I molested one of my students."

Throat constricted, a tension pain surged up the back of her neck. "Oh, Hank, how could anybody say such an evil thing about you? I want you to know I don't believe it, not for a minute. Won't the school say who accused you?"

"No, they have to protect the identity of the person, and in a perverse way, I understand that."

"But, how—how can you defend yourself?"

"I've consulted an attorney. I have a meeting with her early tomorrow morning. Until I talk to her, I can't answer that."

"Is that why you weren't at school today?" Her headache had reached the top of her head and was working its way over her forehead toward her eyes. She rolled her neck and tried to release the steel band of tension.

"Yes. The procedure when a teacher is suspected of molestation is to put him or her on immediate administrative leave. Also, I can't have contact with any of my students and I have to stay at least one thousand feet away from the school. Jesus, I feel like shit!"

Nausea threatened. "Hank, I want to be with you. Can I come to the farm and be with you?"

He groaned. "Oh, God, nothing would make me happier, but it would probably be best if we waited until after I talk to the attorney tomorrow. You'd have to bring Emi, and I can't risk doing anything that would make my situation more difficult."

"Hank, they asked Emi some scary questions at school

today. It was very upsetting to her. She's so worried there is something she may have done to cause you this trouble."

"What did they ask her? What could she have done?"

"One question was about why she was seen, on more than one occasion, riding in your truck with you."

"Jeez, she's one bright kid. The first time I took her in the truck—the day of the science fair—she was anxious about whether the school allowed it. I was so hell-bent to see you that I brushed off her concern." A frustrated groan followed his words.

"They also asked her if you'd ever touched her inappropriately. Can you believe that?"

"*Gówno!*"

"What?"

"It's Polish for—"

Jelly continued right over Hank's answer. "The school counselor must know that a fourteen-year-old girl would understand what that question means. Emi's no dummy. Some kids she knows are having sex already."

"Unfortunately true."

Jelly swallowed at the lump in her throat. "I'm an even bigger freak than I thought when I think about that, Hank."

Hank lowered his voice. "Don't say that, Julie. I love you, and I would never allow anyone to say such a thing about you. You waited, you had standards. I thank God you let it be me."

"Oh, Hank, you're going to make me cry." Tears built, and she swallowed again. She loved him so much and was frustrated at being unable to do anything for him. "I feel so helpless," she said on a sob. "I want to help you somehow."

"My darling Julie, being there and believing in me is worth the world."

"Will you call me after you meet with the attorney?"

"Yes. If she says it's okay. If not, I'll have Mollie or Dom call."

Tears streamed down her cheeks. "I love you, Hank, Emi, too."

"Goodbye, sweetheart."

"Bye," was all she could manage.

Jelly's Kitchen
Late that Evening

Sally Lewis shook her head and slumped next to Jelly in the chair across from Miguel. "I can't imagine a worse accusation being made against a teacher. Not Henry, no, I don't believe it."

Jelly put her head in her hand. "No. Neither do I."

Miguel took a sip of Jelly's cinnamon coffee. "I don't either, sugar, but if I'm going to be any help getting at the truth, I have to withhold judgment for now. These cases can get real squirrelly. Even if he's completely exonerated, that cloud of suspicion will remain in some minds. Sad but true."

Connie nodded to Sally. She reached over and patted Jelly on the shoulder. "Don't get down in the dumps, chica, we'll help you see this through."

"Thanks, Connie. You, too, Miguel. I'm sure Hank is grateful that you're trying to help."

"Miguel, what else can you do?" Sally asked.

"Nothing directly. I put him in touch, by way of a friend, with one of the best attorneys I know. The woman specializes in sexual harassment and abuse defenses. She's got a good reputation for being an effective hard worker on behalf of her clients."

Jelly's smile was hopeful as she looked at Miguel. "Well, that's good news, isn't it? She should be able to prove his innocence pretty quickly. Henry will get a lot of support from everybody who knows him."

"Don't be too sure about that, darlin'."

She didn't think it possible, but Jelly's heart sank even further than before. She stood. "We should call it a night. I don't want Emi to wake up and see you all here. She's very worried about all this."

Miguel came around the table and gave her a hug.

"Thanks, Miguel. I appreciate your help." She set the coffee mugs on the sink.

She smiled at the distressed expressions on the faces of Sally and Connie, her two best friends. "I'll see you tomorrow. Thanks for coming over."

Chapter Twenty-Eight

Big Night Out
Saturday, 5:00 p.m.

"Shall I put up the closed sign?" Emi pointed to the door as the last customer left the shop.

Jelly nodded. "Yes, go ahead. I'll close out the register. Would you rearrange the skirts and pants for me? Make sure everything is in the right size slot? When we finish up, we'll shop for some groceries, maybe pick up a pizza."

Dejected, Emi worked on the racks. She spent all day in the store because, she told Jelly, she was upset about Hank's situation and didn't want to stay home alone. They'd had a long, frank discussion after Jelly talked to him on the phone. Since then, Emi had been uncharacteristically quiet, but Jelly could almost hear the wheels turning in her curly topped head.

She looked across the shop. "Emi, why don't you call Marco and see if he'd like to come over to have pizza with us?"

"He and his parents drove to San Diego for the weekend to visit his brother at Camp Pendleton."

"Oh, that's too bad. Well, shall we go to a movie later?"

Emi turned. "You don't have to worry about me and try to cheer me up. I'll get over it. I just can't stop thinking about Mr. Henry right now, okay?"

Sighing, Jelly said, "I'm sorry. I don't mean to baby you."

"I'm the one who should be trying to cheer you up instead of feeling sorry for myself. Even when you acted perky and smiled at your customers all day, I could tell you were thinking of him."

Jelly walked out from behind the counter and across the shop. She put her hands on Emi's shoulders. "Oh, honey, you do cheer me up. I was so glad you came in with me today. Your company helped a lot."

Emi buried her face in her sister's shoulder. "I wish I could be more like you."

"More like me?" Jelly chuckled and rubbed Emi's back. "I happen to like you just the way you are. We make a good team."

Emi looked up and smiled. "Yeah, we do. You love me even when I'm a brat."

Jelly tilted her head and smiled. "Love, true. Like? Hmm."

Emi laughed at Jelly's reliable honesty. "Let's finish here and get that pizza. There's a Will Smith movie at Regal Stadium. They blow up everything and crash lots of cars. That should make us feel better."

"Sounds like just the ticket."

Regal Stadium Theatre
After the Movie, 9:00 p.m.

Emi pulled Jelly's hand. "Let's walk over to the coffee bar and see which local poets or musicians are making fools of themselves tonight. I could use a decaf cappuccino."

"Okay, let's go." Jelly slung her suede bag over her shoulder and followed Emi to the other end of the mall.

"Dang it, the place is practically empty," Emi said. "Let's go to Thirty-One-Flavors and have ice cream instead." Her big-eyed smile was hopeful.

Jelly nodded and turned. "That sounds even better. They have black walnut this month. I saw it on their ad the other day."

"Yuck."

"Yuck? You've never even tried it."

"It sounds yucky."

"Our mother's two favorite flavors were pistachio and black walnut. I remember how hard she had to coax me to try them when I was a kid." She chuckled at the memory. "Now I love both flavors."

"I like pistachio okay."

"Why not be real brave and taste a sample spoon of the black walnut? I dare you."

Emi cocked her head. "You think I'll do it if you dare me, don't you?"

Jelly merely smiled.

True to form, Emi tried the black walnut on Jelly's dare, but pulled a face and refused to order it. She said her favorite was peanut butter and chocolate, and she saw no reason to change.

Jelly had a double scoop, one pistachio and one black walnut. It conjured happy memories of her mother and the fun they used to have window-shopping and eating ice cream cones whenever Jessie returned from a concert tour. "Come on, let's walk. This is the first warm night we've had in a long time."

"Jelly?"

"Hmm?"

"What do you think will happen to Mr. Henry?"

"How I wish I had a crystal ball. I don't know. He had a meeting with a lawyer today."

"Is he going to call us?"

"He said he would if the lawyer told him it was okay. He can't risk doing anything that will make it worse for him. He's not allowed by the school district to have contact with any of his students."

"But he could call *you*."

"Maybe not. He promised me Dom or Mollie would get in touch if he can't. We just have to wait."

"Where's your cell phone?"

Patting her shoulder bag, Jelly said. "Right here."

"He never did anything to anybody, Jelly. It's not fair."

"We both know that life is anything but fair, don't we?"

Silently, they strolled and ate their ice cream. They sat on a bus bench at the corner and watched the activity at the police headquarters across the street. Not much was going on there for a Saturday night. Some squad cars came and went, a few people entered and left the building.

She was pulled from her musings when Emi said, "Jelly? Can I ask you something?"

"If you let me ask you something first."

"What?"

She faced Emi. "Why did you tell Hank I was a lesbian?"

Emi groaned, put her hand to her cheek, and leaned forward with elbows on her knees. Her cone tipped precariously. "I don't know why I'm so mean sometimes. Soon as I said it, I told him you probably weren't."

"Did you really think I was a—"

"No!"

"What was going on in your head when you told him that?"

Emi rolled her head from side to side. "I could tell he liked you. I was like, jealous. I wanted to keep him for myself, you know, I didn't want to share him with you."

Jelly flinched with shock. Heat rose in her face at the same time a shiver went down her back. "You mean he—did he ever, uh, did he—?"

Emi sat straight. "No! No, I didn't mean it the way it came out! He's my teacher, that's all. He thought I was smart, he, I don't know—he respected me. I didn't want that to change. I was afraid if he got to like you he'd—oh, I don't know what I thought."

"Oh, honey." Jelly slid closer and put her arm around Emi. "Hank tells me how smart you are. He loves both of us."

Emi sighed and rested her head on Jelly's shoulder. "He was kind of like a dad, you know? I didn't want him for a brother. I have Marco for that."

This wasn't the first time Jelly felt sad about how much Emi had missed not having Daddy in her life. As much as Jelly loved their father, she blamed him for not putting her and Emi ahead of his own devastating loss when he killed that awful man. Daddy had a lot to answer for with Emi. She doubted he and Emi would ever have much of a chance at any kind of normal father-daughter relationship. Nearly grown when he went to prison, Jelly knew what it meant to have a father. Emi had only youthful fantasies.

"Anyway, Jelly, I thought Marco was a kind of like a brother. That's what I wanted to ask you about." She stood. "Let's go home."

Jelly picked up her bag, brushed the cone crumbs off her lap, and turned back in the direction of the parking lot. "Okay, let's go. What about Marco?"

"Is it like, possible for a boy and a girl to be best friends? I thought it was, but now I don't think so anymore."

"Why?" Jelly dug around in her bag for the car keys. "Why can't you and Marco be friends?"

"He wants to kiss me and stuff."

Hair prickled on Jelly's neck. "And stuff?"

Emi's bright blush took on a halogen glow in the lights of

the parking lot. "You know, touch me, and other stuff. He thinks we're old enough."

Jelly leaned against the side of the Mustang, stomach churning. It wasn't the first time she felt like she was in over her head, being both mother and father to her kid sister. "Hank and I were talking about that."

Alarm in her voice, Emi said, "You and Mr. Henry were talking about Marco and me?"

"No, just kids your age in general." She unlocked the passenger door for Emi and walked around to the driver's side and got in. "Fasten your seat belt."

Emi pursed her lips and gave Jelly a hard stare.

Jelly threw up her hands. "Okay, okay, I don't have to tell you to fasten your seat belt. You already know that."

"Duh." She clicked the buckle. "What did Mr. Henry say about kids our age?" She looked out the back window. "There's a car coming, don't back up."

Jelly looked at Emi with her eyes crossed. "Duh."

Emi laughed. "I *am* like you. We're both so bossy."

Out of the mall lot and on the road home, Jelly clicked off the car radio and told Emi about Hank's concern that so many kids were engaging in sex play years before they had the maturity to handle the consequences.

Nodding with agreement, Emi said, "That's exactly what I told Marco!"

"Really?" *I must have done something right.*

"Yes. I told him he could go do anything he wanted to, but I was going to stay a virgin like you."

Jelly slammed the brake pedal just in time to avoid going through a stop sign. "You told Marco I'm a virgin! My god, Emi, what is it with you and your mouth?" Her foot slipped off the clutch and her precious car jerked, bounced, and ground to a halt, throwing them back against their seats.

Emi placed a hand against her chest and gasped for breath.

"I think it's neat to be a virgin. Why do I have to do sex just because all the other kids do it? You were one, at least until recently. Weren't you?"

Jelly gripped the steering wheel and dropped her forehead on the top edge of it. "Yes, Emi, I was a virgin...until recently. Okay?"

"Okay, you're old enough, so no big deal." Emi twisted in her seat. "You better start the car and get out of here before the guy behind us calls the cops and reports you for a drunk driver."

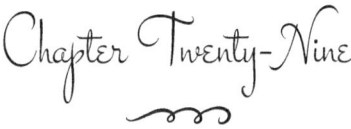

Chapter Twenty-Nine

Jelly's Kitchen
Sunday, 1:00 P.M.

E mi put her glass of lemonade down on the table. "I'm pooped! We got a lot done already. All that's left is my bathroom floor and getting the clothes out of the dryer." She swallowed the last bite of her sandwich.

"You know what? You've been spending too much time on your feet. Dr. Thompson will have my hide if your fracture isn't healing properly. I think you should go rest and read or watch the TV. I'll finish."

"It doesn't even hurt anymore." Emi picked up her plate and glass and carried them to the sink. "I'll sit for a while, though. I've got to start reading a book for English class, ugh, not my favorite subject."

Jelly followed with her own plate and glass. "What book are you reading?"

"*Cold Sassy Tree*, have you ever heard of it? The author is Olive Ann Burns. What a name, Olive Ann. I shouldn't complain about Martha Elizabeth."

"Boy, howdy, that's a wonderful book! I loved reading it."

Emi wrinkled her nose and gave Jelly a quizzical look. "Boy howdy?"

Jelly laughed. "Read the book. You'll see." She turned on the water and rinsed the plates. Glancing over her shoulder, she watched her sister go through the dining room, flop down on the couch, and open the book.

Why hadn't Jelly heard from Hank or his family? She thought about calling the farm but decided to wait a few more hours. He had enough on his mind now, and she didn't want to add to his stress. Who accused Hank, and why? He was one of the most respected teachers at the school.

It was an awful misunderstanding. What other explanation could there be? He'd been teaching there for more than four years. He loved his students. Jelly saw how he interacted so naturally with his nieces and nephews. Hank and kids went together like peanut butter and jelly.

Bodacious Blooms Farm
4:00 p.m.

Henry's stomach churned, his mind a dark whirlpool from which he could barely snatch a single, cogent thought. He paced, took his hands out of his pockets, and shoved them back in. Finally he sat, then immediately rose and paced again.

Dom looked up from the Sunday paper. "For crissakes, Henry! Sit down or go outside to do your prowling. You're giving me a headache."

"Not to take the Lord's name in vain, Dominik," Anka said. "It's the Sabbath."

"Sorry, Mama." Dom rose and tossed the paper. "Henry,

come with me. Let's go to the greenhouse and do some work. You're making yourself and everyone else crazy."

Hank threw up his arms in frustration. "I have to call her, Dom. She's probably out of her mind with worry."

Dom put his hand on Henry's shoulder and pushed him toward the kitchen. "You can't call Jelly. You know that. None of us can have any contact with her until your lawyer finds out who made the charge against you."

"I can't see how a five-minute phone call could matter," Hank said, shuffling reluctantly toward the back door.

"If you're so damn smart, why'd you pay that lawyer a five-thousand-dollar retainer, huh? Come on. Let's get out of the house. We'll drive over to Joe and Dani's place, pick up the twins, and bring them back here to play with the kittens."

Hank pushed open the back screen door. "You go. I'll check the bulb cooler, get my mind off the shit storm I'm drowning in." He turned in the direction of the blockhouse where the bulbs were kept in cold storage. "Anyway," he called over his shoulder, "I'm not going over there because Linda may be hanging around at Dani's. The last thing I need is to bump into her."

Upon entering the cool-house, he slumped down on a wooden crate. Elbows on his knees, he dropped his head and moaned with frustration.

His father's voice startled him.

"You good boy, Henryk."

He dropped his hands and looked through the gloom. "Jeez, Papa, you startled me. I didn't know you were in here."

Janusz chuckled. "I come here get away from you. Bulbs always make calm. Maybe work for you, too?" He gestured for his son to join him.

"What are you doing, Pop?"

"Wishing good luck these ranunculus bulbs. I save them

from last year to plant around front porch. Your mama, she love them best of all."

"I remember."

"Come, you help me check them."

Hank sorted, turned, and examined hundreds of the odd shaped clusters in the cooling drawer. The work calmed him. Pleasant memories of planting bulbs one winter night after Mama went to bed made him smile. He and Aleksy planned a great surprise for Easter but had to reveal their secret when Mama took a notion to till up the area to plant a climbing Cecil Bruner rose.

Her delight when the bulbs burst forth in brilliant yellow, red, and orange blossoms was their reward. Mama's smile warmed Henry's heart like a rainbow after a spring downpour. When he told her about the charges made by the school, her expression of shock and disbelief was foreign to her usual happy demeanor. His memory flash brought Hank back to the reason why he was staying at the farm.

"Henryk?"

"Sorry, Dad, I didn't hear what you said."

"I said is time clean up for supper now. Your mama and Mollie make special dinner to celebrate today."

Puzzled, Henry said, "Celebrate? What are we celebrating?"

"You don't remember is Dominik's birthday? Mollie make big poppy seed cake. Everybody coming for sing and cake after supper."

Throwing his head back and cursing himself, Hank said, "God, how could I have forgotten Dom's birthday? I didn't even get him a card."

Janusz took his son's arm. "Come in house. Mollie buy extra card for you. She know you forget." He smacked Hank on the shoulder. "No curse on Sabbath. You learn better."

Simi Valley
8:00 p.m.

Emi opened her car door. "I enjoyed that." She scooted into the seat and lifted her casted leg to get comfortable. "We haven't gone to Sunday evening mass in a long time. I forgot how many kids I know go here."

Jelly smiled and nodded as she backed up the car and exited the church parking lot. "Do you remember we used to walk the six blocks to church every Sunday after dinner? I'm not sure when we got out of the habit."

Emi shrugged. "I was talking to Melody, and she asked me if I'd like to join the youth group starting next month. Did you see the new junior priest? Father Mike? He's hot."

Jelly laughed and poked Emi in the arm. "What a thing to say about a priest."

"What's wrong with that? Father Ignatius thinks you're hot."

"For heaven's sake, how do you come up with this stuff? Father Ignatius has to be seventy if he's a day. 'Thinks I'm hot.' The stuff that comes out of your mouth. You'd think I'd be used to it by now." She was still shaking her head and chuckling when she pulled into their driveway.

The ringing phone caught their attention as they approached the front porch.

Jelly ran to the door and fumbled with her keys. "That must be Hank calling." She pushed a key into the lock and when it wouldn't turn, she yanked it out and saw it was the key to her shop. "Dammit!"

By the time she had the door open, the phone had stopped ringing. She hurried to the kitchen to see if a message had been left.

Emi caught up with her. "Who was it, Jelly? Was it Mr. Henry?"

Jelly dropped her purse on the table, put her hand to her forehead, and paced in frustrated circles. "I don't know. Whoever it was didn't leave a message. Why don't people leave messages?" She shook the phone, pretending to strangle it.

Emi slumped into a kitchen chair. "You told me that if no message is left, it probably isn't important. If Mr. Henry called, he would leave a message. Don't you think?"

Jelly reached into the cupboard for a water glass. "Yes, you're probably right. It wasn't important. And if it was, they'll call back." She turned on the tap, filled her glass, and drank it dry.

"Doesn't Mr. Henry have your cell number? He'd probably call you on that one first, wouldn't he?"

Jelly grabbed her purse. "I had it off while we were in church. Where is the darn thing? This purse is barely big enough to hold anything. How could I lose it in here?"

Emi rolled her eyes. "It's in the car. You put it in the cup holder." Grumbling, she struggled to her feet. "I'll go get it before you have a cow."

"No you don't." Jelly placed her hand on Emi's shoulder, urging her to sit. "I'll get it. You stay by this one. I'll be right back."

Emi had the top off the Ben and Jerry's Phish Food when her nervous sister re-entered the kitchen and plopped into a chair. Shaking her head at Jelly's anxiety over missing the phone call, Emi said, "This is what you need, Jelly." She rummaged through the utensils for the ice cream scoop.

"It was off. Nobody called. No messages." With a sigh, she placed her cell phone on the table. "Maybe I should go ahead and call him."

Emi set a bowl of ice cream and a spoon in front of Jelly. "Maybe you shouldn't. Here, eat this; it's better than drugs or alcohol. Guaranteed to work every time." She sat across the table and dug into her own bowl, rolled her eyes with ecstasy as the ice cream melted on her tongue, and gestured at the bowl with her spoon. "Mmm, mmm. Don't you just love these little chocolate fishies?" She stuck out her tongue to show one to Jelly.

About to tease Emi for her bad manners, Jelly startled when the cell phone vibrated and jittered on the tabletop.

Chapter Thirty

9:00 p.m.

Momentarily paralyzed, Jelly watched the cell phone jitterbugging across the table. Emi grabbed the shiny candy-apple-red instrument and flipped it open. "Hello. No, it's her sister. Uh huh." She nodded, took a spoonful of ice cream. "Mm hmm." She swallowed. "I guess so." She slapped away Jelly's outstretched hand. "I'll have her call you if she doesn't want to."

Gaping, Jelly demanded, "Who was that!" She snatched the phone and snapped it open. "Whose number is that? Emi?"

Emi pointed to her full mouth. Took her time swallowing the ice cream. "The newspaper wants to know if you're continuing your subscription. What? Finish your ice cream, it's melting."

Aggravated to the extreme, Jelly placed the phone gently on the table, picked up her spoon, took a small bite, and glared at her baby sister. "I think you get some kind of perverse joy out of watching me squirm." She put her elbow on the table and dropped her head into her hand, stirring dissolutely at the growing puddle of Phish Food.

"I don't enjoy it. I'm a teenager. I'm just doing my job. You're always going on how I have responsibilities around here. I'm going to take that seriously from now on."

Cracking open one eyelid to a tiny slit, Jelly spied Emi's puckish grin. Gritting her teeth, she was resolved not to smile or laugh. She slapped her hand down hard; the bowls bounced, and she was satisfied to see Emi jump, eyes agog with surprise.

"Do you have any idea how impossible it is to be a twenty-eight-year-old mother to a fourteen-year-old girl?"

"Nope. I wouldn't be as good at it as you are."

"I'll take that as a compliment." She shoved her bowl across the table. "You rinse the dishes. I'm going to take a nice hot bath. And I'm taking my phone with me."

Sliding down into the silky warm bubbles, Jelly heard the muffled sounds of the TV in Emi's bedroom. MTV was something she could never fully appreciate. If you took away all the gyrating, scantily clad, sexy images and the glitz, the music was pure crap. *God, I sound old. I should like that stuff. It's been around since I was a teenager. Oh yes, I remember. I was busy at the time.*

Unable to wish away the nauseating implications of the charges against Hank, Jelly resolved instead to spend her time planning a way to get in touch with him. She'd call Connie in the morning before she left for the shop. Maybe Miguel would tell her the name of the attorney representing Hank. It was Miguel's buddy who called Hank to recommend the woman. Maybe she could find out from the lawyer if Hank was okay and how long it would be before she could talk to him. There had to be somebody who knew both Jelly and Hank, somebody who could be a go-between, somebody who could pass a message to him.

The image of Linda flashed in her mind. Jelly quickly dismissed it. There was no way she'd give that witch the chance to weave her black magic, to make her anxiety worse.

She told herself to believe that Hank was trying just as hard to come up with a solution to their isolation. The thought of him being as miserable as her gave her a tiny bit of comfort, as perverse as that was.

She snapped to attention when she heard the lush, muted notes of Massenet's Meditation, Mom's favorite piece, the music of Jelly's childhood. Tears sprang to her eyes. Emi was playing the old Perlman CD. Playing it for her.

She turned her head at the sound of a gentle knock on the bathroom door. "Come in, Emi."

Jelly smiled at the sight of Emi in her purple bunny pajamas with feet. No matter how hard she honed her image as a sullen, smarty-pants teenager, Emi had never given up her love for warm flannel with childish prints.

"Jelly?"

"What, baby?"

Face crumpled, tears threatening, she mumbled, "I'm worried about Mr. Henry."

Jelly swallowed. "Me, too, honey."

"Will you sleep in my bed tonight?"

"Just like the old days?"

"Yeah, like when I was little."

"Try and stop me."

Chapter Thirty-One

The following Sunday, 6:45 a.m.
At Jelly's house

Without making a sound, Jelly slid out of Emi's bed. She'd slept there all week. Fuzzy headed, she padded on bare feet to the kitchen and paused at the sink to stare, unthinking, at the eastern horizon. The morning sun was visible through a mist of early morning fog resting just below the crest of the Santa Susana Mountains.

Her feet registered the cold of the kitchen floor. She shivered, put the teakettle on the stove, and then raced to her bedroom to find some socks. A few minutes later, she was sitting on the front porch in her long tee shirt nightgown, holding a steaming mug of hot water with lemon. She watched as the old neighborhood stirred. Lights blinked on in front facing kitchens. The Jensen's car backed out of their garage and slowly turned. They went to early Mass every Sunday. Jelly waved as they passed.

Contemplating the cell phone in her lap, she wrestled with conflicting thoughts and half-baked decisions on whether or not to call Hank despite the no-contact order. Rocking gently, she took a few sips from her mug. She needed to talk to somebody.

Even though it was barely seven on a Sunday morning, she was sure Connie's family would be up. Miguel rounded up the boys early Sunday mornings, took them to IHOP for a big pancake breakfast, and then to church, so Connie could sleep in. Jelly decided no, she wouldn't call. It wasn't fair to get Connie out of bed. Other than transferring some of her anxiety to Connie, what would it accomplish?

She slopped hot water on her wrist when the phone vibrated and spilled the rest of it when she tried to set the mug down on the floor.

With dripping hands, she fumbled to answer. "Hello?"

"Julie?"

"Yes. Who is this?"

"Julie, it's Mollie."

She bolted upright, her heart pounding. "What's wrong, Mollie? Is Hank okay? Is somebody sick? Has something happened?"

"Whoa, Julie. Everybody's okay. I shouldn't be calling you, but Henry is going crazy with worry. I'm sure you are, too. So I'm at a service station using a payphone. The darn thing looks and feels like it was dragged out of a grease pit at Jiffy Lube!"

"Mollie, it's been a week!"

"Look, I'll make it quick. Yesterday, Dom and Papa took Henry up to the cabin on Bass Lake. Henry's been driving us crazy. They figured if they could get him out on the lake to do some fishing he might calm down. Papa and Dom are coming back tomorrow, but they're leaving him there to do some work on the roof. Papa took a big box of shingles and left Henry with strict instructions to find the source of the leak and fix it. He's got plenty of supplies, but no car, so he's stuck up there until Dom goes back to pick him up on Thursday. Now I've got to hang up. Don't you dare tell anyone I called."

"But Mollie—" Jelly said to the flat silence. "Dammit!"

Dominick's Boat, Bass Lake
10:30 a.m.

Dom cut the engine. "Easy, easy, Henry, he'll get off. Give him some slack. Have you forgotten everything Papa taught you about fishing?"

Hank dipped his rod down and pulled some line off the reel. "I didn't notice you catching anything." He slowly wound the line back on the reel, giving the big bass a momentary breather, then yanked up and set the hook. "Got him!"

Dom whooped, "Way to go! Breakfast. Reel him in and we'll get out of here. That sun's getting hotter by the minute."

Hank pulled the big shiny fish into the boat. It flopped, sending water droplets in every direction. "What a beauty, Dom. Look at the color on this big guy. He's at least five pounds."

Dom yanked the engine cord, sending a small puff of black smoke into the air, and turned the boat in the direction of their small dock across the lake.

When they tied up, Papa strolled toward the boat. "I think you boys never come. This lake full of fish. I put coals on the fire two times already. You forget how to fish?"

Hank grinned and held up his catch. "Take a look at this, Pop. He's big enough for breakfast *and* lunch."

"I think is good fishing today." Papa returned his wide

smile. He reached for the fish. "I clean him. You boys wash boat."

Dom grumbled as Papa ambled back toward the cabin. "You were always Pop's favorite."

Hank laughed and punched him in the shoulder. "That's bull, and you know it. Why do you and Alexy always say that?" He stepped out onto the dock and reached for the water hose. "I'm Mama's favorite."

Dom made a grab for his leg just as Henry turned the hose full blast into the boat, soaking him from the waist down. Papa turned, nodded his head, and chuckled at his two grown sons acting out like juveniles.

While wolfing down a breakfast of fresh grilled bass and potatoes fried with kielbasa, the three men discussed the repairs to the roof. Dominik said he should have thought to pick up a new toilet for the bathroom off the back porch. Henry could have installed it when he finished putting on the new shingles.

Henry swallowed. "Yeah, and while you were at it, why didn't you get a load of redwood planks and have me put in a new porch?"

Papa waved his hand. "Stanislaw build new porch when he come with Zofia's husband next month."

"That's a relief." Henry took the last forkful from his plate. He glanced over at his brother. "What's that look?"

Dom leaned back, stretched his arms above his head, and then patted his stomach with satisfaction. "Look?"

"Yeah, that look that says Dom is thinking of ways to get Henry into trouble."

"Oh, I was just thinking that once we complete the repairs on this old cabin, it would be a good place for you to bring Jelly on your honeymoon."

Papa looked surprised as his gaze went from Dominik to Henryk and back again. "You marry beautiful Julie?"

Hank raised his hands and shook his head. "Pop, I have no idea what Dom's talking about. Julie and I have no plans to marry, and for all I know she's finished with me." He stood, pushed his chair back, and picked up his plate. "I'm going inside."

Chapter Thirty-Two

Big Night Out
Thursday, 4:00 p.m.

"Honey, I'm home!" Emi's voice echoed through the busy shop. She waved at Jelly and tugged Marco in her direction. Waiting, as she'd been taught, until Jelly finished with her customer, she tried on a couple of hats and made silly faces at Marco. When Jelly took far too long with the woman deciding on a black or brown skirt, Emi opened her eyes wide and made jerky, barely discernable nods and glances to the back of the shop.

Extracting herself as soon as politeness would allow, Jelly stepped over to them. "What? I'm busy."

Bouncing on her toes, Em whispered back, "I've got good news about Mr. Henry."

"What is it?"

"No, you finish with that customer. I'll see if I can help the other lady. I can't tell you until we're alone."

Jelly glanced at Marco.

"He's okay." Emi pulled off her backpack, handed it to Marco, and pointed to a chair in the corner. "He already knows."

Marco smiled as a blush bloomed in his cheeks. "Yeah." He slung the backpack over his free shoulder, went to the chair in the corner, and flopped down, his long legs creating a traffic hazard in the small shop.

Thursday, 4:00 pm.
At Home

"So, is it positive?"

Jelly screamed. Her arm flew up and the pregnancy test wand sailed through the air. Grabbing the shower curtain to keep from falling, she accomplished nothing more than pulling the expansion bar loose. The entire apparatus, including Jelly, clattered into the empty tub.

Emi caught the wand as it flew in her direction. "Yep, it's positive." She pressed her lips together. "Uh oh."

"You scared the life out of me!" Jelly pressed her hand to her chest. Fighting the curtain and the bar, she crawled out of the tub and slumped on the toilet seat, gasping. Her vision bounced like a small sailboat floating on a choppy sea. Gorge rose in her throat. Gagging, she slid off the toilet seat and got her head over the bowl without a split second to lose. What she barfed up bore no resemblance to the delicious Mexican dinner she'd shared with Marco and Emi to celebrate the good news about Hank's exoneration.

Emi knelt down and put her hand on her sister's shoulder. "Are you okay?"

"No!" Another wave of nausea caught her.

Emi grabbed a washcloth, wrung it out in cold water, and applied it to the back of Jelly's neck. "Does that help?"

"Oh, God, just let me die." Jelly heaved as wave after wave of nausea punched through her. *What a calamity!*

"That's about fifteen dollars down the toilet."

Despite her suffering, Jelly giggled. "Yeah."

Several minutes passed before Jelly slumped back against the side of the tub and sipped the ice water Emi held out to her.

"Better?" Emi asked.

"Considering the fact that I'm an unwed-mother-to-be?"

Emi flopped down next to Jelly. The ears on her bunny foot pajamas bent at comical angles. "Mr. Henry wants you to marry him."

Jelly dropped her head back on the high edge of the old-fashioned tub. "Uh huh."

"So, you won't be an unwed mother. I'm going to be an aunt. Neat!"

A moan escaped Jelly's throat. She made a swift movement toward the toilet.

Bass Lake
Next Afternoon

Sweat blinded Hank. He reached for his water, tipped it over, and watched, dismayed, as the cool water blurped out of the bottle while it bumped and slid to the corner of the roof. It plopped into the rain gutter and rested there, empty. "Damn!"

He crawled to the edge and slung one long leg over the side. A scraping sound caught his attention. He stared in horror to see the heavy box of shingles sliding right for him. One foot rested on the wobbly ladder. He lurched to avoid the box, and the ladder kicked out from under him, crashing to the deck twelve feet below. Unable to grab anything to hold on to, he slipped off the side and hung precariously to the rain gutter. "*Gówno!*"

A screeching sound gave him the good news that the gutter nails were pulling away from the roof just as the box of shingles went over the edge. "Oh, for crying out loud!" He swung his legs, looking for purchase on the side of the cabin, and the gutter sagged some more. "I'm going to break a damn leg if this thing comes down. Hell!"

"Could you use some help up there, cowboy?"

Looking down, Henry saw Linda propping the ladder under his feet. "Linda?" The gutter gave way some more with a gut-wrenching screech. "God, I'm glad to see you."

She stood next to the ladder and pinned him with a sheep's eyes smile. "Why, Henry darling, that's the nicest thing you've said to me in three years." She grabbed one of his dangling feet and shoved it onto a step.

The gutter ripped a big section away from the roof just as he put his other foot on the rung. Losing his balance, his feet bumped down three steps and he struck his chin with a sharp knock. "Dammit it to hell!"

"You're bleeding, Henry darling." She handed him a blue bandana. Here, let Linda kiss your chinny chin and make it all well." She stroked his leg.

He grabbed the bandana and pressed it to his chin. "Back off!"

Linda stepped back and stood with her legs wide apart and hands on her hips. A wicked smile suffused her face. "Now is that any way to talk to the woman who saved your life?"

"Sorry, but what are you doing here?"

"You mean other than saving your life?" She reached out and put a long-fingered hand on his forearm. Her lips puckered in a pout.

"Oh, jeez, cut it out, will ya?" He pulled the bandana away

and looked at the blood. Tilting his chin up, he said, "Am I going to need stitches?"

She stepped closer. "Hmm, I'll clean it up and put ice on it. A couple of butterfly bandages should do the trick." She touched the wound gently.

"Ow, damn it!"

"Don't be such a baby." She turned and walked to the side door. "Are you coming?"

Grumbling and holding the bandana to his chin, he followed her into the cabin. Linda knew her way around the house and went directly to the bathroom to retrieve the first-aid kit.

She pointed to a kitchen chair. "Sit." Her hand on top of his head, she tilted his chin up and peered closely. "It's pretty deep but looks clean. I'll dab it with some peroxide."

"Go easy. My head is pounding. It feels like my lower jaw moved up a couple of inches. It hurts like heck!"

Linda put his hand holding the bandana back to his chin. "Hold this a minute. It still wants to bleed. I'll get you something for the pain."

Henry's gaze followed her shapely behind until it disappeared through the bathroom door. Guilt washed over him. He could remember the times he'd had his hands on that firm butt. He didn't want to think about Linda. Julie was the woman he loved. He reflected on the past couple of weeks. How had his life become such a mess?

Linda handed him two white pills and a glass of water.

He lurched back, eyed her with suspicion. "What is this?"

"Oh, for heaven's sake, Henry, it's acetaminophen. What do you think I'm giving you, roofies?" She threw up her hands. "Do you want my help or not?"

"No. I don't want your help. I can take care of this myself." He swallowed the pills. "What the hell are you doing here, anyway?" He stood, changed his mind, and sat down again. Spots swam in his woozy vision.

She took the bandana, checked his chin again, and said, "It's stopped bleeding. I'll clean it with peroxide and bandage it. Stay still. You almost knocked yourself out." Linda busied herself with the first-aid box, found the sterile cotton balls and peroxide.

"I asked you, what are you doing here, Linda?" He jerked back from the soggy cotton she dabbed on his chin. "Yow! That stings!"

She threw the cotton on the table. "Fine! Finish it yourself. I never knew you were such a wuss." She plopped into the chair across the table from him, casting a look of disgust.

"Can you please answer a straight question, for once in your life?" He picked up a clean piece of gauze and held it to his chin. "Why are you here?"

"Dom has his truck in the garage, and I offered to pick you up and bring you back to the farm tomorrow. That's why I'm here. Why do you think?"

"What I think is I've *never* been able to figure out what goes on in that devious brain of yours." He took a look at the gauze and placed it back on the wound. "Anyway, it's today, not tomorrow. Why are you here today?" *I'm going to shoot Dom!*

She stood and leaned across the table. "Let's have a look."

Henry removed the gauze and tilted his chin.

"I'll put the butterflies on." She picked up a couple of the bandages, tore open the packages, and returned to Henry's side of the table. "I thought you'd be lonely, so I came to keep you company."

"What a crock!" he said through gritted teeth, holding still as a rock while she applied the bandages. It hurt like heck, but he wouldn't give her the satisfaction of teasing him about it anymore. He clamped down on his jaws, which made his head ache worse, and remained stock-still.

Linda's smile was smug. "I just love it when you talk so nice to me, darling. I assure you, my motive for being here is just what I said it was." She emphasized her words by pushing hard on the first bandage. "Nothing more." Then pushed harder on the second. Leaning forward, she quickly planted a small kiss on his nose. "All better now?"

Like a small boy, Henry scrubbed at his nose to erase her kiss. Linda stood back and laughed with delight.

He got up and went to the daybed across the room, stretched out, and threw an arm across his eyes. "Why me, God, why?"

In a matter of minutes, Henry was snoring. Linda busied herself replacing the shingles in the damaged box. She made sure the ladder was on firm footing, then climbed up to have a look at the damage to the rain gutter. Pushing on it, she could see that it could be nailed back into place easily, and nobody would be the wiser. She knew her way around a toolbox and would help him finish the shingles and repair the rain gutter in the morning.

She tiptoed back into the kitchen, peeked to see that he was still sleeping, and then went out to her car to retrieve her overnight bag. She was here for the night, whether he liked it or not. Reaching farther into the trunk, she removed two bottles of wine and a cooked chicken she picked up at Bass Lake Market. Tilting her head from side to side, she grinned with satisfaction.

Bass Lake
Next Morning

Henry looked up from the edge of the roof where he'd just finished nailing the gutter solidly back in place to spot Dom's truck approaching the cabin. The hot dry weather had set in with a vengeance. The truck churned up a long dust trail that drifted across the road and the lake, extending clear to the end of the turn-off.

Raising an elbow to wipe the sweat from his dirty face, he took the ladder rungs two at a time to reach the wooden porch below and dropped the hammer in his toolbox. Several long strides brought him to the parking spot next to Linda's car just as Dom pulled in.

"Get out of the truck."

Dom turned off the ignition and looked at Henry's angry face bent close to the window. He lowered it and cocked his head. "Good morning to you, too, brother."

"Get out of the damn truck!"

Henry's naked anger gave Dom pause. "Why?"

"Because I don't want Mollie and the kids to hear what I have to say." He turned abruptly. "That's why," he said, and walked out to the dock.

Mollie reached out and put her hand on her husband's arm. "I've never seen Henry this angry. I wonder what happened. Did you see the bruises and the bandage on his chin? He couldn't have been in a fight, could he?"

Dom opened his door and threw one long leg out. "I don't know, but I'd better ask him before he comes back and drags me out." He pointed to the car next to theirs. "What's Linda doing here?"

"I have no idea." Mollie stepped out on the passenger side and pushed her seat forward so her two nieces could climb out of the truck's jump seats. "But I'm about to find out."

Dom strolled to the dock, in no hurry to get to his brother. Henry's posture warned him to tread lightly. Hands in his pockets, Henry stared at the opposite shore of the lake, his jaw muscles twitched from tightly clenched teeth.

"Henry?" Dom stepped back and put up his hands when

Henry whirled around. "Hold it right there! I don't know what your problem is, but why are you glaring at me with murder in your eyes?"

Through clenched teeth, Henry growled, "You don't know how close I am to knocking you into this lake, Dom. What in God's name were you thinking sending Linda up here?" His eyes glittered with controlled anger.

Dom jerked back. "What! I never sent her up here. I was wondering what her car was doing here when we pulled in. What happened to you? Mollie thinks you've been in a fight."

"You didn't tell Linda to come here in your place because your truck was at the garage?"

"No! The truck was in for routine maintenance. I told her we were coming up to get you today." Dom waved his hands to emphasize his remarks. "I did not, nor would I, send her up here."

Henry sighed deeply and walked in a circle, working off his tension. "I'm sorry. I should have known you'd never do that." He clenched his fists. "That woman will be the end of me! She won't take no for an answer. Last night she came up with a candlelight and wine dinner. Tried to come on to me."

"She's a piece of work all right." Dom shook his head with wonder. "I don't know why Dani has stayed friends with her all these years." He smacked a big hand on Henry's shoulder. "What the heck happened to your face?"

Henry touched his chin. "I was trying to retrieve my water bottle while I was up on the roof nailing shingles. It rolled down the slope and when I grabbed for it I slipped off the edge and knocked over the ladder, then the damn box of shingles slid down, nearly taking my head off." He suppressed a grin. "Don't you dare laugh! I could still toss you in the lake. I was hanging from the rain gutter when Linda showed up and pushed the ladder back in place."

Dom chuckled. "At least she kept you from breaking a leg."

"I'd almost rather have broken a leg than what I had to put up with last night. The woman's a nightmare, Dom. For the first time since we built this cabin, I wish we'd installed locks on the bedroom doors."

Dom slung a long arm around Henry's shoulders. "Well, brother, I came up here with good news. You're going back to work tomorrow. The whole stink was a big misunderstanding."

Speechless, Henry stopped and stared at his big brother.

Dom glanced away when Henry's eyes sparkled with unshed tears. He was nearly knocked over when Henry let out a joyful whoop and caught him up in a fierce bear hug.

"Hey! Let go, you're killing me." Dom laughed when Henry lifted him off his feet and whirled him to the edge of the dock. He barely had time to close his mouth before they hit the water.

Chapter Thirty-Three

Big Night Out
Thursday Evening

Clasping her hands to her upper arms, Jelly hugged herself with joy. "That's wonderful news!" She threw her arms wide and pulled Marco to her and danced him around the shop.

Emi giggled at Marco's flustered and embarrassed face. He stumbled over his big feet, trying not to step on Jelly. Emi joined them, and she and Jelly hopped around in a circle, laughing hysterically.

"What happened? How did you find out? Where's Hank now?" The words barely left her lips when the phone on the counter rang. "Don't move. I'll answer the phone. Put up the closed sign."

Hand pressed to her heart, Jelly took a calming breath. "Hello? Oh, Hank! I'm so glad to hear from you. When can I see you? Yes, we just closed." She grinned and nodded. "Emi and Marco are here with me. You are?" She pivoted and pointed to the front window. "Yes, I see your truck. We'll be right out." She turned her back to Emi and Marco, shielded the mouthpiece with her hand, and whispered, "I know, me, too. Bye."

Barely waiting for the emergency brake to set, Hank hopped out of his truck and ran to the front of Big Night Out the instant Julie pulled her key from the door. Swooping her off her feet, he planted a big, long kiss on her happy lips.

Emi and Marco looked at each other and grinned. Susan, who'd left her desk at the travel agency when she heard screeching brakes, stood staring through the front window with a big smile and a thumbs-up.

Her feet still dangling a foot above the ground, Julie tried to come up for air. Laughing through the kiss, she went limp and savored the very public moment. A driver searching for a parking space nearly rear-ended a car backing out of one of the prime spots in front of the coffee bar.

Emi nudged Marco's arm. "Uh, Jelly? You don't care if I sleep over with Jenna tonight, do you? Marco and I are going over there to help her study for her UCSB entrance exam." She raised her head to look Marco in the eye. "Weren't we, Marco?"

"Oh! Uh, yeah." He shifted their backpacks. "We're going to ask Mrs. Lewis if we could ride home with her when she gets off work."

Emi tilted her head and winked at him when he came up with the perfect answer. "Yes, we were on our way to the travel agency to see when she'd be ready to leave. Is that okay? She'll stop by the house so I can get my overnight things."

Jelly laughed at Emi's conspiracy, and for the first time noticed the bruises and bandages on Hank's chin. She reached up and touched him tentatively. "Hank, what happened?"

He grabbed her hand and brought her knuckles to his lips. "I'll tell you over dinner. It's funny now, but it wasn't at the time." He extended his hand to Marco. "How's it going old man?" They clasped hands in a firm shake. "You'll see that Emi gets safely to Mrs. Lewis' home?"

Standing tall, Marco replied, "Yes, sir."

Picking Julie off her feet, Hank carried her to his truck, opened the passenger door, and set her firmly in the seat. "No protests, woman, I have plans."

He had plans all right. All the way back to Simi Valley from Bass Lake, Henry tapped his foot on the floor of Dom's truck and his fingers on the passenger door. He was lucky Dom hadn't thrown him out onto the highway.

First plan: Finally getting his hands on Julie. Obsessed with thoughts of her for the past two weeks, his brain now worked overtime planning a fitting reunion. Second plan: Dinner in the new French restaurant everyone was raving about. Third plan: Back to his condo for a night of lovemaking she'd never forget. Then, if they could still walk, he'd take her home. They'd sit on her porch swing and eat ice cream.

Plan one had been accomplished. He grinned across the front seat at her flushed and excited face. Her hand rested on his knee, and it was all he could do to drive safely.

"Where are we going?"

"Henri's *Plat D'Argent*."

"Oh." She cocked her head with big-eyed delight. "Am I dressed okay? I just noticed you're wearing a suit and tie. Maybe I should get out of these clothes."

"Absolutely—but later." He squeezed her hand and waggled his eyebrows with a lecher's leer. "After dinner."

The bright flush rising in her cheeks tempted him to do a U-turn in the middle of the road, skip dinner, and go straight to his place. But no. This was a celebration, and they had the rest of the evening and night to make up for lost time. The waiting would enhance their excitement.

Jelly's House
11:00 p.m.

Julie's porch swing had a squeak like a canary with laryngitis. Hank looked up from his ice cream dish to the ceiling, where the chain was attached to a large eyebolt. "I could fix that squeak if you like."

"No, I like it." She grinned and rested her head on his shoulder. "It's always had a squeak. My greatest stress reliever is listening to it while I sit here early in the morning or at night." She sat straight and looked into his face. "You have beautiful gray eyes, Hank."

"I know. So do you."

"I know. They're the same exact shade as yours."

He kissed the top of her head. "That proves it. We were meant for each other."

"That's silly, but I love hearing you say it."

"What's silly? That we were meant for each other?"

"No. The part about—you're teasing me." She elbowed him in the ribs.

Hank smacked his forehead with the heel of his hand. "I almost forgot. We're having a big family dinner on Sunday. You and Emi are invited, of course. This time, you'll meet everybody. Stanislaw and Zofia weren't there before. They live in Carlsbad."

"Hank, do you have to go home tonight?"

"You want me to sleep here?"

She licked the last of her ice cream from the spoon. "Mm hmm, that too."

His arm around her shoulder pulled her tightly against his side. "You are my wild woman, aren't you? I'd love to stay, but I have to get up by six for an early meeting with the principal and staff."

Julie took the two dishes and set them on the porch. She

rotated around and pulled herself into his lap. "I'm always up by six. And I wasn't a wild woman before I met you. You've been a bad influence on me. Very bad." Her lips brushed his injured chin and trailed down to the hollow at the base of his neck.

His arms crushed her against his chest. "Would you like to be even badder?"

She slid her hand inside his shirt. "Oh yes, very, very bad." The bright moon lit her hair like a bonfire, matching the intense flames burning inside. Wicked with abandon, she dared, "Let's see how bad we can be."

Her *news* could wait a while. It could wait until he got back to work, back to his classroom. Teaching. What he was meant to do. He'd be so happy when she told him.

Chapter Thirty-Four

Bodacious Blooms Farmhouse
Sunday

The dining room table was extended with two leaves and a card table placed at each end. Two different hand embroidered tablecloths covered the battered card tables, and a long, crocheted banquet cloth was draped over the dining table. The hand painted banner hung from the wall above the doors to the patio, declaring in bold red letters: Happy Birthday Rodzic!

Julie placed folded cloth napkins on each beautiful old dinner plate. "Dani, who's Rodzic? Is it someone I've already met?"

Dani paused while carefully positioning the silver knives and forks. "Yes, that's Polish for father. Papa is eighty today."

Flabbergasted, Julie drew in a sharp breath. "Why didn't Hank tell me? I could have brought a birthday card."

"Papa doesn't like a fuss. That's why Zofia and her husband took him on that phony mission to see the tractor that's for sale over at Simpson's place." She chuckled. "If we have it all ready when he gets here, he won't be able to grumble about it. I'm sure by now he's caught on. We do it every year, but we might surprise him this time. His birthday is actually not till Tuesday."

"Still, I wish Hank had told me so I could have brought a card from me and Emi."

"I'm sure Henry has a card for Papa from the three of you. He'd want to do it that way. It's sort of a declaration of his intentions, you know?"

"His inten...?"

"Here's Joe with the flowers." She smiled at her husband. "Put one arrangement in the middle of the center table and one on the sideboard, honey. Those peonies are magnificent, Joe. Papa will love them."

Joe cocked his head in Julie's direction. "Not as magnificent as Jelly looks tonight. The bloom on your cheeks overpowers these peonies. That dress looks familiar. Have I seen it before?"

Julie blushed and did a model's turn. "You may have seen a picture of Jennifer Garner wearing it to the Screen Actor's Awards dinner. I bought a carload of her clothes for the store. She and I wear the same size. I put most of them on the racks, but I couldn't sell this one. I had to have it." *Even though I won't be able to fit into it much longer.*

Dani studied the shimmery sea green dress. It fell just at the knee and had a low cut back. "It looks stunning on you, Jelly. I meant to say something earlier. I'll bet Henry loves it."

Jelly studied Dani's figure and pursed her lips. "We look like we're the same size. You should come by the shop one day and look at the rest of the collection. In fact, with your hair and eyes you'd look great in the gray two-piece outfit with pale printed poppies on the under-layer. It's very filmy and floaty. Perfect for a wedding or fancy party. In fact, I'm going to remove it from the rack and set it aside for you."

Joe hugged his wife and smiled lovingly into her eyes. "That's a great idea, Jelly. Hold it back and I'll bring Dani in to try it on one day next week."

"Oh, Joe, where would I ever wear it? We're such homebodies. We never go anywhere."

"That is a correctible problem, my love. I'll think of something. I'd like to see you in a sexy new dress."

Her cheeks aflame, Dani smacked Joe on the arm. "Make yourself useful. Go bring the folding chairs in and throw a cloth on that picnic table on the patio." She gave him an affectionate shove in the direction of the hallway.

Julie leaned across the table and whispered, "You've got one good-looking husband, Dani. Joe's a dreamboat."

Dani laughed and they busied themselves putting the finishing touches to the table. Candles in the tall silver antique candlesticks were lit. They stood back to admire the beauty of the table and the glow of the room.

During the festive dinner, where Julie happily noticed Linda was not present, Hank told his family the details of his suspension resolution.

Dr. Thompson's receptionist had mistakenly thought Henry had embarked on an improper relationship with Emi. The woman's daughter, a classmate of Emi's, told her that Mr. Henry was dating Ms. Swanson. It was the talk of the school. The woman was horrified when she discovered Henry was dating Julie, and that her mistaken assumptions had prompted Henry's suspension.

Julie already knew the story, but enjoyed the reaction of various family members and the questions that flew back and forth.

"Yes," Jelly said. "The woman tearfully confessed to Dr. Thompson that she grew suspicious because Henry brought Emi to all her appointments. He and Emi seemed too familiar in their behavior, always laughing and animated. She was worried about Emi and other girls, so she called the school."

Henry nodded. "I've been oblivious to the fact that my students knew about my private life, my relationship with Julie. I should have known that few secrets would survive the scrutiny of a room full of bright, curious teenagers."

Julie leaned forward. "Dr. Thompson and his receptionist went to the school to explain what lead up to her call to the principal. She was embarrassed that her presumptuous talk nearly ruined the reputation and career of this good teacher." She pointed across the table at Hank, and mumbles of agreement went from one end of the dining room to the other.

"She offered to reimburse Hank for his legal expenses. He wouldn't take her money."

Henry shrugged. "My main concern was for her daughter, my student. The girl was so humiliated by what her mother did that she wanted to change schools."

Dom reached across the table and topped off Henry's wine glass. "What happened to the girl?"

"We had a long talk. I asked her to go easy on her mom. Parents have a responsibility to their kids. She did what she thought best at the time. I don't have any hard feelings about it."

Papa Januz raised his glass. "We always know Henryk a good boy. He love teaching children. We raise glasses to Henryk and his beautiful Julie."

"Henryk and Julie," rang out from around the table.

Papa smiled. "Henryk bring me most wonderful birthday present of all. Julie and little sister, Emi. Welcome to family, Julie."

Glasses rose again and the toasting went on. Julie cast a

loving look Hank's way. She cocked her head with an unspoken question. *When was this announcement made, and why haven't I been informed?*

He merely winked, grinned, and downed the contents of his wine glass.

Driving Back to Simi Valley
11:00 p.m.

Emi seemed to be sound asleep on the seat behind them. Julie leaned close to Hank and whispered, "Okay, I waited till Emi was asleep. What was your father talking about? Welcome to the family? Is there something you're not telling me, Hank? And if there is—"

"LA, LA, LA, I can hear you, Jelly! I'm not asleep." Emi sat up with her hands over her ears repeating, "LA, LA, LA."

Jelly reached back and smacked Emi on the elbow. "Oh, for Heaven's sake, quit it! I can never have any secrets from you."

Hank squeezed Julie's knee. "It's no secret, I love you. I want us to be a family. You can't possibly be surprised about that."

"I am surprised, Hank, especially since you told your family. We should have talked about it before you announced it to the world."

Hank pulled the truck onto the shoulder. He turned off the ignition and reached for Julie's hand. With his lips to her fingers, he said, "Julie, I love you. I can't live without you. Will you please marry me?"

A ring slipped onto her finger. The darkness of the truck interior couldn't hide the sparkle of the large diamond. Tears sprang to her eyes. She barely had the breath to say, "Yes."

"Do I have anything to say about this?" Emi mumbled from behind them. "Well, do I?"

"No." They spoke over each other.

"Okay, okay." Emi slumped on her side and pulled her jacket over her head. "Get it over with then. Tomorrow's a school day."

Chapter Thirty-Five

Big Night Out
Tuesday, 1:00 p.m.

J oe admired Dani as she modeled the dress Jelly had put back for her. It fit perfectly. As usual, Jelly had a good eye for the best selections for her customers, even though it seemed at times that she hadn't looked in the mirror when she herself dressed for work. This afternoon she wore lime green, form-fitting pants with a pink, polka dot tee shirt that hung to her knees. She'd tied it up in a big knot at the hip. Her shoes were shiny red patent leather with four-inch heels.

"Here, Dani, look. I hope these shoes aren't too big. They're perfect for the dress."

"What size are they?"

"Eight."

"Darn, they are great, but I wear a seven. I'd probably walk right out of them. Do you have anything else? Maybe something with a lower heel?"

"Oh, oh, I know." Jelly reached over to the adjoining rack. She pushed dozens of belts back and forth across the metal bar.

"Look, Dani. If we switch the belt from your dress with this one, then these gray suede mid-heel pumps will be perfect. Here, let's try it." Jelly switched the belts, helped Henry's sister with the gray shoes, and turned. "Joe, what do you think of your beautiful wife now?

He strolled across the shop, stood with crossed arms, and studied Dani. "I think she looks just like she did on our wedding day."

Jelly put her arm around Dani's waist. "That's what I like to hear. Didn't I tell you the dress was perfect for you?"

Linda, who'd been browsing in silence through the purses and scarves, joined them. "It looks great, Dani. Made for you."

Jelly decided when the three of them came into the shop that she'd do her best to be civil to Linda, even though the sight of the woman gave her a piercing headache. "Linda, you're looking well. I see you've been enjoying the sun."

"Yes. I picked up this nice glow when Henry and I were up at the Bass Lake cabin last week."

Dani's mouth dropped open. A menacing glare from Joe, followed by a tight-mouthed headshake, his disgust took clear aim at his wife's old friend.

Ears ringing, Jelly couldn't hear the classical music that always played through the shop's speakers. Jeannie must have turned it off. She stood rooted to the floor. She cleared her throat. "Is that so?"

Tossing her black mane over one shoulder, Linda answered, "Yes, it's lovely up there this time of year. We've been going to that cabin since we were kids. Isn't that right, Dani?"

Dani cast a pleading look at Jelly. "They weren't—he wasn't—"

"You'll have to excuse me. I'm late for an appointment." Viciously twisting at her engagement ring, Jelly tugged it off her finger and thrust it at Linda. "I'm sure you'll be happy to return this to Hank for me."

She turned to Jeannie. "Would you mind closing today?"

Before anyone could react, she walked through the dressing room and out the back door of the shop. Her head swimming, she was halfway home before she realized where she was or that she was driving her car. Once home, she parked the car and walked into the house in a daze. In her bedroom, she sat on the side of the bed, her heart aching. What was she going to do? The man she loved and trusted had lied to her. She was carrying his child.

Chapter Thirty-Six

Halfway to Sacramento
Thursday

Emi slumped sullenly in the passenger seat, her arms crossed. Head turned toward the window. She refused to look at Jelly or speak to her. The atmosphere in the Mustang was cold, silent as a crypt.

Only the weak mewling of the still un-named kitten, in its carrier secured to the back seat, broke the deathly silence now and then. The proof of Emi's anger and disappointment was demonstrated by her dogged refusal to comfort the scared little thing.

Jelly gave up trying to make small talk and even turned off the CD player. They'd stopped only once for gas. "Do you want something to eat, Emi?"

Emi clamped her lips tight, glared at her sister, and stared out the window.

Jelly got back on the freeway and continued the silent drive north. It would be two more hours before they reached Aunt Martha's home.

Her aching heart was a frozen block in her chest, the iciness extended to her back, legs, and arms. Jelly summoned up the will to not cry. She needed to cry, to scream. But she'd do that later in private. Unable to overcome her years of masking her deepest fears and emotions in order to protect Emi, she couldn't switch gears now.

The last time she'd felt such pain and betrayal was when Daddy selfishly killed Norman, thinking more of his own grief than the consequences to his motherless daughters. She'd hoped never to experience a breach of faith like that again.

Tears of humiliation welled in her eyes whenever she thought of the way Hank had played with her trust and love, spending time alone with Linda while she'd worried herself sick over him. *Men couldn't be trusted.* She'd never put her heart in the hands of another man. Hank came along when she had finally come to accept that she'd spend the rest of her life alone once Emi left home. She had no one to blame but herself. She was no starry-eyed teenager. Perhaps Aunt Martha made a wise choice when she never married.

Jelly decided she would look for a buyer for her store, sell the house, and move away from the town filled with too many bad memories. The Napa Valley area might be a good place to open up a new shop. No, maybe not. There were lots of rich people there, but the population wasn't large enough to support a gently-used clothing store. The last thing any woman wanted was to walk into an affair wearing the cast-off clothing of someone she might know.

She always dreamed of setting up shop on Oahu or Maui, but not till Emi was out of the house. Emi needed to be within easy distance to her only other relatives—Daddy and his sister.

Sacramento was out of the question as a viable location. A business and government center, most women wore business suits or conservative clothing during the day. The place was a ghost town at night. Maybe some place near San Francisco or

Silicon Valley. She'd saved enough money. There would be time to make a smart choice. She'd find a place both she and Emi would like that would also be good for business.

Damn you, Hank! Get out of my head!

Her cell phone rang. When she saw Hank's name on the display, she turned it off and tossed it into the glove box. *Leave me alone!*

After another hour of silence, they pulled onto the quiet, dark street where Martha had lived for the past twelve years. Jelly alerted them she was on her way up. Daddy was anxious to meet Emi. He'd last seen her when she was two. Jelly didn't tell them the reason for the short notice visit, but they were happy she and Emi were coming.

Jelly pulled into the driveway and stopped in front of the detached garage.

Emi yanked open the door.

"Take your cat. She's desperate to get out of the car."

"Me, too," Emi muttered as she opened the back door and lifted out the cat carrier, startling the poor creature into a frightened yowl. "Shhh, shhh, it's okay, baby." Emi put her face close to the carrier. "Okay, okay now. I've got you." She reached back for her overnight bag and slammed both doors.

Jelly recalled saying those very words to Emi twelve years ago.

The porch light brightened the path. Emi carried her things toward the house, her limp barely noticeable. When a man opened the front door, she stopped.

Jelly recognized Daddy, put the car in reverse, and backed out of the driveway.

Her voice tinged with panic, Emi yelled, "Jelly, wait. Where are you going?"

Jelly lowered a window. "I'll be back soon. Go on in and meet your father."

"You're not coming with me?"

Continuing to back out, Jelly waved. "No, you'll be fine. I won't be long. There's Aunt Martha."

Tears glittered in Emi's angry eyes. She straightened her shoulders, glaring at her sister with determination. "Fine then, take as long as you want. I don't need you to hold my hand."

Jelly caught a breath when she smiled at her baby sister. "I know you don't, baby."

Aunt Martha called, "Come on in, dear. I have supper waiting. Introduce us to your new kitty." Jelly didn't look back as she retraced her way out of the neighborhood. Once she was about a block away, the floodgates opened. Racking sobs tore through her like hot knife blades. She drove to a nearby park and pulled into the deserted parking lot, avoiding the lighted area. Lowering her face into her hands, she loosed her tears. There was no more holding back.

Splashing cold water on her face in a convenience store restroom, Jelly stood over the sink and let the water drip from her nose and chin. She gripped the edges of the sink, pulled a couple of rough paper towels from the holder, and brought them to her face. After several deep breaths, she studied her reflection in the scratched and dented stainless steel mirror. Her eyes were red, but some of the puffiness had diminished.

Rooting through her handbag, she pulled out the few items of makeup she would use to repair her appearance. Old, she felt old and tired. A deep sadness brimmed over in her soul. *I hurt. I'm wounded. I'm pregnant.*

Moving like an automaton, she re-did her eyebrows and dabbed tinted moisturizer around her eyes, upper lip, and nose. She left off the mascara, knowing what a mess it had made. Even though sure she had no tears left, she wasn't taking any chances.

After applying lipstick, she pinched her cheeks hard to raise some color.

It was after eleven. She had to get to Martha's house now, before they became alarmed. She told them that she would drop Emi off and be gone for a short while, but it had been three hours.

Grabbing a Coke, she settled the tab for that and her gasoline at the register. The disinterested young man gave her a cursory glance, took her money, handed over a receipt, and immediately turned his attention to his textbook.

I must look like an old wreck.

At Martha's house, she turned off her headlights and parked in front. As quietly as possible, she closed the trunk after removing her bag. The porch light was still on, but the living room was dimly lit, and she could detect no activity in the house.

Her shaky fingers had barely touched the front doorknob when her father opened the door from inside. He took one look at her ravaged face and drew her into his arms. "Oh, Julie Lea, I'm so sorry."

She hadn't run out of tears after all. The shoulder of her father's shirt was soon soaked. He drew her to the sofa, and they sat together. He held her tight. "Do you realize, Julie Lea, that this is the first time I've held you in twelve years?"

She nodded against his shoulder.

Aunt Martha tiptoed into the room with a tray holding three mugs of hot cocoa. "Hello, sweetheart, I'm sure you can use this." She anticipated Jelly's question. "Emi's asleep in the guest room. She's fine. She and George had a nice visit."

Afraid to say anything that might start the tears again, Jelly lifted the steaming mug to her trembling lips and sipped cocoa from under the thick layer of whipped cream. George and Martha followed her lead.

After several quiet moments, George set his cup on the

coffee table. "Emi asked me if she could call me George." A rueful smile, lasting only a second, graced his lips. "I told her that was okay with me. She asked me if I had any ideas of a good name for her kitten just before we finally said good night. I promised to think about it. The poor, shy baby extended her hand for me to shake when she went to bed. You've done a wonderful job with her, Julie Lea. I'm so grateful."

"Oh, Daddy, life has been an unkind challenge for us." She looked at Martha. "All of us."

Martha shifted in her chair. "Julie, you should know that Henry Palasczewski has called three times this evening. He's frantic with worry."

Jelly made a dismissive sound as she rolled her eyes and pulled a sour face. "I'm sure."

"I spoke with him last time he called," Martha said. "He wants to talk to you. He sounded desperate."

"Well, I'm not going to talk to him. Ever."

George put down his cup and leaned toward her, elbows on his knees. "Julie Lea, you have to tell him about the baby. He has a right to know. Give him a chance to explain."

Jelly stood. "I need some sleep. Thank you for looking after Emi."

Martha and George shrugged, the twins mirroring each other.

Martha reached out. "Julie—"

"Goodnight."

The muffled sound of a ringing phone woke Jelly. Her head throbbed with every beat of her pulse. She groaned softly when she turned over. Opening her eyes, no more than a slit, she saw the bed Emi slept in was empty. It was after ten in the morning. She sat, squinting in the bright shafts of light coming through the white Venetian blinds. Stretching, she threw back the blanket and sat on the edge of the twin bed. She'd spent countless nights in this room during her many visits to Folsom prison.

When she dragged herself to the kitchen, Martha was reading the newspaper and sipping a cup of coffee. She looked up from the paper with a bright smile. "Good morning, Julie dear. I was about to check to see if you were still breathing." She reached for the coffee pot. "Have some. It always restores my humanity in the morning."

"Boy, do I ever need it. I didn't even have nerve enough to look in the mirror." Jelly plopped into a kitchen chair and reached for the carton of half and half. "Coffee smells fresh. Did you just make it?"

"About twenty minutes ago, when George and Emi left to take a walk."

A mewing sound caught Jelly's attention. She looked around. "Where is that nameless cat?"

Martha grinned. "Right here, all snuggled up in my lap. And as of this morning, she has a name. It's Hanky."

"Hanky! Oh, no. Emi wouldn't name that cat after—"

Martha raised a hand. "No. Emi gave her that name because she said the kitten was better than a hanky for soaking up tears and snot. I practically had to bathe the poor little thing after they left. I did the best I could with a warm washcloth." She reached into her lap and held up the kitten. "Doesn't she look bedraggled?"

Jelly had to smile at the sight of the kitten presented with damp hair sticking out in all directions.

Huge eyes implored Martha to pet and comfort her. When Martha complied, overly loud purring filled the kitchen. "My gosh, this little scamp purrs as loud as a big tomcat."

Jelly chuckled and reached across the table to touch her tiny head. "She is adorable, isn't she? At least Emi didn't name her Kleenex."

"Henry called again this morning, Julie. You really must talk to the man and settle things with him."

"I'm never going to speak to him again after what he did. You were right to stay single. Men are nothing but trouble."

Martha set the kitten on the floor where it lapped at a small bowl of water. "Oh, Julie, how wrong you are. I didn't *choose* to remain single. Deeply in love when Jessie was killed, I was thirty-seven and engaged to be married. My fiancé had just accepted a great job offer in Seattle. We were already packing for the move. I refused to leave with him after George was arrested. He was very patient with me for almost a year, then he fell in love with someone else." Her bleak face showed the depth of her sadness when she related the story.

A pain surged through Jelly's stomach and chest. "Oh, God, I feel so guilty. I had no appreciation for what you gave up for us." She reached for Martha's outstretched hand.

"No, Julie. It was no doing of yours. It was my choice. You have no reason to feel guilty. We've all paid a heavy price for those awful days."

Squeezing her aunt's hand, Jelly noticed how soft and young it looked. It dawned on her that Martha was barely fifty-two years old. Why had she ever have thought of her as old? It was true she had old-fashioned values and manners, but she was still smooth-faced and young. Shame heated Jelly's chest. "I'm sorry, really sorry."

Martha gave her hand a perfunctory squeeze and stood. "You need to eat. I've got some waffles in the oven. They're soggy, but still edible. I'll get you a plate."

"Aunt Martha, why aren't you at work?"

"Oh, I called them when I heard the two of you were coming. They owe me a lot of time off. I'm home for the rest of the week. My boyfriend and I are driving to Muir Woods tomorrow."

Jelly's eyebrows snapped up. "Your—"

"Yes, my boyfriend. Do you think I'm too old to have one? I've still got a lot of living to do, Julie."

"No, no, you're not old. Neither is Daddy." She lowered her forehead to her hands and rolled her head from side to side. "I've been going through life with blinders on. What a selfish jerk I am."

Martha laughed heartily. "Oh, my goodness, Julie, enough. Don't even think that way. You've been living in a self-directed and determined way to make a good life for Emi and yourself, in spite of all you've been through. I don't want to hear any more talk about selfish."

Martha's Neighborhood
7:00 p.m.

The sun's rapid descent in the west was nearly complete. Through the looming darkness, Hank searched the old Sacramento neighborhood for the address of Julie's aunt.

Sally finally gave in to his pleas. She handed over Martha's address when it became apparent that Julie was not going to talk to him or return his calls.

Hank's first impulse upon hearing what happened in Julie's store was to find Linda and read her the riot act. His rage at her action sent him into a mental frenzy. He could only imagine what Julie thought he'd been up to. Exactly what Linda wanted her to think.

He snapped to attention and grinned when he spotted Julie and a man walking down the street away from him. *Wait a minute.* Something wasn't right. He slowed to crawl. She walked hand-in-hand with the tall, slim guy. He reached across and put his arm around Julie's shoulders, leaned down to kiss her on the cheek. *What the—?* Her arm went around the man's waist. They stopped walking, faced each other, and embraced. Julie rested her head on his chest. Hank's gut roiled, his breathing rapid and his heartbeat uneven. He slammed the brake pedal.

Above trembling hands, Hank stared at the couple and gripped the top of the steering wheel so hard he lost the circulation in his fingers. *Who the heck is this guy?*

Julie and the man talked intimately. She tilted her head back, and they kissed.

Sweat bloomed on Hank's forehead. He swallowed against rising bile.

Through the sound of his ringing ears, an accelerating engine caught his attention. He looked through his open side window to see an impatient driver flash a crude gesture as he passed. Hank pulled to the curb. He needed to get a handle on his racing thoughts.

Is this guy the reason for her frequent solo trips to Sacramento? She supposedly came to visit her father in prison. *What is she up to? How long has she been seeing this man?*

Hank's vision blurred. There was one way to find out. He grabbed the handle and opened his door but was welded to the seat as if an anvil sat on his lap. Julie's tinkling laughter pierced his eardrums like shards of ice. Stupefied, Hank gaped as they continued arm in arm along the tree-lined street into the growing darkness, dim old-fashioned streetlamps the only illumination now.

First Linda, now Julie. When it comes to women, I'm a first-class chump!

Nearly back to Martha's house, George stopped and turned to his daughter. "Julie Lea, you do realize that you'll have to return the man's calls and tell him about your pregnancy. Look at me, sweetheart."

Jelly gazed at her father's face, then rested her head on his chest. She sighed and reached around his waist with her arms and hugged him. For the first time in twelve years, she could hug her father. Nothing ever felt better.

Smiling into his eyes, she said, "I do know. I'll call him as soon as I get home. In my heart, I know there couldn't be anything going on with him and Linda. Must have been my hormones that made me hand back my ring and storm out of the store, then leave town on top of that!"

George kissed Jelly on the cheek. "I know you waited a long time for the right man to come along. I trust your judgment of his character and look forward to meeting him."

"I love you, Daddy." On her toes, Jelly planted a kiss on his lips. "And you'll love Hank. He's kind and funny and awkward, but he's so smart and such a good teacher. The kids in his class adore him. I'm sure Emi would agree with me on that, not that we agree on much these days."

They laughed and George turned. They walked arm in arm the short distance to Martha's house. The loud grinding sound of an engine caught their attention. Looking back, they watched a large pickup truck complete a U-turn in the street and head back into the darkness.

Jelly chuckled. "Now I'm seeing things. That looked like Hank's truck. I miss being with him more than I thought possible."

Chapter Thirty-Seven

Henry's Classroom
Two Weeks Later

"Why are you still here, Emi?" Henry's head didn't move as he continued grading papers.

"What's wrong with you?" The silent classroom echoed her words.

"Please leave. It's not a good idea for you to be alone in the classroom with me. We've played that game and it was no fun."

Emi's glare translated to her voice. "Are you blaming me for what happened to you?"

Silence greeted her question. She waited.

"Emi, I'm not blaming you for anything. Classes are over. Please pick up your books and leave." A stiff breeze outside blew leaves past the windows.

"You know what, Mr. Henry? You're no fun anymore. Your class stinks. All the kids have noticed it." She pounded a fist on the lab table. "Please look at me. I'm not leaving till you talk to me."

"I'm sorry you're no longer enjoying the class. I don't think we have anything to discuss beyond your homework assignments." This is just what he needed. As if he wasn't miserable enough, he now had an angry teenager in his face.

"Mr. Henry, if you don't look at me and talk to me, I'm going to count to ten and start screaming rape!"

"For the love of God, Emi!" His pen slammed down on his desk and he put his head in his hands, his fingers spread through his hair. When he looked up, Emi stood in front of his desk. "What?"

Fury and resolve played across her features. Her lips clamped shut, and she shook her head. "I don't know what you did, you big skunk, but you broke my sister's heart, and I want to know why."

"I broke your sister's heart. How did I do that?"

"How would I know? You don't come over, you don't call her, don't answer your phone at home or your cell phone. She cries all the time."

Hank sat back in his chair. This enraged girl standing at his desk, acting like she wanted to kill him, was a constant source of pride, and a constant painful reminder of Julie. How to separate his feelings for Emi as his student and as the sister of the woman who'd betrayed him? He lowered his eyes and sighed with resignation. "Emi, this is really none of your business."

"Of course it's my business. Jelly's my sister!"

"Yes, I know that, but—"

"Why won't you come over? Why won't you talk to her?"

"That's a question for Julie to answer."

"I asked her. She doesn't know why." Kicking the front panel of his desk in frustration, she emitted a frustrated, "Aaargh!" She leaned closer to his face and glared. "She thinks you're back with Linda again. Are you?"

Henry groaned and peered at the ceiling. "I think you really must leave my classroom now, Emi." He stood, walked to the door, and held it open for her.

"I don't care what you think, okay? You better talk to me, Mr. Henry. I'm almost up to ten." She opened her mouth and sucked in a breath as if to scream.

Henry slammed the door. "Stop it! You want me to get fired?"

If possible, her glare was stronger. "I don't care if you get fired or not. If you don't talk to my sister, I'm going to scream. I mean it!"

His head dropped back, and he groaned. "What do you want from me? This is a nightmare."

She stared in disbelief. "I just told you. Are you deaf? Grownups are the most stupid things on the planet. You're the most stupid of all."

"You're way out of line, young lady."

"I'm out of line? You're out of line, *teacher*. You said you love my sister. You asked her to marry you. I was there, remember? Now you act like she's got cooties or something. Your family doesn't know what's going on with you either."

"My family? What are you talking about?" *My family?* "What do you know about my family?"

Her expression said you're-a-moron. "I'm friends with Sharla, okay? Everybody's clueless about what's going on. They're afraid to ask you about Jelly. They're really sad and they don't know why. They want to know what's going on."

"Look, let me explain something to you, then you can go. Whatever there was between your sister and me is over and done with, okay? We no longer have a relationship. That's what's going on." If he didn't get out of this classroom and away from this kid, who was too smart for her own britches, he would start to scream himself.

"Why?"

"Why?" *Do I need to explain myself to this child?*

"Hello-oo. That's the whole point of this conversation, isn't it? I want to know why. Jelly wants to know why."

"Julie knows why."

Emi took a big breath and let out a scream. "Rape!"

Henry leaped forward and put a hand over her mouth. "Stop!" Everybody within a half mile of his classroom must have heard her. Sweat broke out on his forehead. "Are you going to stop?"

She nodded, her eyes huge in her face.

He removed his hand, and she hollered, "Rape!"

His hand covered her mouth again. He said through gritted teeth, "Emi! Do not do that again. You must stop. I'll talk to her, okay?"

Her eyes squinched with skepticism. She blew out a muffled, hot breath against his hand. "You better mean that."

"I mean it. I'm going to take my hand away now. Are you going to scream again?" He had to get her out of here, whatever it took.

She nodded up and down. "You better not be lying to me, because if you are..."

"I'm telling you the truth. I'll talk to her. I'll call her tomorrow."

"No. You'll get in your truck and go over to her store and talk to her right now. Tomorrow is not good enough."

"Tomorr—"

"Now, you big jerk! Jelly didn't do anything bad to you. When she met you, she was a virgin. Now she's—"

Henry's lips twisted as he slowly shook his head. "Now she's what? I don't know what she is. I don't know who she is. I wish I'd never met her." Why God had singled him out for special punishment was a mystery. He hoped that if he ever looked seriously at another woman, somebody would shoot him right between the eyes.

Emi's eyes swam. "I hate you."

"Yeah, well, that's the least of my problems. Now get out of here."

"No way, I'm not leaving. I'm going with you to make sure you're telling me the truth."

With her hands-on-hips posture, she presented the picture of awesome determination. It was no doubt genetic. Henry pitied any man who ever fell in love with this little hellion.

Fisting his hands, Hank hissed, "Shit!" His head bounced with emphasis.

"Teachers shouldn't swear, it's—"

"Don't test my patience further, Martha Elizabeth Swanson. Keep your mouth shut. Pick up your backpack. Walk to my truck in complete silence. I don't want to hear another word out of you. When we get to the store, you stay outside. Understand?"

The look of gleaming triumph in her clever blue eyes infuriated Hank. He would send his résumé to every school in the state of California. Every school beyond a fifty-mile radius of Simi Valley. He'd put his condo on the market tomorrow. He couldn't put enough miles between Julie Swanson and her demon of a little sister.

The bell on the shop door tinkled. Deep into finishing the bank drop bag for the day, Jelly didn't look up. "Is that you, sweetie?" When she heard no answer, she turned.

Her breath caught. "Hank?" She couldn't hide the shock she felt at his appearance.

"Who's sweetie? I don't want to interrupt your plans."

Her attempt at a smile failed. She swallowed at the coldness in his voice. "Emi, of course. Who else would it be?"

"I'm sure I'd be the last to know." The muscles in his jaw bulged from the clamping of his teeth. Jelly faced a very angry man. She steeled herself. Stepping from behind the jewelry case, she faced him.

"What are you saying, Hank? Why are you so angry?"

He fisted his hands and shoved them into his pockets. "I'm not angry."

"You are."

"I'm not angry!" He turned his back on her and strode toward the door.

"Hank, don't leave. Please, we need to talk. I have something to tell you." Heart pounding, she took a tentative step in his direction and stopped short when he whirled around.

"I'll bet you do, Julie. You have a lot to tell me, right?"

Who was this stranger standing before her? This man with a face like thunder, tensed like a steel band ready to snap? "We, uh," she drew in a calming breath. "I wanted to share some news with you. That's why I've called you so many times. What's wrong, Hank? Why haven't you called me? Have I done something?"

He shook his head, closed his eyes. "Just tell me whatever it is so I can leave. I have things to do."

There was no way she could stop her tears. She drew a breath, started to speak, then stopped and dashed them away. She thought she saw the faintest flicker of sympathy in his eyes. "Now is probably not the best time. Go. Do whatever it is you're so anxious to get out of here for."

Anger flared from his face and heated her like a flamethrower. She took a step back from him and raised her hands to hot cheeks. She felt the flush and took another step back. "Hank, you're scaring me."

"I'm not going to hurt you, for crissakes!" He threw up his hands and walked in a circle. "Say what you have to say, Julie. Let's end the agony for both of us."

Her massive attempt to control a sob failed. "Hank, I'm

pregnant. I thought you had a right to know. This is not the way I was hoping to tell you."

Henry's face registered shock. A blush bloomed from his neck. His gray eyes, usually soft and full of love, flashed steely and cold. He said nothing.

She waited. Finally Jelly whispered, "Hank?"

Still, he didn't speak.

"Hank, don't you have something to say?" Hot tears slid down her cheeks.

Muscles in his jaw danced. Flexing his fingers, his facial expression darkened. "What would you like me to say?"

Stunned by his coldness and unexplained fury, Jelly was speechless. Is this stranger the man she loved, the same man to whom she'd given herself willingly, the gentle teacher beloved by his students? Her knees wobbled, and she grasped the edge of the counter and slumped onto the pink vanity stool. Gritting her teeth against more tears, she clamped her eyes shut and drew a fractured breath.

Her response to his question was barely audible. "I don't know, I, I thought you'd be—"

"You thought I'd be what? Brimming with joy?"

"Hank, I'm confused, I feel sick. Please leave." Face in her hands, stomach churning, a sick headache nauseated Jelly.

This can't be happening.

His angry footsteps paused at the door. "Good idea, get your little problem sorted out with whoever the father is. Unless you don't know."

She jerked at his unbelievably cruel words. The door slammed.

Hank brushed past Emi, got into his pickup, and roared out of the parking lot. He drove. He drove for hours. He drove aimlessly.

The scene in Big Night Out played and re-played in his head. The more he thought about it, the more bizarre it became.

How could he have said those cruel words to his beautiful Julie? She betrayed him, played him for a sucker. Blindsided and heartbroken, he drove and drove.

Ink-like darkness surrounded the car. He realized he was driving without headlights and switched them on. *Where am I?* The Pacific Ocean shimmered in the faint moonlight on his left. North, he was headed north, the road narrow and full of curves. Rolling cliffs and hills loomed on his right. He must be on Highway 1. How far had he gone? The gas gauge warning light flashed on the dash.

Highway 1 at night. Not a good place to run out of gas. Eyes darting back and forth, he searched for a turnout. He must get off the road before his gas tank ran dry.

Where the heck am I?

A sign in the distance caught his eye. Hank reduced his speed as he approached the sign. *San Simeon next exit.* San Simeon? No way could he have driven over a hundred-sixty miles in a daze. He switched on the overhead light, checked his watch, and took the off ramp. *Almost nine. My God!*

Chapter Thirty-Eight

Jelly's House
8:00 p.m.

The minute Emi opened the front door for Connie, Jelly broke down. She tried to hold it together for Emi's sake, but the sight of both her best friends offering help and sympathy was more than she could handle. Her racking sobs came from so deep inside, it hurt. Unable to answer them, she pressed a wad of tissues to her lips.

Connie gaped. "Jelly, what happened?"

When Jelly remained silent, Sally answered for her, "I went over to her store as soon as Emi came for me. She was in no shape to drive, so I brought them home."

Connie sat next to Jelly. "Honey, you look like a train wreck. Is there anything we can do?"

They peered at Emi, unanswered questions in their eyes.

"I don't know what happened. Mr. Henry talked to her. He left after a couple of minutes. When I went into the store, she was in the bathroom throwing up. I couldn't do anything."

Desperate worry on Emi's face broke Jelly's heart. If there

was anything left to break. She reached for her little sister's hand and gave her a comforting squeeze. "I'll be all right. Give me a minute." She sucked in some air, straightened her back, and scrubbed her eyes with tissues.

"Okay, I'm better now." Jelly shook her head and wiped away the rest of her tears. "I got myself into a big mess."

Emi knew about her pregnancy, but it would be news to Connie and Sally. Jelly needed the support of her friends and family now that Hank accused her of not knowing who the father of her baby was, then walked out on her.

Relating the story wasn't as difficult as she thought it would be. Sharing it with them lessened her burden. Concentrate on the future, that's what she would do. Make plans and quit dwelling in the dark pit of her misery. It wasn't her style. Look ahead, that was her motto.

Connie sighed and squeezed Jelly's hand. "I'm shocked we were such lousy judges of his character."

"We'll help you through this, Jelly. You're not alone," Sally added.

Jelly's swelling heart nearly brought more tears, but she'd had enough of crying. "I know I'm not alone. I have Emi and I have both of you. Right now, I could use a glass of wine."

"No wine for you, chica, not until December. No good for the baby and you're going to have a beautiful, happy, healthy baby. Look at this as a blessing. It's hard, but I know you. You can't be sad for more than an hour."

Jelly smiled weakly and nodded. "You're right, I'll be okay. The baby will be okay." She leaned against Emi. "We'll be okay, won't we?"

"I hate him. I'm never going back into his class again."

Jelly tilted Emi's chin with her fingertip. "Look at me, Emi. You have no reason to hate Henry. He's a good teacher, and he likes you."

"He was mean to you."

"It's only a few weeks until summer break. Please don't do anything to hurt your grade-point average. All you have to do is go to school and complete your assignments for a little bit longer. Then we'll have all summer to enjoy."

"I can't look at him, Jelly. How can I go back there?"

"You can and you will. I know you can do it."

Connie and Sally nodded encouragement and agreement with Jelly.

By ten, she and Emi were alone in the house. Jelly suggested they wind down by reading for a while; it was nearly bedtime. She picked up a fashion magazine and Emi the book she was reading for her English class assignment. Jelly glanced over when Emi giggled at something in the book, glad she was no longer in such a black mood.

Emi closed the book and placed it on the table between them. "You were right, Jelly. That *was* a good book."

"I remember how much fun I had reading it. How about we get to bed now? Tomorrow's a school day."

Emi grumbled all the way down the hallway to her bedroom. Jelly crossed her fingers that she'd go back to school and finish the semester without too much of a fight.

Chapter Thirty-Nine

End of June,
Friday Night, 7:45 p.m.

"Are you sure you're pregnant?"

"Yes, Connie, I'm sure."

"She doesn't look pregnant, does she, Sally?"

"No, but it's only a couple of months, isn't it, Jelly?"

Strong and slim, Jelly had plenty of energy. "I could tell you to the day, but I won't. Come on, we're almost to the top."

Connie grumbled, "Whose idea was power walking?"

Jelly and Sally shouted, "Yours!"

Still light, the sky glowed robin's egg blue, tinged with amethyst on the western horizon. They paused at the top to watch the old windmill on the hill, then headed down the last leg.

"Daddy took Emi to Knott's Berry Farm today."

Sally smiled. "Gosh, I remember when Charlie and I took the girls there when they were little. Remember Mrs. Knott's chicken dinner, Connie?"

"The best part was the boysenberry pie. Why didn't you go with them, Jelly?"

"I'm happy with the way Emi is warming to Daddy. I want them to spend time alone. He's been visiting for the past week, and I stay out of their way as much as I can. Jeannie and I have tons of work at the store." During the early part of summer, she did a complete inventory, cleared out items that had been on the racks long enough, and sent large bags of clothing and accessories to the local women's shelter. Hard work kept thoughts of Hank away.

"I have a lot to do at home to get ready for our camping trip to Sequoia Park. Mother and Daddy and I used to go every summer. Emi's never been...well, actually she was there when she was one, so that doesn't count.

"Daddy promised to teach her how to fly-fish. They spent hours in the garage a few days ago dusting off his fly rods and checking the reels and lures. He always wanted to teach me, but I wasn't the least bit interested." She chuckled and breathed in the warm evening breeze.

Sally asked her, "Jelly, anything happening on the Henry front?"

"No, nothing." *I wish.* "That's in the past. What he said would be very hard to forgive. I faced reality and moved on." She didn't mention that she'd seen him drive by the house a few nights ago while she sat on the porch swing with her father. Her heart flopped in her chest at the memory. What was he doing driving down her street?

Connie took her hand. "Such a shame, I feel so bad for you."

Jelly gave Connie's hand a squeeze. "Don't worry about me. I'll be fine. The upside is I have a live-in babysitter. The three of us will make a great team."

"You're a hard one to keep down, my friend," Sally said.

"Jenna and Erin will both want to take turns with the little one during breaks from school."

"How can I be down when I have such a terrific backup system?" She slung her arms over their shoulders as they walked the last few paces to their turn. "I'll see you in a week?"

Daddy's rental car was in the driveway when she got home. Emi stepped out carrying a bakery box. "Jelly! You're just in time. We brought your dinner. Do you like my hat?"

A black cowboy hat sporting a big feather dwarfed her head. Emi would never be as tall as Jelly. She hadn't grown an inch in the past year. *She definitely takes after Mom.*

"I love it. I can picture you standing by the King's River in your waders, holding a fishing pole."

"George said it's a rod, not a pole."

Emi had yet to call their father Daddy or Dad. She used his first name, but he seemed comfortable with that. He told Jelly that one thing he learned at Folsom was patience.

Jelly sniffed the box. "Boy, does that smell good. I hope there's some pie in there."

"We brought home a whole pie. I could eat a piece right now." A telltale purple stain on the front of Emi's shirt gave her away.

Jelly pressed her finger on the spot. "I have a hunch you already had some." She took the box and hugged her sister. "Come on, I'm starved. Where's Daddy?"

"He went in to set the table."

Jelly raised her eyebrows. "We're wasting valuable pie-eating time. I'll race you to the kitchen."

George smiled at his laughing daughters, pushing and shoving each other through the door.

"Hi, Daddy." A warm glow heated Jelly every time she saw

her father without a barrier between them. "You two have fun today?"

"That we did. She walked my legs off, didn't you, little girl?"

"I think it's the other way around. I took two steps for every one of yours. Jelly, you for sure get your long legs from George."

They sat at the table. Emi refused to remove her hat, claiming that because they didn't have company, nobody would know the difference. When Jelly opened her mouth to disagree, Emi clamped her lips tight and flashed a warning glare. Jelly took a breath, smiled, and swallowed her etiquette lesson for the evening.

Daddy insisted on washing the few dishes. "Go have a warm bath and relax. I'll finish up here."

She stood, thanked him, and headed for her bathroom. Thoughts of Hank trembled in her broken heart as she sunk low into the lavender scented bubbles. She deliberately forced them from her mind.

Instead, she replayed the scene when Daddy entered her kitchen for the first time since Mom's body was found. Jelly held her breath when he walked through the door. The look of relief in his eyes made her heart squeeze.

Over the years, she'd replaced the original appliances one-by-one and added stone countertops and bright painted walls and cupboards for a new, modern look. She and Emi had removed the old kitchen floor and installed pecan-toned wood laminate. Her greenhouse window above the kitchen sink overflowed with pots of fresh herbs and was her finishing touch. The room bore little resemblance to the one George remembered.

Hank's Condo
Saturday Morning

Henry's doorbell rang twice, followed by knocking that would wake the dead. "Okay, okay, I'm coming." He zipped his flight bag and cursed the airport limo. They were usually late enough to make him worry about missing his flight, but half an hour? *This is new.*

He flung open his door and flinched when he saw his brother standing on his porch. "Dom? What are you doing here?"

"Mama and Papa sent me to find out if you're all right." He gestured to the luggage. "You going somewhere?"

"Yes, I'm—"

"Where?"

"Bozeman. An old colleague and I are going kayaking and wilderness hiking." Henry stepped back and tilted his head to invite Dominik inside.

"What the hell's the matter with you? You're leaving town without letting the family know?"

Guilt washed over Henry. His brother and parents tried to contact him several times in the weeks since school let out. They left many messages on his phone, and worse, he'd ignored a written invitation to Joe and Dani's anniversary party.

"Dom, I—"

"Our parents are worried about you, Henry. Not to mention the rest of the family. We know something happened between you and Jelly. Emi and Sharla are friends. They talk on the phone frequently."

"I don't want to discuss it." Henry walked back into the middle of the living room and picked up his bags.

Dom took the flight bag from his hand and set it on the floor. "Henry, you stubborn S.O.B., have you forgotten we're a family?" Dom ran his hands through his salt-and-pepper hair. "Don't you care that Mama and Papa are sick with worry?"

Frustration and anger built in Hank's gut. Who gave Dom, or any of them, the right to interfere in his life? "Yes, Dom, I care, but this is my problem and I'll handle it. I see no need to unburden my private life on the family." He reached for the flight bag.

Dom put his hand on Henry's shoulder. "Your private life? The past month has impacted all of us. Even some of the younger kids know something is wrong. You quit showing up for family dinner. What happened?" His gray eyes locked with Henry's.

Henry dropped his head and shrugged. The wound Jelly inflicted on his heart was still raw. He wasn't ready to talk about any of it. "Dom, please, I can't—"

Both of his hands on Henry's shoulders, Dom spoke, "Look at me, little brother." When Henry continued to stare at the floor, Dominik tightened his steel-fingered grip. "Look at me, please."

Henry couldn't hide the pain in his eyes. His scalp tingled when Dom's expression showed shock and sympathy. He gulped. "Dom, she cheated on me."

"And you know this how?"

A black snake of pain slithered into his chest. "I saw them together!" He stared at the floor.

Dominik shook him. "Henry, look at me. You saw them when, where?"

Henry clenched his teeth against a wave of deep sadness. "In Sacramento, when I went to find her after Linda's treacherous stunt. I saw them together."

"What did you do? Did you confront them? Are you sure it was her?"

"Yes, I'm sure, all right? And, no, I didn't confront them. I was afraid of what I might do." He clenched his fists when he remembered the moment Julie kissed the other man.

Dom dropped his hands. "This makes no sense. Have you seen her since then?"

"I went to her store one afternoon. She told me she was

pregnant. I said some awful things. A few days ago, I worked up enough nerve to talk to her again. I drove by her place." He smacked a fist into his hand. "My God, Dom, the guy is staying at her house. They were sitting together on her front porch. Cozy as can be."

Dominik shook his head. "Oh, hell, Henry, that's her father."

"Her father?" Hank's laugh was bitter, humorless. "Her father is in Folsom prison."

"He was paroled, Henry. He lives in Sacramento with his sister. He's visiting them for a couple of weeks. Emi told Sharla they were going to King's Canyon on a camping and fishing trip."

Blood drained from Hank's head like a heavy stone dropped in still water. Dizziness unbalanced him, and he slumped onto the sofa. "Oh, God in heaven, what have I done?" He dropped his head in his hands. "Julie, Julie, what have I done?"

Chapter Forty

"Henry, the question isn't 'What have I done?' It's what are you going to do now?"

Hank's head dropped back. He gulped air. "Dom, my brain isn't working. I don't know what—"

The ring of Dom's cell phone interrupted. "Hello, Mollie, yes, he's here. Tell Mama he's okay. May I call you back in a few minutes?" He put the phone back in his pocket and sat next to Henry. "Well?"

Henry rocked back and forth, elbows on knees, head in hand. "I don't know what to do."

"I think you do."

Hank stood abruptly and paced. "I have to go over there. I have to go to her and apologize. What a complete ass I am! I don't know where to start to dig myself out of the hole I'm in." He patted his pockets to find his keys. "I have to call Jim, tell him not to meet my flight. I have to cancel the airport limo."

"Give me the numbers. I'll call for you."

Henry scribbled his friend's number on the back of the limo confirmation, slapped it into Dominik's hand, and went through the kitchen to his garage. He punched the door opener and was inside his truck with the engine running before the door fully opened.

His mind raced. How would he start? What would he say? He wouldn't blame Julie if she refused to talk to him after his dreadful accusation. He'd behaved like an ego-bruised juvenile.

Emi had barely looked him in the eye during the last two weeks of class. Her anger and disappointment in him were unshakable. She spoke perfunctorily when called upon, handed in her homework, and left the instant the bell sounded. He childishly left the teacher comment section on her semester evaluation form blank. Not one word of praise to support the A-plus she'd earned. *What a jackass!*

Why would either of them consider his apology? He clearly did not deserve to have Julie and Emi in his life. Whether they forgave him or not, they deserved his apology.

As he approached Julie's home, Emi placed a bundle in the trunk of the blue sedan parked in the driveway and went back inside the house. He pulled up at the curb, turned off the engine, and sat for a moment. A band of steel squeezed his throat and his heart thudded in his chest. He shook his head with disgust and shoved open the truck door.

Bedrolls and duffle bags lay stacked on the porch, ready to be loaded into the car. Julie's father pushed the screen door open as Henry reached for the doorbell. He stopped abruptly and stared. Gray eyes, so like Julie's, studied him. Henry saw a flash of recognition in those eyes.

"You're Hank Palasczewski."

Henry swallowed. "Yes, sir, Mr. Swanson. Is Julie here?"

Emi's face appeared next to her father. "She's not here. Even if she were, she wouldn't talk to you. What do you want?"

George put his arm around Emi's shoulders. "Let me take care of this, sweetheart." He gently pushed her aside, stepped onto the porch, and closed the door. "Emi's right, you know. I don't believe Julie Lea would care to see you if she were here.

We're going camping. I'm to pick her up at her place of business when we leave here."

George raised his hand when Hank opened his mouth to reply. "Let's move away from the door. Come with me." He strode to Hank's truck, turned, crossed his arms, and leaned back against the passenger door. "Say what you came to say, Palasczewski. I'll pass it on to Julie Lea." The man's steely gray eyes held Hank in his gaze.

"I, uh, I came to apologize. I behaved badly. I made a bonehead mistake. I said some things I shouldn't have."

"Yes. I know."

"I saw you two together, and I thought—"

"Well, you thought wrong, didn't you, son?"

Shaking his lowered head, Hank continued, "I'm so sorry. I love Julie. There's no excuse for what I said."

George nodded. "You're right about that." His lips clamped.

Hank ran both hands through his hair. He closed his eyes. "Christ Almighty, I don't deserve to be forgiven for what I did, what I said."

"You're right again."

"I love her. I don't know what to do."

George pushed himself off the truck and dropped his hands. "I'll pass your comments on to my daughter. If she wishes to speak to you, she will. I think you should leave now." He brushed past Hank on his way to the house.

The screen door snapped shut. Hank stood rooted to the sidewalk, his head spinning. *What do I do now?* He'd start by leaving, as Julie's father requested. He slid inside and fired up the engine. *I'll go home and wait.* He pulled the phone from his pocket, made sure it was turned on. *Maybe she'll call me.*

Chapter Forty-One

Bodacious Blooms Farmhouse
Sunday

She didn't call, of course. He desperately hoped she would but didn't expect her to. When he arrived at his parent's home at mid-day, his mother greeted him with deep sadness in her eyes.

"I'm all right, Mama. You shouldn't worry about me."

"I worry for all my children, Henryk. A mother's heart never stops worrying for her children, no matter whether they are three or thirty-three. You're my youngest son. I want you to be happy."

He caressed his mother's soft gray hair. "I want to be happy too, Mama. I'm going to find a way to get Julie back in my life."

Anka kissed her son's cheek. "Find a way, my son. We all love her. She was meant for you. I think she loves you very much. I saw it in her eyes."

"I'll try, Mama. I promise."

The long day was nearly over. Henry sat in the moonlight

with Dani sharing a last glass of wine. He'd put a smile on his face most of the day for Dani and Joe's happy occasion, determined not to ruin the Ruiz anniversary party. Now he leaned into the cushion on the big Adirondack chair and sighed deeply, unable to mask his sadness any longer. "I've never felt so bad, so lost, Dani."

"I know. I saw it in your eyes all evening. Thank you for trying so hard not to spoil my big day." She patted her brother's knee. "You'll find a way to set things right with her." Barely twenty months separated their birthdays. They'd always been close, always shared each other's secrets.

Henry choked down the last of his wine. "God, how I hope you're right. I can't imagine my life without Julie."

"Have you thought about what you'll do now?"

"I've thought of little else. Whatever happens, I know she'll never forget those contemptible words. I pray that I can still salvage what we had together."

Dani sighed, stood, and took Henry's glass and set it on a table. "It's so nice out tonight with the bright moon. Come, walk me home."

"I thought Joe was coming back for you after he put the kids to bed."

"I told him to wait for my call. Let's walk. Maybe together we can come up with a plan."

The bright gravel path to the Ruiz house was easy to follow, except when a cloud passed briefly to shadow the moon. They strolled, hand-in-hand, silent for several minutes. A good country mile stretched between their childhood home and the house Dominik, Aleksy, Henry, and Stanislaw built as a wedding present for Dani and Joe. Ten years had passed in the blink of an eye. Henry put his arm around Dani's shoulder and hugged her to his side. "Are you happy, sis?"

Her lovely face glowed when she turned her head to him. "Yes, I'm very happy. I'm so lucky to have Joe and the twins. I fell head over heels in love with Joe the first time I ever laid eyes on him." She chuckled at the memory.

"It was the same for me with Julie. I was dazzled, completely floored." He squeezed Dani's shoulder. "I couldn't put two intelligent words together. She said it was the same for her. I never felt anything close to that with Linda."

Dani huffed. "All of this started with Linda. I should have dumped her in the fifth grade. I deeply regret bringing her into the family. All these past years, I overlooked and made excuses for her behavior. Even when I knew in my heart what she was really like. I just didn't want to admit it. I'm really sorry for that, Henry."

"Come on, I was thirty years old when I asked her to marry me. What a clueless dimwit I was. I would never have believed her capable of what she did that day in Julie's store. She's a vicious bitch. I should have seen it coming."

"We know hindsight is great, Henry, but it was me who pushed you two together."

"Pah! I went willingly into her web. There was nothing more I wanted than to possess her, that gorgeous body, that mane of raven hair. I drank her delicious poison. I deserve what she did to me, but what she did to Julie? That was over the top, even for Linda."

The only sound for several minutes was the soft crunch of gravel beneath their feet. Hank's thoughts were of Julie and nothing but Julie. He had to win her back. Had to.

Dani broke the silence. "Do you think it would help if I called her?"

"No. Don't do that. This is something I have to do. If I get her back, it will be because she wants to be with me, not because she's feeling pressure from my family."

"There has to be something I can do."

"Say a prayer for us."

Chapter Forty-Two

King's Canyon Campground
Sunday

Jelly shivered and rubbed her hands. She scooted closer to the crackling fire. "Lord! I'm freezing. I think Emi went to bed early just so she could get warm."

George nodded and also extended his hands closer to the flames. "Once the sun went down, the temperature dropped a good twenty degrees, would be my guess. There's still snow under the bushes by the river. I forgot how cold it gets at night this time of year. Perhaps we should consider shortening our stay."

"Oh, no, Daddy, it's so beautiful during the day. I don't want to leave until the end of the week. We'll just bundle up after dark, that's all." She pulled the fleece blanket tighter around her shoulders and grinned at her father. "We're tough, we're Swansons!"

George mirrored her grin. "You're the tough one, Julie Lea. You got me through the last dozen years. You're my hero, you know."

She laughed. "Some hero. Pregnant, unmarried, and brokenhearted." She picked up a small log and tossed it onto the fire.

George stood and pulled his campstool closer to his daughter. "There's something I want to tell you, Julie Lea." Sparks flew from the campfire when the sap in the new log ignited.

His serious gaze unsettled her stomach. Just about anything unsettled her stomach these days. "What? You look so serious."

He reached for her hands and rubbed them briskly between his. "I never told you that I left your mother when she was pregnant with you, did I?"

If his serious gaze had upset her, his words froze her heart. "No! Daddy, you didn't. I don't believe you."

"It's true. I was twenty-three years old and still in college. Jessie's career had barely got off the ground when she discovered you were on the way. I felt trapped, smothered. I walked out."

Jelly shook her head with wonder. Her memories from childhood were of parents happy and contented. "What did Mama do?"

George's smile saddened when he relived the long-ago moment. "She filed for divorce, said I was an irresponsible child who didn't deserve her or our baby." He shrugged. "She was right."

Jelly saw her father with fresh eyes. She pictured him as a handsome, tall, twenty-three-year-old college student, unsure of himself. Making the first mistake that would alter all their lives.

She squeezed her father's hands. "I suppose most people go through life thinking the world started the day they were born. My memories of you and Mama are of a deeply loving couple with a rock solid relationship. I can't imagine a divorce."

George poured hot water into their mugs and dunked the used teabags up and down. "There's not much left in these, but it'll do, don't you think?"

Jelly sipped the hot liquid. "Daddy, tell me how you got

back together." Her parents divorced? They were made for each other. Mama told her they were soul mates. Jelly didn't fully understand what that meant until she met Hank. Her throat closed against the tea, but she pressed her lips tight and forced a swallow.

Elbows on his knees, he stared into the campfire, then smiled. "Oh, it wasn't easy, I assure you. It didn't take long for me to realize I'd made a terrible blunder. I went back and begged Jessie to withdraw the divorce petition."

"She did, didn't she?"

"Not at first. She wasn't going to let me off the hook that easily. She said words were fine, but I had to demonstrate by my actions that I was ready to be a responsible husband and father. Jessie had a spine, that woman. You got yours from her."

Jelly sighed. "I miss her so much. I never stopped missing her, Daddy."

George put his hand on Jelly's knee. "The reason I told you this, Julie Lea, is because you're in a similar situation with your young man. Think carefully about your choices. Take time to consider the consequences of any decision you make."

Jelly set her mug down on a flat rock at the side of the fire. She pressed her hands to her face, fought against tears. "He broke my heart, Daddy."

"Yes. He broke his own heart at the same time." George scooted over and put his arm around his daughter. "I would give anything to go back and change some of the choices I made. I lost nearly everything with those choices, Julie Lea. We make life much more complicated than necessary."

"I don't know what to do, Daddy."

"Yes, Julie Lea, I think you do."

Chapter Forty-Three

Jelly's House
One Week Later

Weary from the long drive, Jelly realized she didn't have the endless stamina that had been so reliable all her life. She followed her father into the house, dropped the bedroll she carried, and turned back to retrieve more gear from the car.

"You put the groceries away, Julie Lea. Emi and I can bring in the rest." He pecked her on the cheek and passed his younger daughter on his way back to the trunk of his rented car.

The message light on the phone blinked, but Julie continued to the kitchen, opened the refrigerator, and put away the partially used carton of milk and other perishables left over from the camping supplies. She placed the pastrami sandwiches and chips they'd picked up on the table for dinner and smiled because she didn't have to look another trout in the eye.

Emi passed the kitchen door and called out, "The message light is on, Jelly."

"I know. I'll have a listen after we get all our things in the house and I've had a chance to shower." A bubble of worry percolated in her chest. What if none of the calls were from Hank? What if they *were?* Still clinging to deep hurt, she wasn't sure she was ready to talk to him. But she would have to talk to him, wouldn't she? So much remained unresolved between them—whatever the outcome of any conversation, they had to talk. "I'll have dinner ready as soon as you and Daddy get the car emptied."

"Okay, we're almost finished." The snap of the screen door followed Emi's remark.

Jelly heard George's shout. "The tent's all that's left. Don't try to lift it by yourself, Emi, I'll be right there." He stepped into the kitchen with a grocery bag. "The Coke's in here. I hope we have some ice, since it's probably warm by now."

Jelly filled three glasses with ice, put the sandwiches on plates, and pulled open the bag of chips. Emi and Daddy slumped down at the table just as she put out a stack of paper napkins. "Emi, you need to wash your hands before you touch that sandwich."

Emi groaned and rolled her eyes. "She never lets up, George." She went to the kitchen sink and squirted liquid soap on her hands.

Jelly exchanged a silent smile with her father.

He winked. "I need to wash my hands too." He stood and went to the sink. He nudged Emi. "She is quite a nag, isn't she?"

"You don't know the half of it, Dad."

Jelly's ears perked up. That was the first time Emi had ever called their father by anything other than his first name.

George looked over his shoulder and smiled in Jelly's direction. They shared a warm glow at this milestone.

After they finished their sandwiches, George stretched his arms over his head, then pushed his chair back. "I'm going to hit the shower. Hot water is going to feel real good about now. You can't imagine what a luxury it is to shower in private."

Emi sipped at the last of her Coke. "Leave some for us."

Jelly watched their father's muscular back, emphasized by his snug tee shirt. He managed to get some color while fishing in the clear Sierra Nevada sunshine. He was a different man from the one she visited in prison for so many years. He appeared youthful and vigorous.

She saw her father through Hank's eyes. It was no wonder he had come to the wrong conclusion about who Daddy was when he'd seen them together. He made a bad mistake, but that didn't excuse what he said to her. How he said it.

She sighed. *Time to listen to those phone messages.*

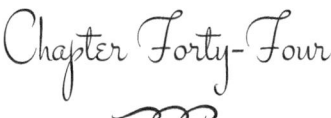

Chapter Forty-Four

Connie's Front Porch
Next Evening, 8:00 P.M.

J elly rocked the glider back and forth, back and forth. "Hank called while we were on our camping trip."

Her remark, out of the blue, brought both Connie and Sally to attention.

Connie smacked her on the knee. "And you're just now telling us?"

"What did he have to say for himself?" Sally asked.

Jelly put her foot down sharply, stood, and walked around the porch, hands on hips. "He left a message, he apologized."

"Please," Connie said, "don't keep us in suspense. Did you call him back?"

"Did you?" Sally said.

Pacing, silent, Jelly did keep her friends in suspense, but not intentionally. Her mind turned Hank's messages over and over. Her stomach churned at the memory of hearing his voice, the voice she loved, the voice that had devastated her.

"Jelly, did you?" Sally asked again.

Her head came up. "Did I what?" She looked from Sally to Connie.

Connie threw her hands up and dropped her head on the back of the glider. "Dios mio!" Her expression of frustration and the huff of air from her lungs brought Jelly back to the present.

"Oh! No, I didn't return his call. Yet. I will, but I'm not sure what to say to him."

Sally stood. "I'm not giving any advice, Jelly. You need to decide what's best for you, my friend." She gave Jelly a hug as she passed her, then crossed the lawn between her house and Connie's.

Jelly raised her eyes and tilted her head in Connie's direction.

"Don't look at me, chica. Sally's right. You gotta do this by yourself." She stood and took Jelly's arm. "Come on, I'll walk you to your corner."

Daddy sat reading the paper and Emi held the phone to her ear when Jelly walked through her front door. She waved and continued toward the bathroom when Emi gestured furiously for her to stop.

Emi put her hand over the phone and hissed loudly, "It's him, Henry. I told him you weren't here. What do you want me to do?"

George looked over the top of his reading glasses. Lips pressed together, he pinned Jelly with a questioning stare. He cocked his head toward Emi, then disappeared behind the paper again.

Jelly sighed. She could put it off no longer. "Tell him I just got home. I'll take the call in my room. Hang up as soon as I answer please."

Emi expressed her disgust with a "Duh."

Jelly sat on the edge of her bed, took a breath, and picked up the phone. "Hello, Hank."

"Julie, we need to talk."

"Yes. Go ahead then."

"No, I mean we need to talk in person."

"I don't know, Hank. It's late and I—"

"Julie, I'm in my truck. I just parked in front of your house. Will you come out and talk to me? Please?"

"We might as well get it over with." She stood, clicked off the phone, and walked back to the front of the house, past her puzzled sister and father and out the front door.

Hank stood next to his truck. She couldn't see his face clearly because the streetlamp in front of her house was out. But she knew him, even in the dim light of the moonless evening.

He bolted to attention and walked toward her, tentatively outstretching his arms.

Jelly stopped and nodded an unmistakable *no.* He dropped his arms and his slumping posture registered defeat. "Julie, I don't know where to start. I'm so sorry. You can't imagine how sorry I am."

She stood tall. Looked him directly in the eye. "You can't imagine how much pain you caused me, Hank. There were only two times in my life when I felt completely defeated and hopeless; when my mother was murdered and when you said those despicable words. There isn't enough sorry in the world to change that."

He raised his hands to his head. "Julie, I love you so much."

She shook her head. "How could you say those things to somebody you love?" She placed a hand gently on her abdomen. "Your child is here, Hank. Your child. Our child."

"Oh, God, Julie, I know. I want to be a father to our baby. I want to be your husband."

"It doesn't seem to me you have what it takes to be a father, let alone a husband." Echoes of words her father had spoken about the near break-up of her parents bounced eerily in her head.

"Julie, everything in my life changed the day we met. It's because of the intensity of my feelings for you that I acted the fool. I know that's a weak excuse, but—"

Instead of answering him, Julie shook her head with slow sadness.

"Is there any way I can make up for what I said, Julie? I wish I could take it back, but I can't. Can you find it in your heart to forgive me?"

"I'd be lying to you if I said yes, Hank. I don't trust you. Not yet, maybe not ever."

He took a step forward. "Julie, I'm begging you."

"I'm sorry. I'm going in now." She turned her back and made her way to the door, opened it, and went inside.

The next morning, a large bouquet of roses was delivered to her store. The note said, "Julie, I love you. Please give me another chance. Hank."

She went through the day mechanically, and the distraction of work was welcome. Only Jeannie knew that the smile on her face and her cheery manner were put there for the sake of her customers. At closing, she tallied up the day's sales and asked Jeannie if she'd do the bank drop.

"Of course I'll do it. You don't even have to ask, Jelly. I only wish I could do more."

"Thank you, Jeannie. I really appreciate that. My father is getting ready to leave, so if you don't mind, I'll take the morning off tomorrow. I'll relieve you at one. You can take the rest of the afternoon off."

As Jelly prepared to leave, Jeannie asked, "Aren't you going to take the flowers home?"

With a sad smile, Jelly answered, "No, they look nice in the store. I'll leave them here." She slipped the note into her purse, tossed her hair, and smiled. "I'm fine, really. I am."

A huge bouquet of flowers nearly covered the top of the dining room table. She spotted it the minute she entered the house, especially since Emi was setting the table with the good dishes and silverware. "What's the occasion?" she asked, a bit wary. Delicious smells wafted from the kitchen.

Acting as if the flowers were invisible, Emi answered, "Dad is leaving tomorrow afternoon. He wanted to fix a special dinner for us tonight. I thought it would be nice to eat here." She went about finishing the settings.

The flutter of unease abated. "Yes, good idea. I'll call Connie and Sally and tell them not to wait for me tonight. What do you want me to do?"

"Nothing, we've got it under control." Emi held up a glass. "I'll get you some iced tea. Go put your feet up."

Jelly smiled. "I kind of like being pampered." She sat on the sofa, raised her weary legs, and put her feet on the ottoman. Hanky hopped onto her lap and commenced purring like a Harley.

Emi arrived with the tea, placed a coaster on the side table, and set it down. "Don't get used to it, Jelly. I can't even remember the recipe for boiled water."

Jelly laughed—a real laugh. It felt good. "I know you're dying of curiosity, so why don't you hand me that card that came with the flowers? I might even let you read it."

Emi scampered to the table, grabbed the card, and brought it to her. "I wonder who they're from."

Jelly twisted her lips. "Very funny." She dropped the card in her lap, removed her earrings, kicked off her shoes, and took a sip of the tea.

"Aren't you going to read it?" Emi did her typical *Emi posture*, hands on hips, accompanied by a challenging stare.

Jelly patted the cushion next to her. "Sit down. I just like to watch you squirm once in a while."

"And you think *I'm* a brat." She leaned toward Jelly, tilting her head for a better view of the card. "Open it."

Jelly gave her a small shoulder nudge. "Okay, but no peeking. I have to read it first." She undid the tucked flap on the back of the card. "Are you sure you didn't read it already?"

"Jelly! Quit teasing me."

The card was from the same florist as the one accompanying the bouquet at Big Night Out. Jelly held it in her hand for a moment, then slowly unfolded the note. She read it, sighed, and handed it to Emi.

Emi snatched it from her hand and peered eagerly at the message. Nodding her head, she said, "Um hum, it's from him, I knew it. He sounds really desperate. Men don't have a clue, do they?"

Jelly whispered, "No, but don't let Daddy hear you say that."

George entered the dining room with a large salad bowl. "I heard. And she's right." He chuckled and returned through the swinging door.

Emi and Jelly mirrored each other by clamping a hand over their mouths. Eyebrows raised, Emi suppressed a giggle.

George called from the kitchen, "Emi, come carry out the vegetables. Julie Lea, take a seat at the table, dinner's ready."

Jelly carried her drink to the table and sat on the long side. She pushed the flower arrangement from the center of the table so she wouldn't have to look at Emi through the stems and leaves. When the flowers were moved, they sent out a big puff of sweet fragrance. Jelly inhaled and nodded her appreciation.

George carried a magnificent crown roast of pork to the

table. He'd decorated it to look as if it came right off the pages of Gourmet Magazine.

Shocked, Jelly exclaimed, "Daddy, that's beautiful. I didn't know you could cook something like that. It smells heavenly."

He set the platter in the center of the table in front of the end chair where he would sit. A smile of satisfaction beamed from his face. "I had a lot of time to read while I was in graduate school, if you get my drift." He took the bowl of steaming vegetables from Emi, set them down, and held her chair.

She hesitated for a split second, gave him a big smile, and took her place at the table. "Boy, what service, huh, Jelly?"

Jelly ate dinner in a haze of exhaustion and what almost felt like happiness. Every now and then Hank would intrude on her thoughts, but she pushed him away and enjoyed the evening with her father and sister. George discussed his plan to work for an old college buddy, Carl Tims. Carl owned a small aluminum-casting foundry near Davis, just south of Sacramento.

"You remember Carl, Julie Lea. You and I spent time with him and his family when you were little, when Jessie was on tour with the symphony."

Jelly was puzzled. "Yes, but, Daddy, you have an engineering degree. What would you do in a foundry?"

"Carl was very generous to give me the job. He needs somebody to honcho the night shift. I'm lucky to get employment at all."

"Night shift?"

"Yes, from eleven at night till seven in the morning. He just won a bid for a huge spare parts order from Boeing. He's going twenty-four-seven. It's something I can do. Carl and I worked for his dad at the foundry for two summers when we were at U.C. Davis."

Davis. That's where Hank went to school. It seemed that no matter what turn the conversation took, it always brought her thoughts back to Hank. Her father was still talking, and she shook her head to focus her attention on him.

"—so I plan to stay with Martha for the foreseeable future. Soon as I scrape enough money together, I'll get a place of my own. I haven't lived alone for so many years. It'll be a welcome change."

"I hope you'll be happy doing that kind of work, Daddy."

"Julie Lea, I have plenty of time to work my way back into a white-collar job. What I need right now is steady employment near my parole officer so I can report in on schedule. A good work history is going to be a valuable asset when I'm ready to stick my toes in the employment pool again. Having a good conduct prison record won't help me in the real world."

Right out of the blue, Emi piped up, "So what about you and Mr. Henry? Are you going to put him out of his misery or let him suffer some more?"

Jelly whipped her head around to face her sister. "I swear Martha Elizabeth, one of these days—"

Emi faced George, a satisfied smirk on her lips. "I get my big mouth from her, you know. She taught me to be honest and straightforward." She stared innocently into Jelly's eyes. "That's the truth, isn't it, Jelly?"

Shaking her head from side to side, Jelly sighed. "I have an idea, Daddy. You can take Martha Elizabeth to live with you and your sister for the next ten years or so."

Before George could respond, Emi screwed up her face and stuck out her tongue. "And give up a free live-in baby sitter? Not a good idea, Jelly. You need me."

Unable to maintain a stern expression, Jelly smiled and shook her head. "Okay, you're right. I need you. I've always needed you, Emi." She stood. "Now I need you to clean up the table and do the dishes, so Daddy and I can take a walk."

"What should I do about Hank, Daddy?" She took her father's arm and leaned against his shoulder. Mist haloed around the streetlamps and dampened their faces while they strolled in the foggy June evening.

George squeezed her arm against his side. "What do you want to do?"

"I want to take him back, but I don't want to be hurt anymore."

"There's no such thing as life without hurt, Julie Lea."

She sighed deeply. "I know."

"Do you love him?"

"Yes. I can't deny it. I do."

"Then, I believe you've answered your own question."

"I don't want to let him off the hook so easy, Daddy. He needs to know how much pain he caused me."

"He knows." George studied his beautiful, flamboyant daughter, so unlike her mother. "Let the rest of your life begin, Julie Lea."

Chapter Forty-Five

Big Night Out
Two Days Later

The flowers kept coming. When the florist delivered yet another bouquet, Jelly picked up the phone.

Hank answered on the first ring. "Julie?"

Her throat grew tight with emotion at the sound of his voice. "Please don't send any more flowers, Hank. My house and my store look and smell like funeral parlors. Today a customer asked me who died."

"Julie, I have to see you. May I see you?" The urgency in his request matched her desire to see him.

"Yes." The cloying scent of the flowers gave her a headache. "We do need to talk."

"Will you come to my place?" The note of hope in his request was loud and clear.

"No. Not tonight, Hank. Tomorrow would be better."

"May I take you to dinner?"

"Yes. We can meet at the coffee bar across the parking lot when I close."

"Five thirty tomorrow, Julie. I'll be there."

Big Night Out
Next Evening

Emi watched Jelly as she arranged her hair at the mirror in the restroom of her shop. "You're going on a date with Mr. Henry?"

Jelly carefully applied a bare hint of blush. "It's not a date."

"Why are you getting all dressed up, then?"

Jelly turned. "For heaven's sake, Emi, these are the same clothes I wore to work this morning."

Emi pointed at Jelly's reflection in the mirror. "Why'd you put all that junk on your face?"

"Don't you have something else to do besides standing here criticizing me?"

"Nope, I'm all yours."

"Wonderful." Jelly surveyed her appearance. The earrings were wrong. She pulled them off and went to the jewelry counter. It contained dozens of pairs to choose from. She slid open the back panel.

Emi stepped closer and reached past her sister's hand. "Wear these. Your face is looking fat these days. These silver ones are long and skinny." She offered them to Jelly.

Jelly pursed her lips and cast a sour, sidewise glance at her sister. "You always know how to cheer me up, don't you?"

"Well, it does. Your stomach is pooching out a little too."

Jelly emitted a "Grrrr," as she walked behind the changing room curtain, Emi a step behind her. "Get out of here! Give me some privacy."

"Sheesh. You don't need to yell."

"Apparently, I do. Now scram." Emi's phony, big-eyed

expression of complete innocence didn't prevent Jelly from giving her a gentle push toward the front of the store.

Emi looked over her shoulder. "Marco's here in his dad's car. We're going for pizza. I hope I don't have to hate Mr. Henry for much longer. I'm getting tired of it."

Jelly waved goodbye. "I'd like you to be home when I get there, okay?"

Emi nodded and put the closed sign in the window as she left the store.

Hank's breath caught when Julie stepped out from her store and locked the door. He swallowed the lump in his throat at the barest sign of her pregnancy, his heart squeezing with love. He stood, transfixed, in front of the coffee bar, watching as she walked across the parking lot.

She stepped up onto the curb and stood in front of him on the sidewalk. "Hello, Hank."

He tugged open the door to the coffee bar. "Hello, Julie. Thanks for agreeing to see me." The smell of fresh brewed coffee greeted them. He gestured toward a window table overlooking the sidewalk; neither of them seemed sure where to start the conversation. Finally, Hank cleared his throat. "I saw Emi leave with Marco. I didn't know he had a car."

"He's driving his dad's car. He just got his driving license. I keep thinking he's Emi's age, but he's sixteen now."

"Emi has a birthday in November, doesn't she?" Hank ordered coffee from the waitress and Jelly asked for ice water. "She'll be asking for a learner's permit once she turns fifteen, I expect."

She glanced at Hank, surprised he knew Emi's birth date. "Yes, November, how did you know?"

"My niece, Sharla, mentioned it. They talk on the phone."

"Ah."

He waited for her to say something else, but she opened the menu and didn't add anything further to her terse answer. "Uh,

Sharla asked me if I'd take Emi out to the farm for her birthday. I told her I'd have to clear it with you."

Without looking up, Jelly shrugged. "I don't see any harm in them continuing their friendship." She turned when the waitress came to the table and asked them if they were ready to order. "Yes, I'll have a roast beef sandwich with double horse-radish, a side of jalapeño fries, and a mocha freeze." She handed back the menu.

"And you, sir?"

"I'll have the same." He risked a small smile when Julie raised her eyes in surprise.

She rewarded him with a faint softening of her lips. "Apparently you don't remember what happened the last time we ate here, and you said, 'I'll have the same.'"

He leaned forward on his elbows. "I remember every minute of that time, Julie. I wish we could start all over from then."

She sat back and looked at him. "We can't though, can we?"

The roar of the espresso machine nearly drowned out his answer. "No, we can't."

The awkward silence between them continued. Julie seemed content to sit quietly, while Hank's uneasiness increased. Now that she was here, across the table from him, he couldn't remember a thing he'd planned to say. Previously certain that his words of apology would soften her heart, her demeanor unnerved him. Julie's natural upbeat, happy temperament, her sunny optimism had been replaced by a quiet coolness, so unlike her. He didn't recognize this new Julie but suspected his actions had played a part in that change.

The waitress served their sandwiches and drinks. Julie sat quietly, her hands in her lap. She cast him a steady gaze, which gave him no clue as to what might be going on in her mind.

She picked up her knife and fork and cut into her sandwich. "This looks good."

"Yes, it does, smells good, too. Although I might have to stop at the pharmacy for some Tums after I eat this." He dared to venture a small smile.

Julie took a long pull on the straw in her mocha freeze. "Gosh, it seems I'm famished every waking moment these days." She shook her head. "Why in heaven's name did you order that? Last time I remember you practically had smoke coming from your nose and ears."

Was that a small chuckle he heard?

His sigh was full of hope. "Lord, I don't know. Showing off? Trying to re-create a happy memory? Julie, I'm completely lost here. We need to open up and talk. Can we do that?"

The misery in Hank's gray eyes softened Jelly's heart. The hands she loved toyed nervously with his straw. It wasn't her intention to torture him, but that seemed to be what she'd accomplished. She didn't want that.

"Yes, Hank, we do need to open up. Neither of us can read minds, and I don't think you realize how deeply you hurt me." She sighed and brushed hair from her cheek.

"Julie, I do, I—"

She shook her head. "No, Hank, you don't know. That's the heart of the problem."

"But Julie—"

"Hank." She took a calming breath. "Please, let me finish. I'm as responsible for going too fast as you are. I was starry eyed with love and desire. I'd never had a relationship before. When I met you, my dormant teenage hormones bloomed into life. I jumped right into your bed. My head was in the clouds. When I look back on it now, I'm embarrassed by how little I understood my own emotions. How naïve I must have sounded to my friends when I told them how I felt about you."

Hank shook his head sadly. "No, Julie. That was my fault. I should have been more careful. I was consumed with passion for you from the moment we met. I'm as much in love with you now as I was then."

"Neither of us got beneath the surface. I didn't give myself time to know you. I jumped to so many conclusions and made so many emotional decisions those first few weeks." She raised her hands. "Yes, you did too. You have to admit that."

"That's true, but it doesn't change what I feel for you now, what I want for us and for our baby." He put down his sandwich and placed his hands on the table.

His declaration, his mention of the baby, sent a pang to her heart. "How *do* you feel, Hank? What *do* you want? Honestly? Think about it before you answer."

"Okay. You're right. Let's finish dinner, and then if you can take the time, we'll go for a walk or a drive." His eyes pleaded with her, his deep baritone sorrowful.

He reminded her of Emi's little Hanky, the way the kitten used her expressive eyes when she wanted to be fed or petted. Jelly couldn't hold back a softhearted smile. "Okay." She nodded. "That's a good plan. But first, I want to go home and check on Emi. We can walk in my neighborhood."

Hank followed her home from the coffee bar. Marco and Emi were there. Julie pulled into her driveway and Hank parked his pickup next to her Mustang. She asked him to wait outside while she changed shoes and checked on the kids.

When she came back outside, she had a tenderhearted smile on her face. He took note of subtle physical changes. Her cheekbones were less prominent, and a new softness plumped her naturally rosy cheeks. Pregnancy agreed with her.

She looked at the sky. "The evening haze has a golden color now that the days are longer. I've always loved this valley. It's beautiful here, isn't it?"

He put his hands into his pockets. "Yes, it is. I love it, too." More than anything, he wanted to touch her, but that would be the wrong move right then.

She knocked the back of her hand against his pocket. "Hold my hand, Hank. We can start by being friends, can't we?"

Hope flooded his chest. He grasped her hand tenderly. "Yes, we can. That would be the place to start, Julie." He told himself to breathe, to consider his every word, to think with his brain instead of his heart.

"Hank, I don't think we're going to get anywhere until I tell you how much you wounded me when you asked me who the father of our baby was." She squeezed his hand.

He felt the pressure of her grip from his neck to his knees. "God, how I wish I could take those words back, Julie."

"You can't take them back. I forgave you, but I still feel the pain. What hurt the most was that you assumed if I was pregnant, I had cheated on you, that I was the kind of woman who slept around. You crushed me to my soul."

He stopped walking and faced her. His gray gaze penetrated hers. "I don't think that Julie. Your openness and honesty are traits I treasure. I love that about you. I acted the jealous fool when I saw you hugging and kissing the man I later learned was your father. If I'd had my wits about me that night in Sacramento, I'd have approached the two of you and learned the truth. Instead, I turned my truck around and went home like a wounded dog."

Sally's Patio
8:00 P.M.

Connie walked to the big umbrella table after a brief conversation with Miguel over the hedge between their back patio and Sally's. She sat across from Jelly. "Looks like he might have to drive all the way back to Parker Center tonight. They picked up a suspect from the murder case he and Bob are working. If they can locate the witness, they're probably going to try and do a line-up tonight."

Joining them, Sally set a bowl of cherries and a pitcher of iced tea on the table. "He's certainly been putting in some long hours lately, Connie."

Connie rolled a cherry around in her fingers and put it in her mouth. "Yes, I hope they can wrap up this nasty case soon. He's getting hard to live with. Poor man hasn't had enough sleep for a month."

Jelly frowned and stared at Connie. "You and Miguel aren't fighting, are you? Is everything okay at home?"

Connie smiled and reached over to pat Jelly's arm. "Don't you worry about me and mi esposo, chica. We've weathered plenty of storms in the past twenty years. This is nothing."

Sally filled Jelly's nearly empty glass. "Don't be troubled about Connie and Miguel, Jelly. We're dying of curiosity. What's happening with you and Henry? You look happier tonight."

Jelly smiled at the concern on their faces. She could always count on these two to be there to laugh with or provide a shoulder to cry on. "Hank and I took a long walk tonight, which is why I didn't show up earlier. Sorry I didn't call, I forgot. I hope you weren't too concerned."

They gave her waves of dismissal and eagerly asked her to fill them in.

"I told Hank how deeply he hurt me, how I was having a hard time getting past it."

Her friends nodded for her to continue, all too aware of how she'd suffered.

Jelly leaned forward. "I didn't know till tonight why he thought I cheated on him."

Connie put down her glass. "What did he say?"

"Yes," Sally added. "How did Henry explain that?"

With a look of wide-eyed wonderment, she said, "He was

frantic when Dani told him Linda came to my shop and said she'd been staying with him in the cabin at Bass Lake. He actually came after me, followed me to Sacramento. He drove along Martha's street and saw me walking hand-in-hand with a man. He didn't know it was Daddy. How would he? Hank jumped to the conclusion I had a boyfriend up there. He turned around and went home. That was the beginning of his refusal to talk to me. That misunderstanding brought on his accusations."

Connie sighed and shook her head. "Men. They'd never admit it, but they're a lot more fragile than women are."

"Absolutely," Sally agreed.

Jelly studied the bowl of cherries, picked a couple, and sat back. "Hank and I have to learn how to be friends who trust each other before we can hope to be lovers again. That opens up a big can of worms, doesn't it? Tell me, what is love, anyway?"

Connie laughed. "We'll all be old and gray before we figure out that one. The only thing I know for sure is the definition changes to meet whatever situation you're in at the moment."

Jelly grinned in Connie's direction. "You're a big help."

Sally agreed with Connie. "She's right. Love means so many things. That's a question for the ages. For me, most of all, it was the nice cozy comfort zone it provided. Pretty much knowing where I stood from day to day. There was no mistrust between Charlie and me. Both of us knew that the most important thing in our lives was each other."

Connie smiled and nodded agreement at Sally's answer. "Right. After a rough patch, you kiss and make up. Right, Sal?"

"Mmm hmm."

"So, what's on the horizon for you and Henry?" Connie asked. "Did you kiss him goodnight? When are you going to see each other again? Soon? What?"

"No, I didn't kiss him. We held hands while we walked. When he said goodnight, I asked him to plan on having dinner with Emi

JELLY'S BIG NIGHT OUT

and me day after tomorrow. He was so happy when I suggested that. He wants to marry me, be a family, be a father to our child." Crickets were at the peak of their nightly songfest. A balmy breeze ruffled Jelly's hair. "We have a lot of talking to do before that can happen. I do love him, but he needs to know and understand what *I* want from life, for me and Emi, and the baby."

Hank and Julie settled into a routine of dinner once a week for the three of them. She had no desire to eat out, preferring the simple fare of home. They encouraged Emi to open up and express her feelings. After dinner, they often took a private walk. Once Jelly, Emi, and Marco went to Hank's condo for a cookout on his small back patio. The atmosphere was relaxed and happy. Hank and Jelly listened as the two teenagers talked about whatever caught their fancy.

Marco and Emi would enter eleventh grade in three weeks. They regretted that Henry would no longer be their homeroom teacher. They would still have science lab with him, and he'd still be running the field trips, so that softened their disappointment.

A couple of weeks later, a smiling Jelly told Connie and Sally that she and Henry had set a date for their wedding. They were delighted when she asked them to be part of the wedding party.

Connie put an arm around her shoulders while they strolled the last stretch of their usual walk. "I'm so happy for you. I think you and Henry will have a great marriage. After what you've been through already, you can weather whatever comes along."

"You and Henry are a good match, Jelly." Sally put a hand on her shoulder. "I'm sure you'll be happy together. This is a lucky little bundle you're carrying, to have you for a mom and Henry for a dad."

Jelly extended her arms, grasped them by the waist, and pulled them in tight. "You two are the best. I mean it. I'm so lucky to have you for friends."

"Cut it out, chica, you'll have us all blubbering."

August

The last week before school started, Hank had to go to Sacramento for a four-day teacher seminar. Julie and Emi rode up with him, and he dropped them off at Martha's home.

This would be their last visit with their aunt and father until Thanksgiving.

George hugged her. "My goodness, Julie Lea, you've put on a lot of weight since our camping trip." He winked and his smile got bigger.

She patted her stomach and grinned. "Daddy, I must have swallowed a chipmunk in my sleep while we were there. I can feel that little wheel running round and round."

Martha hugged her. "What does the doctor say? Do you know if it's a boy or a girl?"

Julie shook her head. "Nope. Hank and I decided we'd rather be surprised. In another four months, though, we'll all know."

Martha raised her eyebrows. She held Julie at arm's length. "Dare I ask what the future looks like for you and Henry? He was all smiles when he dropped you off. And I see you're wearing his engagement ring again."

Emi pursed her lips. "Oh, they love each other and they're going to get married. Jelly just strung it out to torture him and keep him guessing."

"I did not!"

"Yes, you did, Jelly. He wanted to marry you, and you wanted to marry him, right?"

"Yes, but—"

"So the wedding date is set, right?"

"Well, yes—"

"You and Henry and the baby and I are all going to live in our house after you're married, right? You've already started construction on two bedrooms and a bathroom, right? So what's the big deal? Just tell Dad and Aunt Martha the date."

Jelly pursed her lips and threw up her hands. Emi was always one step ahead of her. Amused at the exchange, Daddy and Aunt Martha took it all in, chuckling.

Emi turned to them, shook her head, and raised her eyebrows. "She can be a real pain. Right?"

Chapter Forty-Six

Bodacious Blooms Farm
Thanksgiving Eve

J ulie and Henry Palasczewski turned under the autumn-decorated bower to face the applause of friends and family. Dominik stood at Henry's side as best man. Next to him were their brothers, Aleksy and Stanislaw. At Julie's side her maid of honor, Emi, along with Connie and Sally.

A big white tent had been erected beside the farmhouse to accommodate the large crowd of wedding guests. Henry's neighbor, Gary the DJ, started the music. Henry led Julie to the dance floor. They were quickly joined by Henry's parents and then others from the wedding party. Soon the dance floor vibrated, crowded with happy wedding guests.

Emi and Marco joined Sharla and the twins on the sidelines with the younger guests watching the grownups dancing to "old-fashioned music." Emi sighed and rested her chin in her hands. "This is the best birthday I ever had. Isn't it romantic?" Marco nodded and returned her grin.

Later, at dinner, Dominik offered a beautiful, heart-felt

toast to his youngest brother and his beautiful bride. He welcomed Julie into their family. He, Aleksy, and Stanislaw had nearly finished the addition of two bedrooms and a bathroom to Julie's house in Simi Valley, and he promised it would be ready for the arrival of their newest niece or nephew in late December.

George Swanson toasted the future of his daughter and new son-in-law, expressing his gratitude for the day he'd never expected to be part of.

Henry took Julie's hand and stood. He raised his champagne glass. "I love you, Mrs. Julie Palasczewski." He placed a hand on their pending bundle of joy. "And you too, whoever you are."

She smiled, her eyes shining. "And we love you, Hank-Daddy."

Don't miss out on your next favorite book!

Join the Satin Romance mailing list
www.satinromance.com/mail.html

THANK YOU FOR READING

Did you enjoy this book?

We invite you to leave a review at the website of your choice, such as Goodreads, Amazon, Barnes & Noble, etc.

DID YOU KNOW THAT LEAVING A REVIEW...

- Helps other readers find books they may enjoy.
- Gives you a chance to let your voice be heard.
- Gives authors recognition for their hard work.
- Doesn't have to be long. A sentence or two about why you liked the book will do.

About the Author

Patty claims she's led many lives—oldest of five sisters, baby sitter, drugstore fountain waitress, popcorn girl in the local movie theater, line server in a popular cafeteria alongside her grandmother, telephone operator, executive suite receptionist, hospital admitting clerk, shoulder to cry on for the broken-hearted, pediatrician's assistant, medical billing clerk, travel agency owner, coffee bar owner, and now – author. Somewhere in between all those things, she got an education, married her soul mate, became mother of two handsome sons, two grand-children, and three great-grandchildren. And she's not even tired!

pattycampbell.com
pattycampbellauthor.blogspot.com

facebook.com/Patty-Campbell-Author-536855299661241

goodreads.com/goodreadscomuser_PattyCampbell

Also by Patty Campbell

Wounded Warriors Series

Heart of a Marine

Love of a Marine

Soul of a Marine

Always a Marine

Novels

Risky Business

Forever Amber

Jelly's Big Night Out

Once a Marine (available 2022)